SURVIVING THE DEAD VOLUME 6:

SAVAGES

By:

James N. Cook

COPYRIGHT

Also by James N. Cook:

Surviving The Dead Series:

No Easy Hope

This Shattered Land

Warrior Within

The Passenger

Fire in Winter

The Darkest Place

Whoever fights monsters should see to it that in the process he does not become a monster. And if you gaze long enough into an abyss, the abyss will gaze back into you.

-Friedrich Nietzsche

ONE

Things would have been a lot worse if not for the helicopters.

To the north, the steady *phoom, phoom, phoom,* of artillery thundered through the morning air, while to the south, shells exploded in flashes of fire and black smoke. Hollow Rock—my town, my home—was in flames. I was too far away to hear the screams and shouted orders and desperate calls of people yelling for loved ones. Too far away to hear the cries of the dying, of parents trying to find their children, of those same children sobbing in fearful, choked voices.

I wish I could say it was for them I wept, but it was not. It was for Allison, my wife, the mother of my unborn child. She was down there somewhere, probably running for her life like everyone else.

If she's not already dead.

I tried to surge up from the ground, but Hicks grabbed me across the shoulders.

"Don't," he said. "You'll get yourself killed."

Ignoring him, I struggled to get my feet underneath me. Hicks rose up and snaked an arm through one of mine in a wrestler's wrist tie-up. Unable to use the arm he controlled, I tried to sit through and twist out with my unencumbered arm. He stopped me by putting his full weight across my back. Hicks was heavier than he looked, probably outweighing me by thirty pounds.

"Stop, Eric," he said into my ear. "You can't do anything for her right now."

Still, I struggled. If I'd had my wits about me, I could have gotten out from underneath him. Even pinned as I was, there were techniques I could have used to wrestle my way free. But I was not thinking straight. So instead I bucked and thrashed and called Hicks names I knew I would later regret. All the while he kept talking to me, telling me help was on the way, it was going to be all right, Allison would get to safety. Finally, he grabbed me by the hair, jerked my head up so I was looking him in the eye, and said, "Listen!"

I stopped fighting. Hicks pointed to my old friend, Staff Sergeant Ethan Thompson. Above the din of explosions and the increasing volume of rotors spinning overhead, I heard Ethan speaking into his radio.

"Copy," he said, "Apache engaging, maintain position and stand by for orders." He turned his head toward his squad. "Did you hear that? For now, we hold position. But be ready to move."

"Let the chopper do its job," Hicks said.

I went limp and nodded. "Okay, okay. Get off me."

His weight left my back and I could breathe easier.

I lay with my face close to the dirt, breathing in the scent of pine needles, pulse thumping in my ears. The Apache flew overhead, gaining altitude and banking northward until it went out of sight.

A few moments later, the *hiss-BANG* of a Hellfire missile sounded from less than half a mile away, followed by the chatter of a thirty-millimeter cannon firing in bursts. After the eighth or ninth burst, the cannon stopped and the Apache flew back in our direction. The artillery was silent.

"Roger that," Thompson said into his radio. "Will approach from the south and spread out to envelop the target area. Second Platoon will approach from the east and advise when in position. Over." He turned his head and said to his squad, "Check your weapons and follow me."

Out of habit, I looked to my carbine. Tugged back on the charging handle. Round in the chamber, magazine seated firmly, safety off, trigger finger pointing straight down the lower receiver. I pulled my Kel-Tec from its holster and checked it as well. Ready to go.

Thompson led the way as Delta Squad emerged from the treeline. The other three squads from First Platoon emerged at other points, one north of us, two others to the south. We had split up when fleeing our transport truck to make ourselves a harder target in case the enemy artillery had zeroed our position. Evidently, they had not. I would ordinarily have considered this a good thing, except all the rounds they fired hit Hollow Rock. A glance over my shoulder showed me a breach in the north gate wide enough to drive a tank through. Black smoke rose from the buildings behind. I hoped none of them was the clinic. Or my house.

Shoving thoughts of Allison aside for the moment, I followed Thompson as we met up with the rest of First Platoon.

*****

There was not much for us to do.

Burned bodies lay in death poses near three smallish artillery cannons no more than twenty yards apart. To my left, a charred corpse lay on its back, the skin and clothing burned so badly as to be unrecognizable. Its legs were crossed as though lounging on a bed, one hand reaching skyward, the arm bent at the elbow. I wondered if it would fall off if I went over and kicked it.

The cannon in the middle lay on its side, burned and blackened and misshapen from the impact of the Hellfire. Made

3

sense. As close together as the cannons were, hitting the middle gun would do the most damage to the crews. An artillery piece is just a big ugly paperweight with no one to shoot it.

The cannon on the Apache Longbow had taken care of the enemy troops, save for a handful who ran away. The recon team from First Platoon, along with a few scouts from the Ninth Tennessee Volunteer Militia, had gone after them. Hicks and Holland went along.

After reporting to Echo Company's commanding officer, Captain Harlow, we searched the bodies for identification. As expected, we found none. Chinese AK-47s, side arms I did not recognize, and Russian hand grenades. No hand weapons. Plain black uniforms with no body armor, black tactical vests with no manufacturers tag. Flashlights, spare ammo, and an array of tools common to Outbreak survivors. Bolt cutters, crowbars, flat pry-bars, machetes, entrenching tools, that sort of thing. No food, though.

The bodies recognizable as human all shared the same ethnicity: Asian. They were short, wiry, and save for the fact they were dead, in supreme physical condition.

"What do you think?" Sergeant Isaac Cole said standing next to me. "KPA?"

"Could be," I replied. "Although technically we should call them ROC."

Cole snorted. He sounded like an angry bull and stood almost as big as one. "Call 'em whatever you want, they North Korean. Buncha brainwashed-ass motherfuckers."

"Goddamn suicide troops," Private Fuller said behind me. "Got to be. No other explanation. They couldn't have expected to get out of here alive."

I said, "Tell that to the ones who ran away."

For a while, nothing happened. My eyes strayed anxiously toward home while I stood with the rest of Delta Squad waiting for Ethan Thompson to tell us what to do. On a salvage run, it would have been the other way around. But this was official military business, so I deferred to the federal types.

Ethan looked relieved when his earpiece finally buzzed to life. He pressed two fingers to his right ear and listened. A moment passed before he clicked transmit and muttered, "Roger that."

Turning our way, he said "We're moving out. Walkers closing in from the north and east. We're moving east to intercept. Second will maneuver north. Let's go."

"What about the rest of First?" Cole asked. He was the second most senior man in Delta Squad, so the question begged an answer.

"They'll catch up. Captain Harlow still has Charlie and Alpha patrolling the perimeter. Not sure where Bravo is."

"Right here," Staff Sergeant Kelly called out behind us. His squad followed behind him. Once again, Thompson looked relieved. Kelly had more experience than almost everyone else in First Platoon, and was next in line to be platoon sergeant. He and his squad mates were all seasoned veterans. Good men to have around in a fight.

"You with us?" Thompson asked.

"Yup," Kelly replied. "Horde's moving in fast. We need to get going."

"You heard him," Thompson called. "Double-time."

It was nearly a mile to where the Chinook's spotters directed us to intercept the incoming horde. At the top of the rise, I could see there was not just one, but three hordes coming in. One directly in front of us to the east, one descending from the north, and another closing in southward. Both the eastern and southern walls were still standing, but the north gate was a wreck. I watched the Chinook and the Apache turn in that direction to render air support.

"Okay, men," Kelly said. "Let them pack in against the wall, then we surround in standard crescent formation from behind.

5

Stay low and quiet. The last thing we want is to lure them toward us before we're ready."

The soldiers nodded, most holding their arms above their heads to catch their breath. They were in good physical condition, but running a mile in full combat gear is a strain. Kelly gave them ninety seconds to rest, and to their credit, all were fresh and ready to go when he gave the order to move out.

As they departed, I took a moment to dial my VCOG scope up to its highest magnification and look over the horde. Watching them, I got the sense something was not right. I had seen hundreds, maybe even over a thousand hordes of varying sizes over the years, and something about the way this one moved puzzled me. So I perched my rifle on my Y-stand to steady the image and slowly scanned the mass of walking dead.

And nearly had a heart attack.

"Shit, shit, shit."

In a low scramble, I scurried up to Ethan, stage whispering the whole way for him to stop. When he finally heard me, he radioed up to Kelly to halt the column and waited.

"What is it?" he asked irritably.

I handed him my rifle. "Look carefully," I said. "Pay close attention to their midsections."

He did as I asked. His brow furrowed as he looked through the scope, then a moment later he paled and pulled the rifle away.

"Holy shit." He keyed his radio. "Kelly, we got a problem. Those walkers are rigged with explosives."

A moment of silence. Thompson's earpiece was loud enough I could hear Kelly's reply. "You're shitting me."

"Afraid not. You want to call it in?"

"Yeah, I got it."

While we waited, I said, "Those bombs must be on remote detonators. No way a timer would work; the infected's movements are too unpredictable."

"Yeah, I figured that."

"So what are we going to do about it?"

Thompson looked at me sternly. "Wait for orders."

I hissed in frustration and sat down, checked my rifle for the fifth or sixth time, made sure my grenades were securely in their pouches, and verified all my P-mags were in the proper position for combat reloads. Same for my pistol. All ready to go.

Just as I was about to say to hell with it and volunteer to lead the horde away, Kelly's voice sounded in Thompson's earpiece. I stood up and leaned in to listen.

"Good news and bad news. Bad news, all three hordes are rigged. Looks like every ninth or tenth walker has dynamite or something strapped to it. Probably on remote detonators. If they reach those walls, they're coming down."

"Perfect," Thompson replied. "What's the good news?"

"Howitzer en route to our position. Bradleys and Abrams deploying north and south respectively."

"Any chance the Chinook can air drop some mortars?"

"No time. Right now, we're to flank the horde, whittle their numbers, and try to lead them away from the wall. Have all designated marksmen concentrate fire on the Rot rigged with bombs and have SAW gunners aim for the legs. And tell your grenadier not to be shy with the ordnance. We want to disable as many of these things as possible. We can always pick off the survivors later."

"What about the detonators? There have to be spotters watching from somewhere."

"Recon team and the Chinook are searching for them. They have to be somewhere close. There's no cell connectivity around here, so they're probably using a portable RF transmitter

7

to send the detonation signal. But right now, that's not our concern. Our concern is diverting that horde and killing as many as we can."

"Roger."

Thompson turned and explained the orders to Delta Squad. After a brief conference among fire teams, we followed Kelly's squad in the direction of the horde. On the way, Cole said, "Ghouls rigged with IEDs, man. What will these assholes think up next?"

TWO

We fanned out at ten-yard intervals, steadied our rifles on standard-issue telescoping Y-poles, and waited. That was the hard part. The waiting. Standing still and staying relaxed while a mass of mangled, white-eyed monstrosities bore down with no greater desire than to peel me from the bone. No matter how many times I did it, it was still unnerving.

The horde was relatively small, maybe three-hundred strong. Which made sense considering ghoul wrangling is extremely dangerous, not to mention strenuous. Wranglers have to travel light, which means very little food, water, and minimal weapons and ammo. Mostly they survive on what they can hunt or scavenge along the way. Casualty rates among them are roughly equivalent to a pre-Outbreak nursing home. I could only imagine the amount of effort that had gone into capturing thirty or forty of the things, rigging them with explosives, blending them in with a few hundred of their undead brethren, and leading them hundreds of miles across open terrain to Hollow Rock. And that was just the horde in front of us.

All of which, when taken in context with the suicide troops and sacrificed artillery, told me something as important as it was disturbing. Someone wanted to destroy Hollow Rock, and they wanted it very, very badly.

"Riordan, you ready?" Ethan called to me.

"Yep." I leaned over my rifle.

"What range do you have?"

Using the reticles on my scope and a few mental calculations, I said, "About eighty yards, give or take."

Thompson said, "Riordan and Fuller *only*, fire at will. The rest of you wait until they're at a forty yard standoff, then start piling them up. That includes you, Cole."

"Man, shit."

I spared a glance at the giant. At six foot four and roughly two-hundred-seventy pounds, Isaac Cole handled his heavy SAW machine gun as though it weighed no more than a twig. It was unusual for a sergeant to be a SAW gunner, a task usually assigned to a junior man, but Cole had refused to give up his beloved weapon. Thus far, no one seemed inclined to argue.

Beside me, Private Fuller's M-203 made its characteristic *phump,* a small dark shape hurtled into the midst of the infected, horde. The explosion destroyed a few infected, disabled a few more, and knocked roughly a dozen to the ground. The rest shambled on heedlessly, open mouths belting out high, keening wails of animal hunger. Bloody, ragged hands reached in our direction while ruined legs trudged tirelessly through the tall grass. Most of the ghouls were older, their clothes long since fallen away. Some of them had undergone the change that reduces a walker's skin to a scaly crust that eventually flakes off exposing dark gray muscle tissue beneath. I could also see shriveled internal organs where the muscle had been eaten away, indicating how the infected had died.

The old ones were the hardest to look at. The more recently dead still resembled humans, but the old ones looked like something else entirely. Only their shape and vaguely human-like faces stood as testimony to the people they had once been. I had heard rumors the older infected were capable of healing, that their teeth were harder and less likely to break, and that their bones were stronger and denser than the newly dead. Whether or not this was true, I had no idea. All I knew was my sword and my guns killed them. That was enough for me.

"Hey Riordan, you gonna get busy or what?"

I looked over at Fuller. He had loaded another grenade and was angling for a follow-up shot.

"Right, sorry."

The first infected I lined up on was an old one. Tall, broad, must have been a big man in life. In death, he looked like something out of a lunatic's nightmare. Around his waist, secured by nylon webbing and thick strips of Velcro, was what appeared to be a not insubstantial amount of dynamite. I could see the wiring and duct tape holding the works together, as well as a box in the upper right corner of the vest. Someone had spray-painted the box black, ostensibly to conceal it. I assumed the box was the receiver for the detonation signal, so just for giggles, I shot it.

The vest blew up.

The explosion was huge. The shock of it hit me like an invisible hand, blowing dirt and grass into my face. The force of the detonation caused everyone on the firing line to cover their eyes and take a step back. Ahead, the TNT had taken out not only the ghoul wearing the vest, but more than a dozen others in close proximity.

"Mary, mother of God," I muttered. Turning, I shouted to Ethan. He rushed over and gripped my shoulder.

"What the hell was that, Eric? What did you do?"

I explained about shooting the black box on the infected's vest. Ethan's quick mind found another gear. He turned away from me and began speaking rapidly and concisely into his radio. Moments later, he turned to his squad.

"Everyone back off another twenty yards and maintain that distance. Kill as many infected as you can, but if you see one wearing a vest, aim for the little black box in the upper right corner. Fuller, Cole, go to work. Riordan, keep doing what you're doing."

Understanding spread rapidly. These men had seen more action than most other soldiers in history and did not need to be told twice. Kelly's squad followed the same maneuvering. His

11

designated marksman, a specialist named Thorne, sighted through his sniper carbine and hit the detonator box on another walker. The results were the same. We were still on the retreat and had to cover our heads against a hail of dead tissue and dirt clods.

"Goddammit, Kelly," Ethan shouted into his radio. "Did you not hear the part about falling back twenty yards?"

When we reached a safe distance, the squad turned and opened fire. Cole's SAW rattled angrily as it cut the legs out from under the foremost rank of ghouls. Fuller loaded grenade after grenade into his launcher and sent them flying. The others aimed through their ACOGs and dropped infected as quickly as they could without overheating their rifles. I blew up six more vests with only eight shots. Not bad. The impact of the explosions was less pronounced at this distance, but the results within the swarm were equally as devastating. In less than five minutes, just as the sound of a tank engine and squealing treads came over the ridge, we had reduced the horde by half.

It occurred to me I had not seen any grenades go off in the last few seconds, so I turned to my right to look for Private Fuller. He wasn't there. I had just started to look around for him in the tall grass when something tugged hard at a pouch on my vest. I heard an all too familiar *whup,* and an instant later, a *crack* split the air.

"Shit!"

I hit the ground and found myself lying next to Private Fuller. His eyes were fixed and glassy, the face muscles slack. There was a large red hole where his Adam's apple should have been. A man shouted, "Sniper! Everybody down!" in a voice that sounded remarkably like mine, but an octave higher.

Thompson had been trying to listen to his radio above the noise. When he spun and saw Fuller, his face went blank for the barest of moments, and then he was moving. In seconds, the firing stopped, we were all lying face down in the waist-high grass, and the Howitzer had changed course to get between us and the treeline.

12

I lay with my face close to the ground, desperately wishing I had brought my ghillie suit and a more powerful weapon. With time and luck, I could work my way to the treeline and counter-snipe whoever had shot Fuller. But I did not have my ghillie suit, and my carbine fired standard NATO 5.56 millimeter rounds. So I was stuck breathing in dirt and grass like the rest of the squad and hoping like hell the Howitzer could dismantle the horde and scare off the sniper so I could get away without any unwanted perforations in my precious, irreplaceable hide.

It also occurred to me that with all the body armor in my personal arsenal and in my business inventory, there was no excuse not to wear it. Sure, it slowed me down and made me sweat like a glass of ice water on a summer day, but the discomfort beat the alternative.

My thoughts of weapons and armor ceased as the roar of the Howitzer echoed to the far reaches of the vast field. I wanted to look up to see what kind of damage it had done, but did not dare. If I were in the sniper's position and saw some idiot raise his head, I would smile an evil smile and mutter something nasty while I squeezed the trigger.

A few seconds passed and the Howitzer thundered again. And again. Thompson crawled over to me, spared a glance at Fuller, and asked, "Any idea where the shot came from?"

I looked closely at Fuller's throat. "The wound is in front, dead center. Shooter probably aimed center of mass, but the round went high. That tells me he's above us and directly ahead, due east. Probably in a tree somewhere."

"Any clue how far?" Thompson asked.

I stayed low as I turned Fuller's body over. The bullet hole in front was small, the one at the back larger, about the size of a golf ball. The projectile had hit the young soldier's spine at the base of his skull and scattered it into the grass behind him. He died without a peep, probably before he hit the ground. When I considered how focused the squad had been on the horde at the time, myself included, I understood why no one noticed him fall.

A few months ago, while working for me on a salvage run, Fuller had taken a shot to the ribcage. We shared a two-person room at the Hollow Rock Emergency Clinic while I recovered from a gunshot wound of my own. During that time, stuck in a room together with nowhere to go, I got to know the young man.

He was intelligent, witty, and had an unusual sense of humor. He told me about his parents, his sister, how they died during the Outbreak. How he had survived afterward by scavenging weapons from dead cops and soldiers, pilfering food from abandoned houses, and sleeping on rooftops. He once shot a goose with a crossbow and ate it raw because he was starving and being pursued by a cult of cannibals and could not risk making a fire. A few days later, he saw an Army convoy go by and approached them. The soldiers disarmed him, fed him, and then took him to meet the officer in charge. He took the Oath of Enlistment on the spot, and a month later, he was in basic training.

And now here he was, at the age of twenty-three, laid out dead in an empty field in Western Tennessee. It was a familiar story.

Fuller, like so many others, had endured hardship that would have been unimaginable before the Outbreak. He had found reserves of strength and courage he probably had not known he possessed. He had fought like a mad animal to stay alive, and succeeded. And despite the odds, despite the bitter struggle his life had become, despite the darkness all around him, he had tried to make a difference in this shattered, crumbling excuse for a world. He had fought to preserve what was left of a once-great civilization and give his fellow survivors a shot at some kind of a future, no matter how bleak. But for all his courage, for all his endurance, for all he had strived to do, his story was at an end. Throat torn out by a sniper's bullet. Blank eyes staring lifelessly at a blue expanse of impartial sky.

"Thirty caliber projectile," I said, wiping a hand across my face. "And damned powerful. Probably not a seven-six-two by

14

fifty-four like most of these Alliance and ROC assholes use. It would have hit lower and done more damage."

"How does that help us?" Thompson asked.

"The shot was almost perfectly centered. Meaning centerline of the body, where all the vital organs are. That sniper out there is good, knows his business. Probably accustomed to firing Dragunovs, or whatever the hell they use. But now he's using something unfamiliar, something more powerful than what he's used to. That's why the round hit high; he expected more drop from the projectile. If it was a seven-six-two by fifty-four, it would have hit Fuller in the chest and made a much bigger exit wound because of the slower speed of the bullet. More kinetic energy would have transferred into the body cavity. But it went straight through at very high speed and didn't take much tissue with it. Which meant it had enough power to tear through flesh and bone without slowing down very much." I paused a few seconds, thinking. Thompson stared at me impatiently.

"Well?"

"I'm thinking the sniper is using a .300 Winchester magnum. I'd say he's between five to six hundred yards away, judging by the wound and the distance to the treeline, and straight across the field from us."

Thompson responded by keying his radio and relaying what I told him. Moments later, the long barrel of the Howitzer repositioned and began firing again. After four rounds, I risked a glance upward. The big gun pointed at a high angle, laying down a rain of high-explosive fragmentation rounds over a wide area at the range and bearing I had specified. The tall, old-growth trees in the distance splintered and shattered under the barrage, thick limbs crashing to the forest floor. If the sniper had taken position where I suspected, he was having a very bad day. The thought put a smile on my face.

"Eric, I need you to do something for me."

I looked at Thompson. "What?"

15

"Use the Howitzer for cover and take a look at the horde through your scope. I need to give Captain Harlow a sitrep."

The smile died. "Can't the guys in the tank do that?"

"Not without exposing themselves. You'll make a smaller target in the grass. Like I told you, use the tank for cover."

When I hesitated, Thompson reached out a hand. "Give me your rifle and I'll do it."

"No. I got it."

I hugged the ground as I snaked my way toward the tank, once again wishing like hell I had brought my ghillie suit. My clothes and gear were a light desert tan, which matched the color of the grass. So at least I had that going for me.

A minute or two later, I stood up behind one of the Howitzer's treads and, just for kicks, rapped my knuckles against the outer surface of the crew compartment. Or whatever it's called. I may as well have knocked on a mountain. I had expected a hollow ringing, like hitting the side of an oil drum, but only got a dull thunk. I doubted the men inside could hear.

I should have asked Ethan if he radioed the crew. Now would be a really bad time for the driver to put this thing in reverse.

I waited half a minute with my hands pressed tight against my ears. If the gun went off with me this close, the best I could hope for was the mother of all migraines. There was also the recoil to consider. The crew had not bothered to put down the Howitzer's spades, so if they fired, I was going for a ride. And not the fun kind.

Another minute went by. No boom. I knew Ethan was not stupid, but one can never be too careful. After taking a deep breath and letting it out slowly, I stood and balanced my rifle atop the tread. The scope magnified the pine stands a few hundred yards distant, bent and twisted trunks and limbs still falling against one another. I did not see the sniper, but that did not mean he was not still out there. If he had half a brain, when the first artillery shell went off, assuming it did not kill him, he

16

would have scrambled for cover. Then again, the frag rounds had shredded the better part of an acre of forest and sent lethal shrapnel over a much larger area. If the sniper had been anywhere in the vicinity, he was hamburger.

I searched some more and waited. I still did not see the sniper. No shots came my way. At the very least, we had forced him to keep his head down. Hopefully he would stay that way. Shifting position, I turned my attention to the horde. The big gun had eliminated all but maybe thirty or forty undead, only one of them rigged. They seemed disoriented, walking in wide, unsteady circles. I wondered if the concussion from the blasts had thrown off their equilibrium. The undead hunt primarily by sound, so maybe the gun had blown out their eardrums. An interesting theory. I lined up a shot at the last ghoul rigged with a bomb and detonated its vest. Its limbs were still pinwheeling through the air when I hit my belly and started crawling back to Delta's position.

"Horde is toast," I told Ethan. "Only a few dozen left, none of them rigged."

"Good. Thanks, Eric."

"Anytime."

He got on the radio and gave a sitrep, then told us we were to head south to meet the other half of First Platoon en route via Chinook.

"Expect the southern horde to be rigged as well," Sergeant Kelly said. "Riordan, try to detonate as many vests as you can. Everybody stay behind the Howitzer on the way down there. Never know if there might be another sniper. Let's move."

The mobile artillery piece pivoted in place and turned toward the south wall at the speed of a slow run. As we followed it, I said to Thompson, "What about Fuller?"

The lines of his face were tight and sharp. "We'll come back for him."

17

I spared a glance at the fallen soldier. He lay where we had left him, no breathing, no nervous twitches, no movement at all. The total stillness of death.

Rest easy, amigo. Your fight is over.

THREE

Half an hour later, the southern horde was a scattering of dead bodies in a field.

The Apache, Second Platoon, the Ninth TVM, and a contingent of town guardsmen had eradicated the horde pouring in from the north. But it was only a temporary reprieve. The battle had been loud, and every walker within ten miles was undoubtedly on its way to Hollow Rock.

While First Platoon trudged behind the Howitzer toward the north gate, I said a quick goodbye to Thompson and set off at a run for the southern wall. Once there, I hollered until a guardsman noticed me, recognized me, and lowered a rope ladder. Climbing over the wall was not the safest way to get into town, but it was the fastest. And it put me on the ground a few hundred yards from my house.

The streets on my side of town were lined with houses and trailers in roughly equal proportion. Looking around, it did not appear as if any of the artillery shells had landed nearby. All the smoke and shouting came from the north, closer to the gate.

I surmised the north gate had been the suicide troops' primary target, the buildings behind merely collateral damage. And it was a lot of collateral. The north gate was the entrance for trade caravans. Consequently, new buildings had popped up close to it to serve the needs of visitors and traders. There was a livery, three outfitters, food stands that served grilled meat and roasted vegetables, a clothing exchange, public latrines and showers, a feed and tack shop, a guardhouse, and more than a dozen trading stalls. Gabriel and I owned two of them. One for general goods, and one for weapons and ammunition. They were not manned today, being that no caravans had been spotted heading toward Hollow rock for the last week and a half. But there was a strong possibility both my stalls, and the inventory inside several metal lockboxes, had been destroyed. I did not care. The only thing that mattered was finding Allison.

My boots crunched in the gravel driveway as I sprinted to the door. I tried the handle and found it locked. For a moment, I debated unlocking the door and going inside, but decided against it. Allison was not home. If she had been when the fighting started, she would have left by now. She was not the town's only medical doctor anymore, thanks to the Phoenix Initiative, but I knew she would not stand idle when people were hurt and dying.

Next to the house Allison and I share is the place her grandmother lived until her death a few years before the Outbreak. Gabriel lives there now. He has made a number of improvements to the property, including a half-acre corral and a small barn where he keeps his horse. I jogged into his back yard and entered the barn through the open front entrance.

The barn smelled of hay, grain, piss, shit, and sweaty horse. Red was in his stall, head up, prancing and whinnying, spooked by the explosions. I walked over to the five-foot wall that contained him and spoke soothingly.

"Easy now, big fella. Easy now ..."

I put my hand under his nose and scratched and rubbed his neck just below the ear. He calmed quickly. Red was an agreeable horse most of the time, but tended to bolt when startled. Fortunately for Gabe, Red did not startle easily. I grabbed a lead rope and clipped it to one of the rings in Red's halter, opened the door to his stall, and led him to the dirt-floored tack room. A western saddle hung over a sawhorse in the corner, along with blankets and reins. I laid a blanket over the horse's back, saddled him, and connected a bit and reins to his halter. He accepted the bit without complaint.

"Come on, big guy," I said as I swung into the saddle. "Let's see what you can do."

Red walked slowly out of the barn and paused a few seconds to sniff the air. I had ridden him enough times to know he was not one to be rushed. Impatience nagged at me as I gently kicked his haunches, urging him forward. He walked, then began to trot. I kicked harder and he picked up to a light gallop. I kicked with more insistence. When Red finally realized my hands were loose on the reins, he opened his stride and gained speed. I kept urging him on until we were flying over the grass bordering Seminary Street toward the north side of town. Red might have been slow to get started, but once he got going, he could really move.

The smoke grew thicker as I rode closer to the gate, orange tongues of fire lapping angrily in the near distance. My eyes watered and I had to put my goggles on and pull my scarf over my mouth and nose. Red did not seem bothered. I tugged the reins to slow him down as we approached the clinic.

Through the black and gray haze, I could see nurses and volunteers moving in front of the entrance. I dismounted Red, turned him toward home, and slapped him on the haunches. He took a few clattering steps, swung his big head in my direction, and gave me a mildly offended glare.

"Go on, Red. Go home."

He snorted and set off at a trot.

I jogged toward the clinic, rifle clutched, gear bouncing on my vest and belt. The smoke had been thick when I arrived, but the wind shifted direction and I could see better now. Near the gate, low wooden buildings burned furiously amidst shattered rubble. I glanced toward where my two stalls were, and sure enough, they were smoldering slag heaps. There might be something salvageable, I thought, but it would have to wait.

"Allison!" I shouted. No one answered. I yelled again. Same result. A nurse I knew named Brett Nolan walked past and I grabbed him by the arm.

21

"Brett, where's Allison?"

"Inside," he said, prying my hand from his arm. "She's busy. There are a lot of wounded."

"But she's okay?"

"She's fine."

Relief flooded through me. I had to put my head between my knees until a bout of lightheadedness passed.

"You okay?" Brett asked.

"Yeah. Just catching my breath." Feeling better, I stood up straight.

"We could use some help," Brett said.

"What do you need me to do?"

"Drop your gear in the lobby and go talk to Samantha. She's in the storage room behind the reception desk."

"Will do."

I put my rifle, vest, and web belt on the floor behind the counter and poked my head in the storage room. "Sam?"

Samantha Walcott, physician's assistant, stood up and faced me. She was in her early fifties, over six feet tall, lean, weathered, and hard as an iron chisel. "What?" she snapped.

"I'm here to help."

"Take these," she handed me a bundle of clear plastic bags. "Bandages. Give them out to the nurses, then head to the gate and help the guardsmen look for wounded."

"Where's Allison?"

"Busy." Sam turned around and began sorting through boxes again. I was dismissed.

I went back to the parking lot. More bodies came in on carts, on horseback, in the Sheriff Department's lone electric vehicle, on litters born by weary, frightened townsfolk. Some of the wounded walked themselves in, bleeding and limping and crying out in pain. A boy of no more than fifteen stumbled, fell, and was still. A nurse ran to him and checked his pulse, then rolled him over. There was a piece of shrapnel the length of a man's forearm protruding from his chest. His eyes were wide open and fixed, glassy, lifeless. The nurse closed his eyes, dragged his body into the grass, and moved on.

Nurses took the bandages from me. When my arms were empty, I ran for the north gate.

*****

Mayor Stone's paranoia was Hollow Rock's saving grace.

I remember once going to see her at town hall on some small matter of public affairs she had asked me to look into. As I entered her office, she sat facing a window, feet perch on the sill, silhouetted in warm morning light. She turned when she heard me knock and asked me to sit down.

"Something on your mind, Elizabeth?" I asked.

"There's always something on my mind."

"What's the topic of the day?"

"The wall," she said.

"What about it?"

She laced her fingers over her stomach. "Too many people in this town take it for granted. Especially on the north side of town where it's all concrete and steel. I look at the wall and I think about the Outbreak. I think about all the military hardware leftover from units that were overrun. I think about grenades, and bombs, and rocket launchers, not to mention all the materials that can be used to make improvised explosives. All just lying around waiting to be snatched up. I think about that, and I think about the Alliance, and the ROC, and all the raiders and marauders and assorted scum out there, and I think about how easy it would be to plant something ugly and volatile against the wall and watch from a good safe distance while it lit

23

up the night. I think about that, and I wonder what we would do if it ever happened."

"I've lost sleep a few nights dwelling on that subject myself."

She spun around in her chair. "Did your contemplations yield any useful insights?"

I looked down at my fingernails. "The way things are going, I don't think it's a question of *if*, Liz. It's a question of when. And how bad. You should talk to Ethan Thompson about it."

"Why Thompson?"

"He told me a war story once about a place back in North Carolina called Steel City. Went there to stop some lunatic from leading a horde around and attacking small settlements. Ask him about the layout of Steel City. Might give you some ideas."

She nodded twice, turned back to the window, and looked steadily toward the east wall while I gave her my report.

I did not get much sleep that night.

*****

By two in the afternoon on the day of the attack, everyone that could be saved had been. Forty-eight people lost their lives, including Private Fuller, a sheriff's deputy on the force less than a month, and two men from Second Platoon on duty at the main gate when the first shells hit. In less than ten minutes, a small band of ROC suicide troops had killed more than twice as many people as the Free Legion did in over a year of raids.

I was filthy, sweaty, and exhausted by the time I helped pull the last of the bodies out of the rubble and ashes. The town's sole functioning fire engine put out most of the fires, while crews with shovels and buckets kept the isolated ones contained until they burned out. To the north, the sound of gunfire tattooed the air as all of Echo Company and the Ninth Tennessee Volunteer Militia, reinforced by the Sheriff's

24

Department and a hundred town guardsmen, engaged the infected attracted by the fighting.

Mayor Stone appeared out of the dissipating smoke near the entrance to the clinic. She was speaking to Allison and one of the doctors from the Phoenix Initiative, Sudesh Khurana. Dr. Khurana was a small man in his late forties, balding, dark brown skin, rimless glasses, and sharp, intelligent eyes. His manner was brusque, but according to Allison, he was a highly skilled and eminently competent surgeon. An education at Johns Hopkins had that effect on people, evidently.

Allison spotted me on my way over, stopped talking mid-sentence, and ran into my arms. The mayor looked on with kind impatience.

"You're all right," she said.

I had to clear my throat before I could speak. "Yeah. I am."

Her arms tightened and we stood that way for a few seconds, holding each other. I kissed the top of her head and then her lips and tried very hard to breathe against the constriction in my chest. I let her go and held her at arm's length.

"How are you holding up?"

"I'd say I've seen worse, but that would be a lie."

"And the baby?"

A small smile. "The baby is fine, Eric. I'm only five months pregnant. It'll be a while before it's big enough to cause trouble."

I looked down at the slight bulge in her trim stomach. Anyone not as familiar with her body as I was would not have noticed it. But I did. I stared at it often, and covered it with my hand when we slept at night, and wondered with a mix of fear and anticipation what the little person growing in there would be like when they came out. Would we have a boy or a girl? Would he or she look like me, or Allison? Either way, I hoped the baby had blue eyes. I have always liked having blue eyes.

"Doctor Laroux," Sudesh Khurana said. "We have patients."

25

Allison nodded and stepped away. "I don't know when I'll be home," she said.

"Me either. I'm going to go help out with the infected. Could be a long fight."

"Be careful."

"Always. Mayor, I assume you've set that contingency plan we discussed into motion?"

"Deputy Glover is coordinating as we speak," Elizabeth Stone said. "But the forklifts and propane are in storage on the other side of town. When you reach the lines, tell Captain Harlow we need twenty minutes to get the containers in place and probably another half hour to fill them with ballast."

"I'll let him know."

"Thank you. I'll send a rider when the breach is secured."

"I'll let him know that too."

Allison's cheek was covered in soot, but I kissed it anyway. Then I retrieved my rifle and gear and made my way toward the sounds of combat.

FOUR

Gabriel, Captain Harlow, and a radioman I did not know stood atop the command vehicle. Gabe and the captain peered through binoculars at the battlefield. Gabe made suggestions, which Harlow passed to his radioman, who passed them on to platoon COs and squad leaders. I announced my presence by joining them on the roof of the Humvee.

"Something I can do for you, Mr. Riordan?" Harlow asked without lowering his binoculars.

"Message from the mayor," I said. "Repair crews need about fifty minutes to move the shipping containers into place at the north gate and fill them with ballast. Think you can buy them that much time?"

"I hope so," he replied, still not looking at me. "Depends on how many more infected show up."

"I heard about Fuller," Gabe said, turning to face me. "He was a good kid."

"Yes, he was."

"Is Allison all right?"

"Yes. She's at the clinic right now."

Gabe wiped the back of his neck. "Good to hear. How many casualties do you think?"

"Forty-eight, I believe."

"Jesus. Including Fuller?"

27

"Yeah. Two other troops from Second Platoon as well."

Harlow finally lowered the binoculars. "Are you sure of that?"

"I was the one who found the bodies."

His face fell and he cursed softly. The radioman said, "Should I notify Lieutenant Chapman, sir?"

"No, Private. I'll do it myself, later. For now, I want Chapman focused on fighting the infected."

"Yes sir."

I said to Harlow, "You have a plan, or are we playing by ear?"

"Oh sure, I have a plan," he said. "You see those infected out there? I'm going to have my men shoot every one they see. Infantry will hold the middle ground while tanks and Bradleys cover their flanks. The Apache is grounded for now, so the Chinook's going to fly back and forth making ammo drops and searching for hordes. When the crews in town get the gate patched up, we'll retreat to Fort McCray and regroup. And come up with a better plan."

I tried to think of something to add, but under the circumstances, there was not much else to be done. So I said, "What can I do to help?"

"I need marksmen on the line. Recon team is still out in the woods."

"Sure. Where's First Platoon?"

"Not with them. Over there." Harlow pointed to a bucket lift being offloaded from a HEMTT.

I said, "Are we sure there aren't any more snipers within striking distance?"

"No."

"Great. Sounds like fun. What about you, Gabe? You staying here?"

"For now," Gabe said. "Probably be in a bucket on the other flank pretty soon."

"At least I won't be the only one with my ass dangling in the wind."

I climbed down from the Humvee and went toward the bucket lift. I did not run. My legs were too tired from dragging dead bodies and carrying wounded toward the clinic. Besides, it was not as if the infected would be leaving any time soon.

*****

The repair crews bulldozed the broken concrete and twisted reinforcement bar from the north gate, moved shipping containers into place with forklifts, and poured dirt into them through holes pre-cut through the top for the purpose. The dirt came from piles placed near the gate months ago. Two long human chains passed buckets from the piles to the gate and back again. The whole operation took forty-four minutes, six minutes faster than projected.

When Harlow ordered the retreat, I was on the ground taking a bandolier of loaded thirty-round magazines from a runner. The projectiles from all but a small amount of my personal loadout currently resided in the skulls of permanently dead ghouls. My rifle's barrel was hot enough to give me a third-degree burn, my stomach grumbled angrily, and if I did not piss soon, I was going to need a new pair of pants.

As I was stuffing mags into my vest pouches, the crackling of gunfire ceased. Squad leaders shouted instructions to their men, one of them close enough for me to understand.

"The gate is secure," he said. "We're to fall back to Fort McCray, double-time."

"Aren't there ghouls between here and there?" one of his men asked.

29

"Yes. Armored cavalry is going ahead to clear the way. Don't engage a revenant unless you have to. Just outrun 'em. Everybody clear?"

I held the bandolier out to the runner. "Guess I won't be needing this."

He pushed it back in my direction. "Keep it. You never know."

"True enough. Thanks."

I fell in with the nearest squad and ran with them back to Fort McCray. They gave me a few looks, but said nothing. I was well known in Echo Company: Eric Riordan, the civilian with no prior military service who infiltrated a rogue militant group calling themselves the Free Legion. Even the vaunted Green Berets had trouble tracking them down. He was held prisoner and beaten daily for months, I sometimes heard them say. When I did, I corrected them that it was not nearly that long. He worked in the dark digging tunnels and starving, they said. That part was mostly true. He entered a tournament where men were forced to fight to the death. He won, they said, and that was how he earned the Legion's trust. It was not to the death, I told them. Although in truth, I did accidentally kill a man. And I never actually earned the Legion's trust, they were always suspicious of me. I just managed to play the charade long enough for Gabriel Garrett to find me and get me away from them. Without him, none of what followed would have been possible.

No one outside of Delta Squad quite knew what to make of me. He must be CIA, or what's left of it, they said. Some kind of spook, anyway. Or maybe he is part of the Phoenix Initiative—they must have a militant wing. People trained to deal with the kinds of unconventional threats that arise in a post-apocalyptic world. I tried to dispel these rumors, but soldiers like to talk, and nothing spreads slower than the truth. The man they described was actually a lot more like Gabriel than me, but good luck convincing anyone of that.

The truth is Gabriel taught me everything I know. I learned a little hand-to-hand stuff on my own, but it was Gabe who showed me how to really make myself dangerous. To turn my body into a weapon. To shoot, to use a blade, to make and disarm explosives. He taught me combat tactics, close quarters fighting, how to employ a variety of weapons, and, most importantly, the art of the sniper. I was well renowned among Echo Company for my marksmanship. They may not have fully trusted me, but they had no qualms about letting me help them out of bad situations. If I showed up at the enlisted club on base, I could always count on someone buying my first drink. Usually someone whose life I had saved at one point or another.

But outside a small circle of close friends, the soldiers did not consider me as one of their own. I was an interloper, a sometimes useful outsider who had a tendency to show up when needed and then go away. Mostly, they knew me for my business interests. G&R Transport and Salvage was one of the most successful ventures in Tennessee. Or anywhere, for that matter. Almost every soldier in Echo Company had an account with us. I ran the company's operations, for the most part, while my best friend and business partner, Gabriel, supervised the Hollow Rock General Store, the customer-facing part of G&R.

Retail was only part of our business. Most of our money—or trade, as it had come to be known when money disappeared— came from wholesale and business-to-business transactions. And the military, specifically Echo Company, was our biggest customer. As a result, I was privy to knowledge of secret operations most civilians never knew about. And because of my martial skills, I participated in some of these missions on a contract basis.

It was illegal for soldiers to scavenge for salvage—not that this rule stopped them—but the prohibition against scavenging did not extend to informing civilian salvage companies as to the location of trade goods spotted in the field. Nor did it prohibit salvagers from buying fuel from the military at discount prices, reserving municipal transport vehicles, and bartering found goods to the Army. If a soldier's information turned out to be significantly profitable, there were no rules against paying them a finder's fee. And even when I traded what I found at a steep bargain compared to value, it was still profitable because the salvage business has very low overhead. A good arrangement all around.

As I thought of this, running on weary legs, the tall brown grass gave way to a gravel path leading from Hollow Rock to the main gate at Fort McCray. I trotted along, keeping pace with the soldiers ahead of me, boots crunching over half-buried rocks. Near a grove of trees, a small ghoul emerged from the treeline and moved quickly toward me.

A little one, I had time to think, and then it was nearly on me. I stopped and aimed a steel-toed boot at its chest. The kick sent it rolling backward, but it was on its feet in a flash. Without thought, my rifle came up, canted so I could look through the iron sights mounted forty-five degrees from my scope, and fired twice. The dead kid had enough speed that when it fell, it skidded several feet over the rocks. I kicked it over. No older than five when it died the first time. The little ones are much faster than the adults, and much harder to look at. I dragged it by its feet away from the path and wished I had a blanket or something to drape over it.

Even after over three years of killing revenants, some things just never got any easier.

I killed two others along the way. One was an older Hispanic woman, recently dead, most of her left arm and the left side of her face eaten away. When she opened her mouth to howl at me, I saw she had no teeth. I shot her in the head anyway. Even toothless, the infected are still dangerous. The last ghoul I killed was a gray, one of the long-dead with no skin. My first shot grooved a furrow around its skull and exited without causing significant brain damage. A rare occurrence, but not unheard of. I let the ghoul come closer and fired twice more at point blank range. This time, it went down.

Finally, I reached the gate to Fort McCray. The soldiers ahead of me kept going, headed for their revenant-proof barracks. Overhead, on the catwalk, I heard gunfire rattling.

32

Sharpshooters were keeping the undead away from the gate, allowing their brothers in arms to get through safely. I heaved my way up a set of stairs and asked the officer in charge where he needed me. He glanced at my rifle and the bandolier of magazines across my chest, recognized me, and said to take position on the left flank near the eastern guard tower.

Once settled, I went to work. There is a rhythm to the letting out of breath, steadying of the rifle, gentle squeeze of the trigger until the crack and the recoil and waiting to see if the target goes down. It has a hypnotic quality. Looking through the scope creates a feeling of separation, of detachment. I am here, but I am not here. The me who thinks, loves, laughs, and worries is somewhere else. Somewhere quiet. What remains is a creature of function, of necessity.

These are not people in my sights. They are things. They hunger, are dangerous, and have to be put down. One cannot scare them. Cannot intimidate them. Their morale cannot be damaged because it does not exist. They do not have to be fed, bred, or led like living people do. They recruit from their victims. They hunt because it is all they know how to do. And they will never, ever stop. They are legion. They destroyed the world. The fact that I, or anyone else, have lasted so long against them is nothing short of miraculous.

I did not hear the call to cease fire. A hand swatted me firmly on the shoulder, breaking me from my trance.

"Hey, dickhead, cease fire!" It was the officer in charge. His nametag read Ramirez. His eyes were dark and angry.

"Sorry." I flipped the selector switch to safe, stood up, and nearly sat right back down from dizziness. Ramirez gripped my arm to steady me.

"You all right? You hurt?"

"No, just tired. Been a long morning."

The dark eyes narrowed. "You bit?"

"No."

"You sure?"

"I think I would have noticed."

Ramirez called two of his men over and had them watch me while he checked me for bites. He started with my hands and forearms, and then looked at my lower legs. Not finding anything, he searched the rest of me. His men looked on silently, hands loose on their carbines. They did not point their weapons at me, but could have very quickly if they had wanted to. I gave them no reason to do so.

"He's clean," Ramirez said. The soldiers relaxed and began walking away.

"Can I go now?"

"Yeah. Sorry 'bout that. Can't be too careful these days."

"No harm done. See you around, Lieutenant."

Before I started down the stairs, Ramirez called out, "Hey, Riordan's the name, right?"

"Last I checked."

"That was good shooting. I heard you were a sniper, but I didn't believe it."

"And now?"

"You got the goods, that's for sure. Thanks for the help."

I made my way slowly back to ground level. The rail was made of galvanized steel and held my weight without complaint as I leaned heavily on it. At the bottom, I stood and stared at the bustling, agitated men going about the small forward operating base. I needed to use the latrine badly, and after that, I would figure out what to do next.

FIVE

I spotted Caleb Hicks and Derrick Holland on the way to the headquarters building. They heard me call out to them and waited as I approached.

"What did you find?" I asked.

"Bunch of dead ROC troops," Holland answered. "Looks like they realized we had 'em surrounded and took pills. I'm guessing cyanide."

"Take any prisoners?"

They both shook their heads. "We found the sniper that took out Fuller, I think," Hicks said.

"Dead?"

"In several pieces. Infected got ahold of him. What was left was tore up pretty bad. But we found his rifle. Three-hundred Win-mag, just like you said."

"Is that it?" I pointed to a barrel protruding above Hicks' right shoulder.

"Yep," he said. "Not sure what to do with it. I know it was used to kill a friend of mine, but it seemed wasteful to leave it. I don't think Fuller would mind."

"No, he wouldn't. Especially if you use it to take out some ROC types."

Hicks nodded in silence, eyes looking past me.

I said, "Seen Gabe around?"

"He's at headquarters. Heard it over radio chatter."

"I need to talk to him. Catch up with you two later."

The headquarters building looked like all the other buildings at Fort McCray. Cinder blocks painted a hideous dull brown, no windows on the ground floor, reinforced steel door that only opened outward and could be secured with heavy bars from the inside, narrow windows on the second floor, and a three-foot cement battlement surrounding the roof. I saw several soldiers with field glasses patrolling above me, eyes scanning the inner part of the base for any sign of infected. Their carbines had heavy barrels and were chambered in hard-hitting 7.62 NATO. The Nightforce scopes were not merely for show, nor were the spare magazines on the troops' MOLLE vests.

One of them peered at me through his field glasses and said something into his radio. When I reached the door and knocked, a sergeant with a Mossberg shotgun and a pistol on his chest opened a small panel and asked me to identify myself.

"Name's Eric Riordan. Same as last time, Wally."

"Sorry. Protocol."

"Sure."

Wally opened the door. His name was Wallace, but he went by Wally. He did not look like a Wally. Well over six feet tall, black hair shaved down to a nub, steely black eyes over a nose that had been broken at least three times. When he smiled, there were a few teeth missing. His voice spoke of New England origins—Massachusetts, if I had to guess. His hands were large and brutal looking and the knuckles were covered in scars. There was scar tissue in his eyebrows and forehead, and his ears had the cauliflower swelling of a prizefighter.

I had asked him once, months ago, while waiting to see Captain Harlow, what he did for a living before the Outbreak. He smiled his gap-toothed smile and said, "A little of this, a little of that."

His manner had been pleasant, but the smile did not reach his eyes. I did not ask again.

36

"Captain's expecting you," Wally said. "You know the way."

"Sure, thanks. Always a pleasure, Wally."

He sat down in a chair facing the door and said nothing. I went up the stairs and around the corner. The lower part of the building was mostly dark, but there were a few lights on upstairs. I did not hear the low drone of the generator at the far end of the building, meaning Captain Harlow must have switched over to the solar panels. I nodded to his secretary, went down the hall to his door, and knocked three times.

"Yes, come in."

I entered. Gabriel and Lieutenant Jonas sat in armless metal chairs facing Captain Harlow's desk. There was one chair left, so I took it.

"Captain," I said, and then nodded to Jonas and Gabe.

"We're short on time," Harlow said, "so I'll get straight to it. I just got off the horn with Central. Our orders have changed. All of Echo Company and the Ninth TVM are to remain on station to guard Hollow Rock while the townspeople make repairs to the gate. We also have about two thousand infected to dispose of, wounded to provide for, and dead enemy troops to examine. Sheriff Elliot and a few of my men are investigating what happened today. I doubt they'll learn much."

"Agreed," Gabe said. "It was a well-planned attack."

Harlow looked at him. "Any other observations, Mr. Garrett?"

"If I had to guess, I would say the enemy troops were North Korean Special Forces. They carried the same weapons and gear we keep seeing on insurgents and marauders from the Alliance. They didn't hesitate to commit suicide when faced with overwhelming odds. The troops manning the artillery knew they were going to die. They had to have known about the armored cavalry and helicopters, but they carried out their mission anyway. You don't see that level of brainwashed loyalty in most militaries."

37

"Not to mention the hordes and the artillery," I added. "And the fact that they got so close without a patrol spotting them. Doesn't exactly give me a warm fuzzy feeling."

Jonas said, "Which leads us to a few obvious questions."

"First," Harlow said, holding up a finger, "did they plan to attack the same day we deployed, or was it just coincidence?"

"Couple of possibilities there," I said. "One, they planned it that way. Which means they knew when we were leaving. Which means somebody, somewhere along the line, is passing classified information along to our enemies."

"Or," Jonas cut in, "as Captain Harlow suggested, it was coincidence."

"I don't buy that," I said. "We know those troops were KPA, so-"

"We don't know that for certain," Harlow interrupted.

"Who else could it be?"

No one said anything. I went on. "If they're KPA, that means they had to come all the way out here from the west coast. That would have taken weeks, if not months. Anyone want to spot the hole in that logic?"

"We just got orders to move a few days ago," Harlow said. "This operation has not officially been in the works for very long. A week at the most. And that's at the command level."

"They could have flown out," Gabe said. "We know they have aircraft."

"But do they have fuel that is still usable?" Harlow said. "It's been three years since the Outbreak, so unless they have access to refining facilities and strategic oil supplies, any fuel they brought over from Asia would have gone inert by now."

"I don't know," I said. "Properly stored and treated, fuel can last up to a decade."

"That's true," Harlow said. "So we acknowledge it as a possibility, but an unlikely one. Radar and satellite coverage is still pretty good. It would have been damned difficult for KPA forces to fly an aircraft big enough to haul those cannons without being detected, even if they split them among several aircraft."

"But not impossible," Gabe said.

I stood up and went to the window. Outside, the sun was high above the horizon. Warmth radiated from the wire-reinforced glass, telling me it was going to be an unseasonably warm day.

"It's a moot point anyway," I said. "Even if they flew the men and artillery out, that doesn't explain how they managed to capture over a hundred infected and rig them with explosives, round up nine hundred more, and then march them all the way here from Alliance territory. Even working around the clock it must have taken them at least a week."

"They could have rigged them in advance," Gabe said. "Hid them somewhere within a couple days' march."

"That sounds more like the Alliance's way of doing things," Jonas said. "And we know the KPA, or ROC, or whatever the hell they call themselves have been in-country for well over a year. Plenty of time to move men and equipment to Alliance territory. Could have been staging an attack for months, just waiting for the right opportunity."

I considered the possibility. It fit. It fit very well. So the KPA had a presence in Alliance territory. So they rigged the infected and staged them somewhere close. The Hollow Rock patrols only covered a five-mile radius around town, and they could not be everywhere at once. Say the suicide troops were twenty miles away with the artillery. Say the infected were corralled somewhere close by. How long would it take them to move into position? The cannons, when they attacked, were two miles away as the crow flies. I turned to Gabe.

"What kind of guns were they?" I asked.

"The artillery?" Gabe said. I nodded.

"Heavy mortars. Sani 120s."

39

"As in a hundred-twenty millimeter shells?"

"Yes."

"What kind of range are we talking?"

"Effective out to four and a half miles."

I whistled. Two miles was well within range. "How heavy are they?"

Gabe scratched his three-day growth of beard. "Five hundred pounds, give or take. Not to mention the ammo."

I thought back to the artillery emplacement. "The guns were on wheels, and I think I saw a couple of boxy metal things on wheels as well. Probably for ammo. Could they have rolled all that in from, say, twenty miles out?"

"Very possible," Gabe said. "It would have been a hell of a lot of work, but it could be done."

"Did the recon team spot any animal tracks?" Jonas asked. "Horses, oxen, that kind of thing?"

Harlow shook his head. "No. I thought of that and had that tracker of yours look around. Hicks, I think his name is. Didn't find anything but human prints."

"So they wheeled the mortars and shells in on foot," I said. "How many rounds did they fire at the wall? Do we know?"

Gabe closed his eyes and did his memory trick. If he concentrated, he could remember anything he saw. A useful talent. "Eighteen," he said after a few seconds. "Six per gun."

"Any shells left over?"

"We found four," Harlow said. "But more could have been destroyed by the Hellfire."

I looked at Gabe. He nodded. "Makes sense. Three guns, maybe thirty shells. Have them on standby no more than twenty miles away. Same with the infected. Plenty of places to hide hordes out there. Spread 'em out over a few miles in small clusters. The order comes down maybe a day or two ago, and they move into position."

40

"Which brings us back to the question of timing," I said. "Riddle me this: why attack Hollow Rock? Why not attack the convoy directly? Or Fort McCray? Wouldn't they be higher value targets?"

No one said anything. Outside, birds called to one another over the noise of men running and shouting. A bee hovered briefly in front of the window, then flew away. Gabe looked at his knees and tapped a finger against the side of his jaw.

"I see where you're going with this."

"Well I don't," Harlow said. "Care to enlighten me?"

Gabe looked at me. There was no amusement in his pale gray eyes.

"Let's explore a few known quantities," I said. "Fact: the attack happened right as more than a hundred troops, as well as heavy armor and helicopters, started an expedition north to deal with border incursions into Kentucky. Fact: the infected and the enemy troops came in on foot. To hit us when they did, they had to set out from no further than roughly twenty miles away. Fact: whatever the Alliance is doing in Kentucky, they've gone to a great deal of trouble to make sure we don't interrupt them. From this, we can garner a few logical assumptions. Take it away, Gabe." I waved a hand at him.

"There are any number of reasons for the Alliance to stage the guns and ghouls," he said. "Maybe it was an insurance policy. Maybe they were planning to attack at a different time, but caught wind of the Union's plans to defend the border. Either way, they chose to attack right as we were leaving. I can't see that being a coincidence."

Harlow let out a long sigh. "No. I don't think so either."

"Which means they knew *what* we were doing and *when*," I said. "Which means someone in either Echo Company or Central Command is talking."

At this, Harlow frowned, but did not argue.

41

Jonas said, "But that still doesn't explain why they attacked Hollow Rock and not our forces."

"I suppose you have a theory about that?" Harlow asked, looking at me.

"I do, actually. I don't think whoever sent those men expected them to destroy Hollow Rock. Think about it. Why attack us in daylight when we're still close to town with tanks and air support? It would make much more sense to attack at night. Gabe said something about an insurance policy."

Harlow sat up straight in his chair. "Son of a bitch."

I waited.

"That's why they targeted the main gate, and why they attacked in broad daylight. If those rigged ghouls had blown the walls, we would be evacuating everyone in town to Fort McCray as we speak. And even if they had attacked Fort McCray directly, they knew we could fight them off. Call for reinforcements. That would be the opposite of what they want. They don't want to take us on directly, not until they can attack in large numbers. They just want us to stay put. Crazy bastards sacrificed their own men to keep us here."

"We got lucky," Gabe said, "if not for Eric's sharp eyes, those hordes would have destroyed the wall. And if not for the Apache, those mortar crews would have blown the main gate down to rubble."

"And your men would be stuck here longer than they already will be," I added.

"It was all a smokescreen," Harlow said, standing up and beginning to pace his small office. "The Alliance doesn't want Hollow Rock. At least not yet. They just want to make sure Union forces near their territory stay occupied while they expand southward."

"And it's working," I said.

Harlow stopped pacing. A slow smile spread across his face. "So we let them keep right on thinking that."

42

Jonas said, "Do you have an idea, sir?"

Harlow unlocked a drawer in his desk and extracted a satellite phone. "Step outside for a minute, gentlemen. I need to make a call."

SIX

Night fell over Hollow Rock.

I stared at my little corner of the world and had an oppressive feeling of things ending. It was a rotten emotion, like the time a very polite and appropriately subdued officer with the Charlotte-Mecklenburg Police Department called my cell phone and told me my parents had been involved in a car accident.

Are they hurt? They're at the hospital. Okay, but are they hurt? They're at Presbyterian Main, uptown. Your mother is in surgery, I believe. How bad is it? I'm afraid I don't know the extent of her injuries. Fine, what about my father? I'm sorry, Mr. Riordan. He was pronounced dead at the scene.

That same hollow feeling. Like the ground under my feet moved and rippled and fell away. Like I had nothing inside me, no lungs, no heart, no organs of any kind. My blood was smoke. My breath was ashes. Something precious, something irreplaceable, was gone. Taken away from me.

Allison is still alive, I told myself. And my baby. Okay. As long as I have that, I'll be all right. But what about home? What about the sense of safety and belonging? If the Alliance really wanted to destroy Hollow Rock, they could. Maybe not all the way, but enough to make the place uninhabitable. We could rebuild, but they could come right back and do it again. And again. So what was there to do?

Leave, was my first thought. Call in every favor. Spend whatever I had to spend. Pack up everything, head for Colorado, and start over. Allison is a doctor, and I can fight. We would have no trouble finding work in the Springs. Or somewhere

44

else, maybe. I'd heard from acquaintances that for the right price, I could buy a plane ride to the Florida Keys, and from there, a boat to the Caribbean.

That part of the world was doing comparatively well, if the rumors were to be believed. Cuba, Barbados, Jamaica, St. Lucia, all safe places. Plenty of weapons, stable government, sustainable food supplies, and most importantly, no infected. Everything a person could ask for.

But what about Gabe, and Elizabeth, the Glover family, and all the other friends I had made? I couldn't just leave them. Could I? They were all capable survivors. They did not need me. I would miss them, but I could live without them. Right?

The smell of food cooking reached my nose. Not surprising considering I was sitting on the roof of the chow hall. The smell did not entice me. I had no appetite. Probably would not until I was back home with my wife. Then we would talk and figure out what to do next.

I stared across the long field leading to Hollow Rock. The only movement I could see was wandering infected. The moon was almost full and the sky was clear, allowing me to see all the way to the north gate. Hollow Rock was quiet. Fort McCray was quiet. No lights, no laughter, no loud voices coming from the enlisted club. Everything but the barracks and the chow hall were closed. The sentries on the perimeter wall carried suppressed rifles and wore NVGs. Noise discipline was in full effect. Same for Hollow Rock. It had taken a while for things to settle down over there, but they finally did.

So what now, Riordan? What's the plan?

For right now, I sit here and try not to think too much. Eventually I will get tired, and I'll see if I can scrounge up something soft to sleep on. Tomorrow, I'll find Gabe and grill him for information. Or the guys in Delta Squad. Or Captain Harlow. Or someone.

It was late in the night before I got tired. A supply sergeant who owed me a jar of instant coffee—no small debt in a world where coffee grew rarer by the day—earned himself a chunk of

45

credit by issuing me a ground mat and a sleeping bag on the promise I would return them in the morning.

When I slept, I dreamed I was on a small boat and Allison was on a distant shore. There was a swarm of infected approaching at her back. The forest behind them was on fire. Allison did not seem to notice. She smiled, and waved, and rubbed her large round belly with our child in it. I screamed at her to look back, but she did not hear. The boat drifted farther away, the fire blazed higher, and the moans of the undead grew louder. I tried to jump overboard and swim to her, but my legs would not respond. I screamed until my voice died in my throat, to no avail. I did not understand why Allison could not hear me, why she didn't sense the danger. Then the boat was being tossed by heavy waves, and voices shouted at me from under the water, saying, "Hey, wake up!", and I could not breath, and …

My eyes opened. Someone had clamped a calloused hand over my mouth. In the dim half-light, I saw a face wearing NVGs with a finger over its lips. I relaxed and nodded.

"Sorry," I said when the hand let go.

"S'okay. Happens all the time."

The soldier stood and turned to walk away. "Does it happen to you?" I asked.

He stopped. "It used to."

"But not anymore?"

"No. I wish I knew why."

The door to the drill hall closed gently as the sentry went back out on watch. I lay with my hands behind my head and watched the high windows turn blue, then gray, then pale yellow. With the morning came birdsong—high, melodic, and unapologetically disinterested.

*****

"I don't care how many infected are out there," Gabe said. "I'm going home."

"Sir," the sentry at the gate replied, "I can't open the doors."

"I'm not asking you to."

"How are you getting out, then?"

Gabe pointed at the catwalk along the wall. "I have rope."

"But the infected will be on you in a heartbeat. We're not authorized to use live ammo right now."

"Got it covered," Gabe said. He hooked a thumb at me. I raised my rifle and tapped the suppressor at the end of the barrel.

"But you can't-"

"I'm not military," I said. "I can use all the ammo I want. And with this suppressor, I won't attract any more infected. We don't need your help. We just need you to get out of the way."

"What about him?" the guard said, inclining his helmet toward Gabe. "He doesn't have a suppressor."

Gabe drew his falcata and held it up. The polished blade gleamed in the morning light. "Got that covered too."

The guard eyed the Sword of Gabriel warily and took a step back. "Fine," he said. "Your funeral."

We stepped past him and ascended the stairs to the catwalk. Gabe unslung the coil of rope across his chest and tied it around his legs and hips like a rappelling harness. I took the loose end and passed it around a section of steel railing, doubling the rope for easy retrieval. Gabe connected the anchor end to a carabiner, stepped up onto the battlement, and began easing his weight backwards.

I looked around the perimeter wall. There were no sentries on patrol. The only guards above ground level hid behind camouflage blinds in guard towers. Captain Harlow did not want the infected to see them and crowd against the wall, as if the ambient noise of more than three-hundred soldiers was not enough to attract them.

I peered over the edge and settled my carbine against my shoulder. The VCOG was set to its lowest magnification. Only a few infected clawed at the wall, but their moans would soon attract others. There would have been many more undead if not for an intrepid old fellow by the name of John Wollodarsky.

Wollodarsky owned an ultralight helicopter he built from a kit before the Outbreak. He told me about it one day while foraging around my store for something to make a fuel filter out of. The ultralight was his backup plan in case he ever had to bug out of Hollow Rock. He cranked it up once a week to make sure it still worked.

On the night of the attack, the crazy bastard convinced Sheriff Elliott to lend him some fuel and proceeded to fly a few laps around town. When he had the ghouls' undivided attention, he led them three miles away before heading for one of the many safety towers surrounding Hollow Rock.

The safety towers were a recent innovation. I wish I could say they were my idea, but they were not. A caravan leader told Mayor Stone about a town in Kansas that had built fifteen-foot towers with retractable ladders at various locations along nearby trade routes. The idea was to give travelers a place to wait out the infected if they became stranded. It was so simple, and so logically sound, I was ashamed I didn't think of it myself.

I looked southward and hoped John Wollodarsky had brought enough food and water to last a couple of days. I hoped he was sensible enough to lie quietly until the grunts and groans faded into the distance. I hoped he waited an extra couple of hours in case a ghoul with its throat ripped out stuck around when the others left. Most of all, I hoped he had enough fuel to get back to town safely. Any man who demonstrates uncommon valor deserves a free libation of his choosing. And I intended to buy him one. Or twelve.

"You ready?" Gabe asked.

"One second." I fired four times, clearing a space for Gabe to touch down.

"Go," I said.

He went. One bounce off the wall and he was on the ground. Four seconds later, the rope hung limp and Gabe had drawn his sword.

It was a hell of a thing to watch the big man fight. At six foot five and two-hundred fifty pounds, the veteran Marine scout sniper and ex-CIA operative could lay down an impressive ass kicking. His blade flicked out almost faster than the eye could follow, each swipe sending a section of cranium sailing through the air. He killed three ghouls in the same time it takes to say the words.

"Sometime today, Eric," he said, not looking back. More ghouls were approaching.

"On my way."

I pulled the trigger five more times. Nine rounds. Twenty-one left in the mag. The tactical sling made a zipper sound as I moved the M-4 around to my back and secured the barrel with a fold of Velcro attached to my web belt.

Unlike Gabe, I did not bother making a harness. There was not enough time. I grabbed the rope, lowered myself over, and clamped it between my knees and boots. Friction heated my gloves painfully as I slid down. Once on the ground, I flapped my hands a few times to cool them, then pulled the rest of the rope from the railing. Gabe glanced back at me.

"Forget the rope," he said. "We'll find more."

Gabe was right. Several dozen infected were lurching toward us, attracted by the noise we made. I dropped the rope. Some lucky soldier, probably someone on overwatch in the guard towers, would retrieve it. Nylon rope is rare these days. Valuable. I hated to leave it behind, but I was not about to die for it.

I took point, Gabe running a few steps behind on my left side. I held my rifle in a right-handed grip, my most comfortable shooting position, which was strange considering I am mostly left-handed. I can do most things with either hand, but with some activities, writing and eating being chief among them, I am an irredeemable leftie. Many years ago on a date, I tried eating right-handed with a pair of chopsticks. My date laughed at me and said I looked like I had a brain injury. I did not ask her out again.

A small ghoul weaved around slower moving adults. I took aim and fired three times before I finally brought it down. Moving targets are difficult to hit on the run. Gabe angled a few feet away from me and knocked another ghoul down with a jumping front kick. The force of the blow sent the skinny creature tumbling ass-over-heels into two more that tripped over it. Three running steps later, Gabe was back in position.

We kept moving, my rifle emitting muted barks and Gabe exerting his impressive reserve of brute force and swordsmanship. The undead seem slow, but are faster than they look. They began to crowd around us. When they were too thick to keep going ahead, we doubled back and ran a hook pattern to the west. This forced the infected to cross paths and bump into one another, slowing them down. Two-hundred yards later, we executed the same maneuver in the opposite direction. Now there was a maelstrom of ghouls whirling and thumping like a pen of blind, drunken sheep.

The horde, such as it was, thinned out ahead of us. As long as we maintained a steady pace, the ghouls behind would not catch up. I slowed to a fast walk as Gabe came up beside me. We were both breathing hard and sweating in the growing heat. The tall grass pulled at my legs and forced me to step high to make sufficiently swift progress.

"Nice work," Gabe said between deep breaths. With his longer legs, he was not having nearly as much trouble.

I checked my rifle. The slide was locked to the rear on an empty magazine. I ejected it, stowed it on my vest, and inserted a fresh one. Hit the release. *Clack-chop* of a round going into the chamber. A comforting sound.

"Look there," Gabe said, pointing with his sword.

My eyes followed. Wollodarsky's ultralight crossed the sky ahead of us, blades beating against the air as it cleared the wall and vanished into the open space at the center of town. I hoped the old man got a hero's welcome, and I hoped the infected were too far away to track him.

"Crazy old fucker," I said.

"No crazier than us. At least he's above the fray."

I aimed at a ghoul blocking our path. "Good point," I said, and fired.

SEVEN

The clinic was a buzz of activity. I stopped to stare at it.

"She's probably still there," Gabe said.

"I know."

"You going to see her?"

I hesitated. "I don't think it's a good idea. She's probably busy."

"Well, I'm going to see Elizabeth."

I clapped him on the arm and started down the road. "See you in the morning."

"Yeah."

On the way home, I saw a pile of horse manure on the side of the road and remembered I had let Red out of his stall and had not told Gabriel. Gabe would not be happy if Red was missing when he got home. A sense of alarm told me to run, but I was too tired. A brisk walk was the best I could manage.

I turned the corner on our street and saw Red with his head down munching grass in my front yard. He still wore the saddle I had put on him. His long tail switched at fat flies trying to land on his flanks. He did not seem to be in any discomfort. I called to him and walked closer.

Red nuzzled my chest, sniffed at my face, and left a smear of horse snot on my forehead. I laughed and wiped my head across his shoulder, leaving a sticky smear in the reddish-brown coat. "Bet you're hungry, big fella."

I led him to the barn by his halter and removed the saddle and blanket. After tossing them over the sawhorse, I put Red back in his stall. He went along willingly—a human putting him in his stall usually meant feeding time. The padlock securing the feed room was clamped shut, so I threw a big wad of hay into Red's stall to give him something to munch on and went home to get the spare key to Gabe's place.

As I came up the drive, I heard voices coming from inside the house. A boy of about eight years sat on the front porch feeding pieces of dried fish to a stray cat. I stopped. Thoughts swirled in the old gray matter until a reasonable explanation presented itself. Nonetheless, I rested a casual hand on my pistol.

"Hi," I said to the boy as I stepped onto the porch.

"Hi," he said. He was thin, like all kids are now, and most everyone else for that matter. The boy had dark hair and eyes, and did not seem put off by my arrival.

"When did you get here?" I asked him.

The boy looked down and fed another scrap of fish to the stray tabby. I noticed the cat was missing one eye and half its left ear. Another hardened survivor.

The boy said, "Yesterday. Our house burned down. One of those bombs landed on it."

"Everyone in your family all right?"

"Yeah. None of us were home. One of our neighbors died, though. Mrs. Steadman."

"I'm sorry to hear that."

The boy shrugged. "She was mean. Her and my dad argued a lot. He had to send for the sheriff one time when he caught Mrs. Steadman stealing out of our garden."

I did not know how to respond. The boy reached out to the cat with both hands, one holding fish, the other gently scratching at its ears. The cat began to purr.

"I'm Eric, by the way. I live here."

53

"I know who you are. Everybody does."

"You got a name?"

"Brandon."

"You staying here now, Brandon? You and your family?"

"Yeah. Doc Laroux said we could stay here until we can get a new place. Lots of folks are staying with other people now."

I winced, and was immediately glad the cat held Brandon's attention. I liked my house. I liked that it was just me and Allison. I liked our privacy. But the house had four bedrooms, and we only used one. There were two guest rooms and Allison's office. The office could be cleared out to accommodate more people if necessary. Whatever disruption our new guests might cause to our lives was small compared to what they were now going through. I could only imagine how much they had lost.

Don't be selfish, Riordan. Go inside and introduce yourself.

I went in. The foyer opened into the living room. The couch and recliner and fireplace were right where I left them. Atop the dining room table were plates, flatware, and the remains of a recently-eaten meal. I remembered making love to Allison on that tabletop and determined it best if my guests remained ignorant of that information.

"Hello?" I called out.

A man in his late thirties emerged from the kitchen wiping his hands on a towel. He was short, broad shouldered, and had the same face as the boy on the porch, aged thirty years. He smiled and came over to offer me a handshake. His eyes registered recognition.

"Hi, Arthur Silverman. Call me Art."

I accepted the handshake. It was calloused, strong, and gritty like sandpaper. The hand of a farmer. "Eric Riordan."

He smiled. "I know who you are. Sorry to barge in on you like this."

54

"Your son told me what happened to your house. I'm sorry."

The smile went away. His eyes dropped and he nodded. "Yeah. Burned all my crops too. I only had a few acres and some chickens, but we made it work. Don't know what I'm gonna do now. Might have to sign on with a caravan and head someplace else."

"There's always the military."

"No, I've been down that road already. Four years in the Army. Infantry. '04 to '08. Served in Iraq."

I held back a grimace. "I know some folks who served around that same time. Tough years, from what I understand."

"Tough enough I don't ever want to go back."

I unslung my rifle and hung it on a hook by the front door, followed by my MOLLE vest. The shirt underneath was soaked through with sweat. A long pull from my canteen eased the burn in my throat. I stared at my gear and worried over the fate of my pack. There were valuable things in it. But like everyone else, I had left it in the transport when the bombs started flying. Now that things had calmed down, I hoped someone from Delta Squad found it and kept it safe. If one of the troops from Second or Third Platoon realized it was a civilian contractor's pack, it was as good as gone.

"I'll get this mess cleaned up," Art said. He began stacking plates in the dining room.

Normally I would have offered to help, but right then all I could think about was filling a bucket with water, wiping myself down with a sponge, putting on clean clothes, and sleeping for ten hours. After I gave Red his dinner, of course.

"Thanks," I said. "By the way, how many of you are there?"

"Me and my two kids," Art said. "My boy Brandon, and my daughter Jenny. She's outside using the facilities."

By 'facilities' he meant the outhouse. I'm proud of my outhouse. A friend of mine, who in my opinion is the Michael

Jordan of carpenters, helped me build it. By post-Outbreak standards, it is downright posh.

"Take whichever rooms you like," I said, "except my bedroom. I'm afraid that one is reserved for me and Allison."

Art laughed. It was an awkward laugh, like he was out of practice. His expression held a kind of guilty tension I had seen on many faces since the Outbreak. The notable absence of his wife likely had something to do with it. He held up a hand.

"No argument here. I'm just glad to have a roof over my head tonight. Been plenty of nights me and the kids didn't even have that much."

I grabbed a towel from the linen closet and headed for the bathroom. "Make yourselves at home."

*****

Allison came home late. I did not hear her come in, nor did I hear her cleaning up in the bathroom. She could have stomped into the bedroom with a knife and stabbed me and I would not have noticed. I did notice, however, when she slid in bed beside me and kissed me on the side of my neck.

"You awake?" she asked.

"I am now." I rolled onto my back and pulled her into my arms. She slid against me like fine silk and lay her head in the hollow between shoulder and chest. Her left hand moved slowly over my lower stomach and she put her lips close to my chin. I knew what she was thinking, what she wanted. It was a stress response. Many people have experienced it, myself included. Tired as I was, I did not object. But I knew not to rush things. Best to let her set the pace.

"How are you holding up?" I said.

"Better than most of my patients."

56

I ran gentle fingers through her hair and kissed the top of her head. "You did everything you could Allison. You can't save them all."

"I know. I still hate it."

We lay quietly a few minutes and listened to the night sounds outside our bedroom window. I had opened the window to let some cool air in. Spring was rapidly headed toward summer, and the days were getting warmer. The nights, on the other hand, would still be refreshingly brisk for a few more weeks. As much as I hated facing a Tennessee summer with no air conditioning, it was good to know the nuclear winter of the last three years was finally abating.

"So many of them were children," Allison said. "I see that, and I can't help but think it could happen to our child too."

The movement of soft fingers dipped lower and brushed at my waistband. Despite the topic of conversation, I felt myself beginning to respond. "I'd like to tell you I would never let that happen, Allison, but I think we're both realistic enough to know that's not possible. False bravado only gets people killed. All we can do is be smart and take as few risks as possible. I'll do everything I can to protect you and the baby. And I know you'll do the same. That's all we can do. It's all anyone can do."

The hand stopped moving. Her breathing slowed. I knew she was working her way up to say something she did not expect me to like. "Eric," she said, "I think we should leave."

Color me surprised. "You mean leave Hollow Rock?"

"Yes. But not yet."

"Okay," I said slowly. "When?"

"Somebody has to do something about the Alliance. And the ROC."

I blinked. "Okay. I agree completely. But what's that got to do with us leaving town?"

"You remember the other day when you told me you were going with the expedition?"

57

"Yes. My memory is pretty good when it comes to people throwing things at my head and shouting at me."

She sat up and looked me in the eye. She did not smile. "I was wrong. You were right. You belong in this fight. There's a reason I'm telling you this. I overheard Captain Harlow talking on his satellite phone. He and General Jacobs are planning to send a strike team to meet up with Task Force Falcon."

"Jesus, you heard that? Talk about lousy op-sec."

Still no smile. "Do you know anything about it?"

"No, but Gabe and I have a meeting with Captain Harlow tomorrow morning. Did you hear anything else?"

"Yes. He wants you and Gabe on the team."

I was quiet for a long moment. I knew Captain Harlow respected my abilities, but he did not like me very much. The feeling was mutual. We often traded salvage and other goods, but always kept things strictly business. No banter. No jokes. No friendly handshakes to seal a bargain. And while he had hired me in the past for sniper work and recon and such, he had never tried to recruit me for something this high level. It made me nervous. "What else did he say?" I asked.

"They're going after the Alliance's leaders."

I laughed. "Yep. That sounds like General Jacobs. Listen, I appreciate the heads up, but what are you really trying to say? I sense a subtext to this discussion."

"I want you to go with them, Eric. I want you to help them. The Alliance is weakening. Remember, they're not really a country, just a loose federation of city-states. And a lot of people living in Alliance territory don't much care for the way things are being run. They don't like antagonizing the Union, and they don't like North Korean commandos in their communities. They don't like that the Alliance central government legalized slavery. Most Alliance citizens are still angry at the Union government, but they still see themselves as Americans. Foreign occupation doesn't sit well with them, nor does the slave trade. Take out the leaders, and the Alliance will fall apart. If that happens, the individual communities will have to turn to the Union for help. And when they do, the ROC will be out of options. They'll have to surrender, or face all-out war. They're already being hard pressed by resistance forces in California and Oregon. They'd be facing a war on two fronts, and it would be a war they couldn't win. But to make that happen, General Jacobs is going to need the best fighters he can get. Fighters who can end the Alliance for good." She kissed me on the side of the mouth. "And you're one of the best there is."

For the first time I can remember, I was stunned speechless. I stared at my wife and felt like I was seeing her for the first time. The eyes were different. The usual gentle honey-browns glittered in the dark like slices of amber. I remembered seeing a look like that before on a six-hundred pound Bengal tiger.

When the circuitry in my brain finally rebooted, I said, "You know, for a country doctor, you sure know a lot about politics."

Her smile finally made an appearance. It was not a warm one. It was a surgical incision with pretty white teeth. "I'm a very smart country doctor, Eric. I have a disarming smile and an excellent memory. People trust me. They tell me all kinds of things. Doctor-patient privilege and all that."

She laid her head back down. Her left hand went below my waistband and did some wonderful things. My hips began to move involuntarily.

"Is this how you plan to convince me?" I breathed.

"No," she said. "I know you'll go. What I'm doing now is getting you hard because I've had a very stressful couple of days, life is fleeting, and sometimes a girl just wants to get fucked."

As usual, I could find no fault in her logic.

EIGHT

Captain Harlow was kind enough to send a Bradley to pick us up at the gate. A few salvos from the 25 millimeter guns cleared the infected long enough for Gabe and I to hop down from a shipping container and clamber into the armored vehicle. At Fort McCray, M-240s laid down cover fire as the Bradley drove into the courtyard. Or parade ground. Or whatever the hell it was called. I am familiar with some military terminology, but I am still a lifelong civilian and have only learned so much. Sometimes I listen to soldiers jabber at each other, and it's like they're speaking a foreign language. And don't even get me started on all the damned acronyms.

The good captain was waiting for us as we exited the Bradley. He shook hands with Gabe and gave him a respectful nod. He did not offer me the same courtesy. He glanced at me briefly, then looked back to Gabe and said, "Glad you two could make it. We have a lot to discuss. If you'll follow me, please."

He led us to a golf cart and climbed in the passenger seat. Wally drove. Gabe took up most of the back seat, leaving me dangling from the little cushion mounted to the rear and trying not to fall off. Story of my life.

As we drove, a Blackhawk roared overhead and dropped slowly toward the helipad. I put on my goggles and scarf to ward off the swirling dust and looked to see who had arrived. A tall, familiar figure emerged. I did not need to see the star emblem on his uniform to know who he was. When a man sits in your living room and drinks tea with you, recognizing him is not difficult. Even from a distance.

60

"Methinks shit just got real," I said to Gabe.

He glanced toward the chopper with an expression that would have looked blank to most people. The hard lines, angles, scars, and those cold gray eyes could hide a lot. But not from me. I knew him too well, and I knew Gabe was thinking something along the same lines I was. The finely-crafted gears of his finely-crafted mind were spinning, calculating, going through the permutations.

The golf cart stopped in front of headquarters and we all got out. Wally went ahead of us and unlocked the security door. When we were all in, he closed it, barred it, locked it, and informed the sentry to allow no one but General Jacobs and his entourage inside for the remainder of his watch. The sentry said, "Yes, Sergeant. No one but General Jacobs and the people he authorizes, Sergeant." Wally nodded and said, "Good." I was surprised he did not pat the kid on the head.

We tromped up the stairs to Harlow's office. Wally stayed outside to make sure we were not disturbed. I doubted anything short of a Tyrannosaurus with a machine gun would be capable of getting past him.

"I hate to keep everyone waiting," Harlow said, "But General Jacobs is on his way in. He has something very important to discuss."

"And what would that be?" Gabe asked. He had been around the block. Marines, CIA, the works. He did not like to be kept waiting by mid-level officers.

"The General wants to give the briefing personally."

Gabe frowned, but did not push.

A few minutes later, I heard footsteps in the hall. Four sets of them. Words were exchanged between Wally and someone whose voice I did not recognize. Then the door opened and General Phillip Jacobs walked in.

He was a tall man, very lean, standing about six-foot-four. His silver hair was cut short and he was clean-shaven. He wore fatigues and boots polished to a high sheen. There was a scar

61

over his right eye from a piece of shrapnel that had hit him during the early days of the Outbreak. There had been a bandage over the scar the first time I had seen him, which had been on CNN, viewed from my home in Charlotte, North Carolina. He had been a colonel then, and was leading a column of National Guard troops toward Atlanta. And here I was, three years later, about to be briefed by him on a secret military assassination mission to prevent another civil war. Strange are the paths life takes us.

"Gabriel. Eric," he said and shook our hands in turn. "Good to see you again. I wish it were under better circumstances."

Gabe and I offered greetings and agreed the circumstances were less than desirable. The General acknowledged Captain Harlow, who behaved with more obeisance than I had ever seen him display. To me, the general was just a man. A powerful man, granted, but still just a man. I considered him a friend. Gabe was more reserved in his opinion, and had good reason to be. Captain Harlow, however, was looking at someone who could make or break his career with the stroke of a pen. He was being appropriately careful.

Jacobs sat down in a chair that had been wheeled in for the purpose and looked around the room. "You're probably wondering what all this is about," he said. "I won't keep you in suspense. First of all, the expedition to Kentucky was a bluff. Our analysts at Central have long suspected that the Alliance has been staging assets well inside Union territory. Their suspicion, which I share, is that the Alliance and the ROC are planning a series of coordinated attacks at a date as yet unknown with the intention of crippling the Union's ability to prosecute a war. I also share the suspicion that they intend to inflict massive damage to as many secure Union communities as possible. Create chaos. Much like they've done here at Hollow Rock."

"So the expedition was just a ruse to draw them out?" Gabe said. "Confirm your suspicions? Give you a little actionable data to please the suits in the Springs?"

"Yes. I sense you disapprove."

62

"Forty-eight people are dead, General. Including three soldiers, one of them a friend of mine."

The general's hard gaze softened. When he spoke, he was either genuinely regretful, or the best actor I had ever seen. "I'm sorry, Mr. Garrett. I never intended for that to happen. I knew I was taking a risk-"

"A risk with other people's lives," Gabe growled.

"Yes. And I have to do it every day, Mr. Garrett. If you think I never feel the weight of it, you're fooling yourself. I can't tell you how sorry I am about the people that were lost yesterday. But whether we like it or not, we are at war. And in war, people in positions like mine have to make difficult decisions."

"Tell that to the families. To the kids without parents and the parents without kids and everyone else."

Jacobs shook his head. "As I said, I'm sorry. I really am. And I'm here today to make sure their deaths were not in vain."

"By risking more people's lives."

I spoke sharply. "Gabe."

The blistering energy of his glare swung around and settled on me. Most people he inflicted The Look upon began sweating and stuttering and backing slowly away. Not me. I was used to it.

"What?" His voice sounded like a badly tuned diesel motor.

"Do you really think you're helping right now?" I said. "You think arguing with the general is going to fix anything? Bring anyone back?"

Still the glare, but no answer.

"Didn't think so. So maybe pipe down and let the man say what he has to say."

The glare stayed a moment longer, then lowered. "Fine. General, let's hear it."

A sigh. "As I said, the expedition was intended to force the Alliance's hand. Make them show their cards. And as you said,

63

Mr. Garrett, it confirmed our suspicions. Now we have the information we need to act. That's where the two of you come in."

He paused for effect. I resisted the urge to wiggle my fingers in the air and say, "Oooooo, dramatic."

After a moment, Jacobs said, "Task Force Falcon is still conducting operations along the Alliance border. They are in contact with an intelligence asset with access to the Alliance's leaders."

"When you say asset," I said, "you mean a spy, right?"

"Precisely. And not someone we sent in. Someone who turned on their own and came to us."

"And how do we know he or she is not just feeding us bogus intel to throw us off?"

"A lot of reasons, not all of which I can discuss just yet. Suffice it to say, they have very good reasons for wanting to bring the Alliance down. And everything they have told us thus far has turned out to be accurate. The asset has already helped us do severe damage to the Alliance's leaders by helping us expose what they're really up to. This has undermined their popularity among the Alliance citizenry, which is why the Alliance is on such shaky ground right now. And we have the asset to thank for most of it."

I nodded, figuring that was as much answer as I was getting for the time being. "Fair enough," I said. "Go on."

"Our plan is to insert a strike team into Alliance territory and take out a number of high-value targets. The asset will feed us the locations of the people we're after. If the mission succeeds, chances are very good the Alliance will crumble. If it fails, the asset will make sure the Alliance does not cover up the attempt, which will force them to acknowledge publicly that they have not normalized relations with the Union. Which, in turn, will likely have the same effect as if the mission succeeded, although to a lesser degree. Either way, the asset remains in place, and we have the leverage we need to continue exerting pressure on the Alliance."

"A win-win for you," I said.

"For all of us."

"Sounds like a suicide mission," Gabe said. "I never agreed to that."

Jacobs pinched the bridge of his nose for a moment before responding. "It is *not* a suicide mission. We have a plan to get you in and get you back out alive. That said, there are always dangers. You know this as well as I do."

"Better," Gabe said.

The general let the barb go. "What do you say?"

I looked at Gabe. I knew about his bargain with the general, and I knew why he had made it. But he was right; he had never agreed to a suicide mission. My answer had already been decided, although Jacobs did not need to know that, but I wondered what Gabe would say.

"If you're sending us as a sacrifice play," Gabe said, "then you better make damn sure the Alliance kills me. Because if they don't, I'm going to come looking for you, General. And sooner or later, I *will* find you."

General Jacobs' expression did not alter, but I thought I saw something shift far back in the granite-colored eyes. One does not take a threat from someone like Gabriel lightly. Not if they like breathing.

"As I told you, Mr. Garrett, this is not a suicide mission. Whether you choose to believe me or not, losing people really does hurt me. Badly." He looked in my direction. "Mr. Riordan, how old do you think I am?"

"I don't know. Mid-fifties, maybe?"

He chuckled sadly. "I'm forty-eight."

My eyebrows went up. He was not much older than Gabriel, but looked like he could be his father. When I said mid-fifties, I was trying to spare Jacobs' feelings. "Christ," I said.

Back to Gabriel. "Does that satisfy you, Mr. Garrett?"

"No. But I'll accept the mission. I owe you. But after this, we're square."

Jacobs nodded. "I may ask for your help again in the future, but you will be under no obligation to accept. If you do, you will be well compensated for any assistance you provide."

"Understood."

"And you, Mr. Riordan?"

I shrugged. "Got nothing better to do. Count me in."

The corners of the general's mouth creased into a smile. I could feel Gabe's eyes boring into the side of my head. I glanced at him and said, "We'll talk about it later."

"Yes. We will."

Jacobs said, "Now, on to the next matter. Task Force Falcon consists of eight operators. You two make ten. We have another man on the way from Central as we speak. I'd like at least one more. Do you have a recommendation?"

"I do, sir," Captain Harlow said. I jumped a little. He had been so quiet throughout the conversation I had forgotten he was there.

"Yes?" Jacobs said.

He slid a manila folder across the desk. General Jacobs took it and opened it.

"The man you're looking at, sir, is one of Lieutenant Jonas' men. Specialist Caleb Hicks. His CO and his platoon sergeant both personally recommended him for promotion to sergeant. His service record is exemplary. He's only been in the Army two years, but he already has a Bronze Star and multiple letters of commendation. Jonas thinks he would be a good fit for the mission."

"Awfully young, isn't he? Says here he just turned twenty-one."

"He is young, but he's very capable, sir. I've seen him in action myself. I would not want to be downrange of him."

Jacobs scanned a few more pages. "It also says his service in the Army is compulsory. A judge in the Springs offered him a deal to avoid a prison sentence on felony assault charges."

I had to strain very hard to keep my shock under control. Caleb was what one might call the strong, silent type. I had never asked him anything about his past, and he had never offered. Finding out he had a criminal record rocked me. Caleb was a friend. A friend I knew almost nothing about beyond what I had seen in combat and on salvage runs. He was dangerous, that was for certain. But he had always seemed so in control of himself. I wondered what could have happened to make him hurt someone badly enough to end up in front of a judge.

"I've spoken to him about that, sir" Harlow said. "Apparently it was a drunken dispute that got out of hand."

Jacobs looked at him. "Any other incidents since he enlisted?"

"None that I am aware of, sir."

The general looked dubious. "Just because you aren't aware of it doesn't mean it didn't happen, Captain. I started out as an enlisted man. Fights get covered up sometimes."

"Sir, if he had done anything like what's described in that file, I would have found out about it by now. It would be extremely difficult to cover up."

Jacobs shrugged. "If you say so. Well, Mr. Garrett, Mr. Riordan, what do you think? Do you know Specialist Hicks?"

"We do," I said. "He works for us sometimes."

A raised eyebrow. It made the scar on Jacobs' forehead crinkle. "Works for you?"

"Salvage work. Part time. Volunteer only. We're picky about who we bring along."

"Who is we?"

I waved a finger between Gabriel and me. "We're equal partners in a salvage company. Captain Harlow allows us to employ his troops' services on a fee basis. The Ninth TVM helps out too."

Jacobs looked hard at the captain. "Are you sure that's wise?"

"As he said, sir, it's volunteer only. Helping Mr. Riordan run his salvage business provides us with much needed resources without having to requisition them through Central Command. Saves us time and saves the government money, so to speak."

"Hm. Not a bad idea." Harlow looked relieved. Jacobs went on. "So you've worked with Specialist Hicks. Have you been in combat with him?"

"I took him with me earlier in the year when I went after Sebastian Tanner, AKA Blackmire," Gabe said. "He's solid."

Another rustling of paper. "He's also recovering from a wound to his leg."

"Seems pretty recovered to me," I said. "He looked just fine during the attack yesterday."

"The wound wasn't bad," Gabe said. "I dressed it myself. A through-and-through on the outside of his thigh. Missed the femoral artery, the femur, and the common peroneal nerve. He got lucky. A couple of inches either way and he would have been in bad shape. As it is, I wouldn't be surprised if he's fully recovered by now."

"So you're all in agreement?" Jacobs asked. "You think he's the one for the job?"

We all nodded. Harlow said, "Yes sir."

"Good. Bring him in and I'll speak with him. Just to be clear, this mission is for volunteers only. I don't want anyone on the team who doesn't want to be there. This mission is too important. That said, any suggestions how I could convince him?"

Harlow said, "I was planning to promote him anyway. Just tell him the promotion comes with acceptance of the mission."

I gave Harlow a hard look. "Caleb is a friend of mine, Captain. I don't like the idea of you using leverage against him. If you want to promote him, fine. Do it. But don't hold the sergeant's stripes in front of him like a carrot on a stick. He is not a fucking donkey."

The captain went red in the face. He was not accustomed to being addressed in such a manner. But I wasn't one of his soldiers, so fuck him. Harlow opened his mouth to retort, but the general interrupted.

"I agree," he said. "We'll give him the promotion before we discuss the mission."

When Jacobs saw my expression, he said, "Look, I need good people. You ever buttered someone up before asking them for something? Even if it was dangerous?"

I let out a breath, counted backwards from ten, and said, "Yes."

"Then don't criticize me for doing it. Anyway, any other suggestions?"

"I don't think you'll have much trouble convincing him," Gabe said. "I know the kid. He lives for shit like this. He'll go willingly and with a smile."

"I hope you're right." Jacobs closed the file and handed it back to Harlow. The captain stopped trying to kill me with his eyes long enough to take it.

"Do you have anything else you want to ask? Anything at all?"

Gabe said, "Where are we on logistics?"

"Still working out the kinks. Captain Harlow and I will wrap that up as soon as we're finished here."

"Timeframe?"

"Still working on it. But definitely within the next week to ten days."

Gabe looked at me. I shook my head. He said, "Then I guess we're done for now."

"Do you mind staying on base for the rest of the day?"

"Define the rest of the day," I said.

"Let's say until 1800 hours."

I did the conversion in my head. 1800 was 6:00 PM. "I can do that. How about a ride home later?"

"Of course."

"Thanks."

Jacobs stood up. "I'll send runners if I need anything else from you. Where should they look?"

"We'll hang out at the enlisted club," I said. "Either there or the chow hall."

As Gabe and I stood up to go, Jacobs said, "Gabriel, one more question."

Gabe looked over his shoulder. "Yeah?"

"If you don't mind me asking, how did you lose your finger?"

NINE

General Jacobs only sent one runner. He came into the mess hall where we were eating lunch with Delta Squad and asked if he could speak with me in private for a moment. We stepped outside, and he asked me how much experience I had with the AK-47 rifle platform.

"None," I said.

He seemed surprised. I asked him if there was anything else. He shook his head, thanked me, and took off at a jog. I watched him go until he was out of sight. He was a short guy, maybe five-foot-six at the most. His arms and legs were thin but full of stringy muscle. He wore a dry-fit shirt that must have cost a small fortune, running shorts that were barely long enough to be considered masculine, and a pair of worn down zero-drop sneakers. I noticed he ran toe-to-heel instead of heel-to-toe.

I read a book once about a tribe of natives in Mexico who ran the same way. They could cover fifty miles at a go as easy me walking down my driveway. I wondered if the runner had read the same book. I also wondered how much trade he earned in an average day. When I first got to Hollow Rock, so many people wanted to work as runners the mayor started making them apply for business licenses. As time went by, the cream rose to the top, and the really good ones put the lazy and the slow out of business. It was still competitive, but a good runner could make far better trade than your average farmhand or full-time guardsman.

Then there were the Runners with a capital R. More of a tribe than an occupation. They transported goods and messages

71

from one community to another, sticking to the wilds and supporting each other through a network of hidden campsites and safe-houses. Tough people. Slow to trust, constantly armed, and if they took a contract, they fulfilled it or died trying. Gabe had gotten in with them by saving one of their lives, and explained to me their practices. Each Runner had a name known only to other members of the community. Gabe had one, but refused to tell me what it was. Consequently, I did not feel bad about occasionally borrowing his horse without asking.

Back in the mess hall, I sat down and went back to my food. Roasted chicken, beans, squash, greens, diced cucumbers, and damn good bread. The bread was the best part, thick and crusty with plenty of bite. The vegetables were local, but the chicken was imported from Kansas. Chickens were big business out there, along with goats and a burgeoning beef trade. I hoped the beef ranchers were successful. Most of the cattle in the US had been devoured by ghouls in the years since the Outbreak. Only a few had survived, but the population was on the rebound. I liked chicken, but the thought of eating an honest to God cheeseburger was enough to make me misty eyed.

"Fuller's memorial service is tomorrow at sunset," Thompson said. His eyes were bloodshot, and he looked like he had not slept much. Dark circles, beard stubble, slight tremor of the hands and voice, all the classic signs.

The mood around the table had been subdued. Only sporadic conversation, simple questions and answers with no enthusiasm. A lot of pushing food around with listless forks. The squad had lost people before, but it did not get any easier with repetition. Fuller had been one of the good ones. He would be missed.

I looked down the table at the survivors. Ethan, Cole, Cormier, Page, Hicks, Holland, and the newest addition, Smith. No more Fuller. His absence felt like a sinkhole, sudden and empty. I thought about Justin Schmidt, formerly of Delta Squad. I had met him back in North Carolina in the same abandoned textile mill where I had met Ethan Thompson. He was sufficiently tech savvy he had been selected and transferred to a mobile task group assigned to the Phoenix Initiative. In exchange for his services, his wife and three-year-old child had been transferred from Fort Bragg to Colorado Springs. I remembered the day he left. I remembered the hoarseness in his voice. I remembered everyone telling him he was doing the right thing for his family and wishing him luck. I hoped he was still alive, wherever he was.

"I'm getting tired of this shit," Holland said. "Tired of losing my friends. We're down to seven now."

Cole patted him on the shoulder. He did not offer words of comfort. They were not necessary. Everyone knew what everyone else was thinking and feeling. No use wasting his breath on the obvious.

"He didn't leave a will," Thompson went on, "so LT asked me if he ever said how he wanted his remains handled. Buried, cremated, whatever. Anybody know?"

"Cremated," Cormier said. "We talked about it once over drinks."

I looked at Cormier. He was my age, in his very early thirties, one of those who enlisted after the Outbreak. He was five-foot-ten, which put him at two inches shorter than me. Dark hair, brown eyes, olive skin, the strong build of a former football player. He did not talk much, but he fought well and pulled his weight.

"Okay," Thompson said. "Good enough for me."

We finished eating and went our separate ways. At 1800, Gabe and I made our way back to the headquarters building. Wally had arranged for transport back to Hollow Rock in another Bradley. There were infected along the way, but not as many as before. Starve them out long enough, and they set off for fleshier pastures. The guardsmen on horseback conducting regular extermination raids didn't hurt either.

Allison was not home when I got there. Neither were Art or his kids. A note stuck to the corkboard in the dining room said they had decided to stay with a family on the west side of town.

A lot of small-time farmers over there. Probably signed on as laborers. There were worse jobs.

I bathed, ate some dried chicken and cold flatbread that was just next door to stale, and went to bed.

*****

After Fuller's memorial service, I spent the next few days seeing Allison in small doses and running my business. Caleb Hicks, as expected, leapt at the opportunity to join us on the mission. The guys in Delta Squad threw him a muted celebration for making sergeant, which I attended. After everyone finished their last drink and went back to the VFW hall for the night, Caleb asked if he could come over to my place and talk. I agreed, and off we went.

Allison was still at the clinic, so I poured us a couple of nips of the increasingly rare pre-Outbreak stuff. We sat down in the living room, the dead television staring at us, its blank black screen reflecting the light from a pair of oil lanterns. Why I had not yet removed the TV I did not know. Laziness, maybe. Or maybe I still had enough pre-Outbreak sensibility the living room would feel empty without it.

"Miranda's going to be pissed," Caleb said as we sat down. I took the recliner, and he sat down on the sofa. "She gets me back, thinks I'm not going anywhere, and now I'm leaving after all."

"Start with the promotion," I said. "It'll soften the blow."

"She's gonna be pissed at you too, you know. Gabe as well. Leaving her to run the store by herself ain't gonna go over too good."

I downed a bit of Kentucky's finest. "Yeah. The thought occurred."

"So what's your plan?"

74

"We'll have to hire somebody. Been meaning to anyway. I ask too much of Miranda and I'm starting to develop a conscience about it."

"You have a conscience?"

"Allegedly. Christ, man, I have no idea who to hire. Maybe I should post a help wanted sign in the window."

"You'd have half the town at your doorstep."

"I know. Can't think of anything else, though."

"I might know somebody."

My ears started to grow little points. "Who?"

"Guy named Johnny Green. Served in Third Platoon. Supply. Got discharged last month, been working as a guardsman and general laborer ever since."

"No place to go back to? Family?"

"None of the above. Lost it all in the Outbreak. He deserted for a while, went home to some little town in Ohio, and found his family had all been infected. Had to put them down."

"Jesus. Tough break."

Caleb sipped his bourbon. "Lot of that going around these days. Anyway, he came back to the Army when the last president announced the amnesty period. Served out his enlistment and took his walking papers."

"Can you vouch for the guy? I mean, if I hire him and he steals from me, or if he's a screw-up, I'm blaming you."

"He's the only supply weenie that never tried to extort anything out of anyone. Doesn't seem to care too much about trade as long as he can keep his belly full and shoes on his feet."

"Okay. Can you get in touch with him and send him by the store tomorrow?"

"Sure. Any particular time?"

"I'll be there until six."

75

"Can do."

Green showed up at two in the afternoon. 1400 hours in military parlance. He had a fresh shave and haircut and wore clothes that before the Outbreak would have been considered business casual. Now, it was practically formal wear. He was about my height, slender, mid-to-late twenties, dark tan on the face and hands, light brown hair thinning on top. He would be bald by the time he was thirty.

I stood up from my stool behind the counter. "What can I do for you today?"

"My name is Johnathan Green. Caleb Hicks said you might have some work for me."

"He called you Johnny."

"Yeah, I usually go by Johnny."

"Works for me."

I hung a sign in the window with a drawing of a clock numbered in ten-minute increments. Above the clock, the sign read: BE BACK IN…

I put the little red hand at thirty minutes and locked the door.

"Come on back," I said. "We'll sit down and talk business."

We sat down at the little table in the storage room where Gabe, Miranda, and I eat our meals when we mind the shop. I offered Johnny some water and he accepted. I explained my business. I explained we were busy and needed help. I explained that running a general store on the barter system is a lot like running a pawn shop used to be. You have to know what is valuable and what is not, and how to make a fair trade while still turning a profit. I explained we did not accept federal credits, the monetary system by which soldiers were paid. If they wanted to spend credits, they could buy something at the PX at Fort McCray and trade that. Otherwise, they were out of luck. He said he could handle that.

"Okay then," I said. "Time for a little test. Let's say I come in with a dozen eggs, a dead chicken, and a basket of tomatoes. How much do you offer me?"

"Depends on a few things," he said.

"Such as?"

"First I have to inspect the goods. How fresh are the eggs? Are any of them cracked? How long has the chicken been dead? Are the tomatoes ripe? Are they in good shape, or have bugs been chewing on them? Also, what is the customer asking for in exchange?"

He was doing well so far. "In this scenario, assume you know the customer wants ammunition for his hunting rifle. How do you evaluate his goods?"

He went through a list of things to look for and hit all the important points. I gave him a single nod of approval and presented him with a few more scenarios. In each one, he knew how to make the trade. His only fault was he was a bit too honest. He wasn't used to pushing to turn the trade in his favor. I explained this to him, and we tried a few more times. I pretended I was the customer, and told him to get a little more out of me than he was getting. In all but one negotiation, he came out ahead. We could work on that.

"I have four hard and fast rules," I said near the end of the interview. "One: Miranda Grove is off limits. You can be friends, but that's as far as it goes. You make a pass at her, and I'll throw you out on your ass. And I mean that literally. We clear?"

A nod. "Crystal."

"Two: you steal from me and I'll fucking kill you."

He almost laughed, then realized I was serious. "Mr. Riordan, I've never stolen a thing in my life. Not since I was a little kid, anyway. My dad caught me putting a pack of gum in my pocket and whipped my ass something fierce. I was too young to even realize what I was doing was wrong, but I never did it again."

"Keep that attitude. Okay. Rule number three: be nice to the customers, even when they're being assholes to you. This job requires a thick skin. People are going to get mad at you, call you names, curse at you, all kinds of shit. Smile and take it and make the trade. If someone tries to put their hands on you, you have a right to defend yourself. Anyone attempts something like that, you tell me and I'll ban them for life. Fair enough?"

"Fair enough."

"Last, but definitely not least, rule number four: Be. On. Time. When you show up late, I miss out on trades. That costs me. This is a business, not a pastime. The purpose is to turn a profit. Don't interfere with my ability to do that."

"I learned all about punctuality in the Army," Johnny said. "It won't be a problem."

We worked out a few more details. His work schedule, the half hour he had for lunch, and lastly, his pay. We decided to negotiate his compensation on a weekly basis based on how productive he was. I told him I paid my employees well, but expected them to earn it. He said he was okay with that. Finally, we stood up and shook hands.

"Mr. Green, I think you'll do. Come by tomorrow morning at six and Miranda will show you how the inventory system works. Keeping the books will become part of your job eventually, but we have to get you trained up first."

He smiled. He had good teeth. That would help him with the customers. "Sounds good to me, sir."

"Knock off that sir shit. Call me Eric. Or Mr. Riordan if it makes you feel better. Anything but sir."

"Will do."

He left and I reopened the store. I had a good feeling about him. It was the last good feeling I would have for a long time.

TEN

Word came down a week after Gabe and I met with General Jacobs.

We rode horses to Fort McCray. The guardsmen had cleared out most of the infected left over from the attack, but we all knew more would come. They always did. Luckily, things were relatively quiet that day. Gabe sat astride Red, while I tottered unhappily on a rented pony so short my feet nearly scraped the ground. On the way over, the big man finally got around to asking me why I accepted the mission so quickly, and why I showed no physical signs of the thrashing Allison must undoubtedly have meted out. I explained how Allison had overheard Captain Harlow on the sat-phone, and our conversation afterward. I left out the part where she seduced me.

"Three things occur to me," Gabe said. I looked up at him. Between his height and Red's, he looked like a skyscraper. "For starters, Allison is being very understanding. She usually tries to murder you when you take on a dangerous mission."

"Must be the baby. Hormones."

"Maybe. The second thing is someone really needs to have a conversation with Captain Harlow about operational security. Loose lips sink ships."

"Why don't you do it? He probably wouldn't listen to me."

"I think we should keep this one under our hats. Which brings me to my third point." He looked down the arm's length between his head and mine. "Why didn't you tell me?"

"Because I had no verification."

"You don't trust Allison?"

"I do, but I wasn't there when she overheard Harlow on the phone. She may have misinterpreted something. I didn't want to send you into the meeting with preconceived notions that might be wrong. I figured I would hear the general out, and if anything he told me didn't jive with what Allison heard, I'd tell you as soon as we were out of earshot."

"So everything Jacobs said was in line?"

"Exactly."

Gabe turned it over for a few hundred yards. "Okay. You have a point there. I'm not mad, but I still think you're an asshole for not telling me."

"You think I'm an asshole no matter what I do."

"Good point."

A ghoul emerged from the brush ahead of us, howled, and started in our direction. "You want it?" I asked.

Gabe drew his pistol, screwed on a suppressor, and fired one-handed. The ghoul dropped. "Come on," he said, urging Red to a trot. "There'll be more."

I kicked the pony. The dumpy little thing picked up to a frustrating canter that left me looking at Red's hairy ass all the way to Fort McCray. Once we were through the gate, I was not sorry to see the pony go. I hired a runner to ride it back and arranged with a civilian quartermaster to get a proper horse for the return trip. Gabe told me I was wasting time and trade. I told him to go smoke a turd in hell.

Wally led us up to Captain Harlow's office. He was not there, but General Jacobs was. He looked up from behind the desk. There was a stack of manila folders in front of him. "Come on in," he said. "We have a lot to discuss."

"Let me guess," I said. "This is the boring part where we go over the mission specifics in exacting detail until my brain melts and oozes out of my ears."

Jacobs smiled. "You sound like you've done this before."

*****

Three hours later, I was standing fifty yards from the helipad and wishing I had brought a flask filled with some of Mike Stall's surprisingly smooth grain liquor. The mission briefing had been interesting at first, then turned mind-numbing as we went over the details again and again. I knew the mission inside and out, but the effort had earned me a headache and my eyelids felt like sandpaper. Gabe did not seem much better. Jacobs looked like he could do it all over again and smile the whole way, the bastard. Afterward, we went outside to wait for the operative from Central Command to arrive.

"So who is this guy?" Gabe asked. "What's his background? SEAL, Green Beret, what?"

"He's what you might call an independent operator," Jacobs replied.

Gabe looked at him. "Like Eric here, or from the intelligence community?"

"Just wait until he gets here. All your questions will be answered." Jacobs wore a little smile.

"What's with the smirk?" I said. "You look like you just banged the preacher's daughter."

He laughed, but said nothing more. A few minutes later, the distant thumping of rotors reached my ears and grew steadily louder. I turned and saw a small dot slowly become a Blackhawk helicopter. The Blackhawk bathed us in dust and rotor wash as it touched down.

I covered my eyes out of instinct even though I was wearing goggles. Through the maelstrom, a figure emerged from the chopper's cargo bay. Goggles and a scarf covered his face, but I could see his hair was shaved into a narrow black mohawk. Immediately, I thought he looked familiar. Tall, about six-three,

81

maybe two-thirty, broad shouldered. He wore black fatigues and tactical gear with no insignia of any kind. In his hands was a SCAR 16 rifle. A shotgun was strapped across his back and he had a pistol in a holster on the left side of his tactical vest. At his waist, tucked through his web belt, was a tomahawk that looked roughly two centuries old. I had seen that tomahawk before.

The helicopter took off with no fanfare. No one else got out. As it thumped away, the operative removed his goggles and scarf. I smiled and held a hand out to a man I never thought I would see again.

He said something that sounded like 'ya-a-tay', and shook my hand. "It is good to see you again, Irishman."

"Well if it isn't my old pal Lincoln Great Hawk," I said. "How the hell are you?"

*****

Great Hawk had already been briefed. Gabe and I had planned to go back to Hollow Rock immediately after meeting with General Jacobs, but decided to stay on base for a while. The three of us reconnoitered to the enlisted club, took a booth, and ordered drinks.

"Correct me if I'm wrong," I said, "But that haircut does not look regulation."

The big Apache nodded slowly. "You are correct. It is not."

"Your enlistment up?" Gabe said.

"Yes. Six months ago."

"Who you working for now?"

Great Hawk waved a dismissive hand. "Some government agency with an acronym for a name."

"The same one I used to work for?"

"Possibly. I honestly am not sure. It is hard to tell who is who anymore."

"How'd they rope you into signing on?"

"There was no rope involved. The lord high shitbird of whoever visited me personally. Made the usual promises. Better pay, more autonomy, contract work. You know how they do things."

Gabe almost smiled. "Yes I do."

"I had planned to go home to Arizona. Try to find my people. I am still not sure why I did not. Perhaps I am afraid I will find only infected that were once my family and my nation. Perhaps it was all the people who told me going to Arizona alone was suicide. Perhaps, like all people, I am afraid of being alone."

He took a bite of stew and chewed it without haste. I had seen Great Hawk in action, and knew the slow act was just that—an act. He was like a desert snake, only expending energy when it really counted. And when he did, it was swift and deadly.

"It is entirely possible," he went on, "that I am the last of my people. I hope this is not true, but I acknowledge the possibility. Perhaps the reason I have not returned home is because I do not want to know for certain. If it is true, and I am the last, I do not know if I would want my life to continue. So I took the job. Perhaps it makes me a coward. Right now, I do not care."

I pointed my spoon at him. "You are a lot of things, Lincoln, but a coward is not one of them."

The face did not move, but somehow the obsidian eyes looked amused. "That is kind of you."

"So how are things in Colorado?" Gabe said.

"Improved. The first time I was in the Springs it was a dangerous place to live. Now, things are better. Safer. Too many refugees, though. Not enough resources. Salvage hunters have taken everything between Denver and New Mexico. There would not be much work for you two. Not unless you like to travel."

"Caravan guards?" I said.

"Yes. It is still a lucrative occupation, assuming you survive the journey. Many do not. Other than that, unless you are a doctor, tradesman, or engineer, work is scarce. Even farm work. The Army does very well during recruiting drives."

"I heard a whole new city has sprung up around the perimeter wall," Gabe said.

"That would depend on your definition of a city. If a squalid collection of shacks built from scrap can be called a city, then yes. Otherwise, it is an unwelcome refugee camp that refuses to go away. The kind of place you can indulge any vice."

Gabe grunted. "Sounds lovely."

"It is not."

"What about farming?" I said. "Isn't the government issuing land grants?"

"Yes. There is ample land between the Springs and the Illinois border. Not all of it will grow anything. If it does, there is the constant threat of infected and no walls to keep them out. If you know how to farm, can obtain seeds, dig irrigation ditches, survive if your crops do not, and are comfortable being anywhere from ten to three-hundred miles away from the nearest government outpost, you can do well for yourself. Some people have banded together to work large plots and are managing. There are many subsistence farmers who scrape by. Far more have made the attempt and failed. And this new world punishes failure harshly."

"What about ranching?"

"A slightly more viable option. Slightly."

"And here I thought they were doing brisk business out there."

"I am not saying the land is not productive. It is. I am simply saying it is not nearly as easy as some would have you believe.

84

You have done well for yourself here in Hollow Rock. I suggest you stay."

I stared at him in silence. Gabe gave me a funny look. I said, "You're probably right," and turned my attention back to my stew.

ELEVEN

I got home late.

Allison was getting ready for bed. She met me in the kitchen and put her arms around me. I hugged her back and said, "Honey, I love you, but if I don't eat this sandwich my stomach will climb out and eat it for me."

She let go and leaned against the counter. "So when do you leave?"

"Three days."

I put leftover chicken, lettuce, and hard white cheese on flatbread, folded it, and took a bite. Now that I did not live in a world overrun with salt, fat, and every spice known to man, I found I had learned to appreciate the more subtle tastes of natural food.

"That's not much time."

I let out a sigh. "No it isn't."

"So tell me about the secret government operative."

"Turns out it's not such a big secret. I bet you can guess who he is."

"Based on what?"

"I've worked with him before."

"Hm. Grabovsky?"

"Good guess, but no."

She tapped a slender finger against her lips. I found it distracting. Her lips were very interesting. "Is it Great Hawk?"

"Got it on the second try. Nicely done."

"You're kidding."

"Nope. Surprised the hell out of me. I got to say, though, he seems to be going through some personal issues."

"Really? Great Hawk? Does he even have feelings? I only met him once, but if he stood still, I would have mistaken him for a statue."

"Evidently he's deeper than you give him credit for. He's worried about his family in Arizona. Seems to think he might be the last of his people."

"The Apache?"

"His sect of them, anyway."

"Poor guy."

I looked at my wife in amusement. Only Allison, she of the infinite compassion, would call a hardened killer like Great Hawk 'poor guy'.

"And that's why I married you."

"Huh?"

"Sorry. Thinking out loud. How was your day?"

She closed her eyes, shook her head, and showed me the palm of one hand. "Don't ask."

"That bad?"

"I told you not to ask."

"Yes you did."

I poured myself a cup of water, took my sandwich into the living room, and sat down on the couch. The sandwich was gone in four bites. I washed it down with the cup of water and sat back. My eyes closed on their own and I felt sleep begin to pull me under.

"Hey."

"Yes, dear."

"You just started snoring."

"Didn't realize I was asleep."

Allison grabbed my chin and pointed my face toward the clock. "It's been ten minutes since you sat down."

"Son of a bitch. All right, let's go to bed."

Allison put the moves on me once the lantern was out, but it was no use. I was just too damn tired.

*****

The days leading up to a mission are strange ones. They go by in a blur. I tried to make the most of my time, but it slipped by so much more quickly than when life was relatively normal. I lay awake at night, usually after some gymnastics with Allison, and wondered what I could have done differently. If it turned out I was amidst my last days on Earth, had I used them like I should have? There was never an answer. What could I do but live my life as if I had a future? I had to assume the world was going to continue its warbling spin around the sun, and I was going to be a part of it. If I did not, I would wind up doing the worst thing of all, which was nothing.

During the daylight hours, I helped Miranda train Johnny Green while Allison was at the clinic. She issued a decree to her coworkers that she was leaving at four o'clock the next few days because her husband was going out of town. She did not need to point out I was headed into danger. Anyone who left town did so at enormous peril. And I had a reputation for throwing myself into awful situations at every turn.

Work continued on the north gate. Gabe and I managed to salvage some of the trade locked in storage there, but most had been destroyed. Volunteers cleared away the rubble, while the engineers from Third Platoon figured out a way to shore up the gap. The shipping containers were a good temporary fix, but something more permanent was needed. Rumor had it the plan was to erect a wooden palisade between the salvageable sections of concrete and reinforce it with the dirt-filled containers. There was certainly enough lumber around to make it work. But the townsfolk who had helped build the gate were unhappy about the engineers' solution. They had worked hard in those hectic early days, all their hopes pinned on building a wall around their home to keep the infected out. The tree-trunk poles would look hopelessly fragile next to the concrete pillars, reinforced or not. The new gate would be a constant reminder of what had been lost, and how much more they had to lose.

Finally, the morning arrived. I woke up early and made breakfast. It turned out to be a waste of time. Allison and I sat across the table from one another with not a scrap of appetite between us. My wife's eyes were red from crying the night before. Her hand strayed often to her stomach.

"This is ridiculous," I said.

"Which part?"

"All of it. Let's go sit down on the couch."

"What about this stuff?"

"Fuck it."

"Okay."

We sat on the couch and did the best thing either of us could think of, which was to hold each other and wait for the knock at the door. I pulled my wife close and put a hand on her stomach.

"How you holding up in there junior?" I said. "Doing some pushups? Jumping rope on your umbilical cord? Keep it up. Mommy needs you to be good and strong so you can come out quick. Nobody around here wants a long delivery. No slacking."

She laughed a little and wiped her eyes. "Just come back," she said. "That's all I ask, Eric. Just come back."

"That's a relief. I thought you wanted me to find some diapers while I was out there."

A smile. "Well, if you happen to spot any …"

And then I heard it; *knock, knock, knock*.

"Shit."

Allison sat up. "You should answer that."

"Are you sure? It's not too late. I can still back out."

"Yes, and feel like a coward for the next ten years. No, Eric. We both know this is something you have to do.

knock, knock, knock "Mr. Riordan? Are you home?"

"Yeah," I shouted. "Just a minute."

"Sorry sir."

"I'm going to slap that fucker. I hate being called sir. Makes me feel old."

Allison smiled. Everything I wanted in the world was in that smile. Now that I knew what it meant to love, really *love*, with everything I had and everything I would ever be, there was no going back. Without Allison, there was no life. No world. I kissed her softly.

"I love you, Allison."

"I know. You're the best man I've ever known. You can be a knucklehead sometimes, but I love you. Come back to me."

Something changed inside me, then. I had felt it before. A soft spot in my chest turned to ice. The tension of leaving fell away. There was no more fear. I wanted to get out that door. I wanted to face the Alliance on their home turf and hit them where they lived. I wanted to get there as soon as I could. And when I did, I would do everything I could to burn them down.

"I will."

Allison looked closely at me, searched my eyes, and nodded to herself. "Go on. I'll be all right."

I hugged my wife one last time, kissed her, and left.

"What's with you?" Gabe asked.

"What?"

"You haven't said five words since you got here."

I looked at my old friend. "You want me to start talking?"

"Not really. It's just not like you. The silence."

I went back to staring at the helipad. I was sitting on a rucksack and holding an Alliance style AK-47. The last three hours had seen me put nearly a thousand rounds through it—first at the target range, then at the close-quarters combat facility. It had more recoil than my M-6, but hit harder. The sights weren't terrible. I could ping a ten inch steel disc at a hundred yards without a scope, and do it reliably. Gabe thought that was good enough. Afterward, he showed me how to take the AK apart and clean it. I practiced until I could do it without help. My shoulders were sore from recoil, I had the beginnings of a headache, and my ears felt grimy from three hours of wearing double hearing protection and sweating.

"Great Hawk hasn't spoken much either. You don't seem concerned about him."

If the Apache heard me, he gave no indication. He was lying on the ground, head propped on his pack, reading a hardcover copy of *The Brothers Karamazov*. Gone were the black fatigues and tactical gear, replaced by stained and threadbare traveling clothes and sturdy hiking boots. Same for Gabe, Hicks, and me.

"Yeah, but he's not the talkative type. You are. Usually. So what's the deal?"

"I don't know, Gabe. Maybe it's the fact I'm leaving my pregnant wife behind so I can go sleep in the dirt for a couple of weeks and get shot at by a bunch of Alliance assholes. Or, maybe it's the prospect of crossing open territory on foot with God knows how many infected around. Possibly, it's both."

"Sorry I asked."

I picked up a blade of grass and started tearing it into little pieces. Hicks stood up, said he had to use the latrine, and walked away.

Gabe was right. I was not myself. The sharp, icy feeling in my chest had not left. It seemed to be expanding. The reasons I gave Gabe for acting the way I did were bullshit. I was not worried about leaving home. I was not worried about anything at all. I was impatient. I was ready to fight. And I wanted to do it *now*. But I couldn't. I had to sit near this helipad and ignore the looks passing soldiers gave us. I could have waited at headquarters or the mess hall, but I was used to spending most of my life outdoors and wanted to be outside. Gabe, Hicks, and the Hawk had come along without being asked.

Calm down, idiot. Pretty soon, you'll have all the fireworks you can handle.

We sat in silence and waited. Night fell. The stealth Blackhawk was practically on top of us before we heard it. The chopper landed in the dark and the three of us picked up our gear and headed toward the open bay door. Crewmen in black fatigues with painted faces ushered us in wordlessly and made sure we were strapped in before taking off.

As quiet as it was outside the helicopter, it was a cacophony inside. I put on a headset and, after flipping a switch, found I could talk to the others and the flight crew. We did a quick mic check and then rode in silence.

It was not my first time in a stealth chopper. The last time had been on an infiltration mission. I had worked for weeks with a friend of mine, who was now dead, to develop my cover. It worked. I did not like to think about the rest of it. The tunnels, the beatings, starving in the dark with other gaunt men, accidentally killing a man in a fight—a man who had done nothing to deserve his fate. Or maybe he did. I don't know. Our only interaction was to fight, and that ended with him lying in a pool of his own blood. Didn't exactly leave much time for conversation.

It took us an hour to reach the rendezvous, so I figured the Blackhawk must have been cruising at about a hundred and fifty miles an hour. A swift bird. When we were close, the crewmen helped us into rappelling harnesses.

While training to infiltrate the Free Legion, Gabe and my dead friend, Captain Steven McCray, had taught me how to fast-rope. I still practiced once a week, partly to maintain proficiency, and partly because I thought it was a good time. Hollow Rock is a nice place to live, but a den of pleasures and delights it is not. A man has to entertain himself somehow.

The chopper hovered over a clearing in the middle of a broad swath of green known as the Apple Creek Conservation Area. We were a few miles from the Mississippi River on the Missouri side. We were to hike to a specific area marked on GPS and meet two operators from Task Force Falcon. According to General Jacobs, they had a boat waiting for us. I hoped he was right. Swimming was not an option, and we did not have time to build a raft.

The pilot hovered patiently while we harnessed up, donned our NVGs, and fast-roped out of the cargo bay. Gabe and the Hawk descended one side while Hicks and I took the other. In seconds, our boots hit terra firma, we dropped our harnesses, and the helicopter slid off into the night.

We needed to orient ourselves, but first, we had to get out of sight. When entering enemy territory via air, it is critical to move away from the landing zone as soon as possible. No telling who might have seen us.

I turned off my NVGs momentarily and flipped them up. The night was nearly pitch black despite the fact we were only three days from a full moon. I looked at the sky and saw low heavy clouds scudding along under dim pewter luminescence. Hardly any light reached the ground. Good. Unless someone had been watching this specific area with a night vision scope, we most likely had not been seen.

Before leaving for the mission, I had talked to General Jacobs regarding my concerns there might be a mole in either

Echo Company or Central Command. I told him it was a bad idea to have a pre-determined LZ. Somebody might talk, and I had no desire to be captured as soon as I hit the ground. Furthermore, it would be best if he did not reveal the mission specifics to anyone until we were already well within Alliance territory. He assured me the only people who knew the plan were him, me, Gabe, Hicks, and Great Hawk. Everyone else involved was a bit player. They knew their part, but not the whole picture. He would keep a lid on everything until it was done. I told him if someone was smart, and was monitoring the goings-on there at Fort McCray, they might see a pattern. They might send a message just to cover their ass. He told me I was appropriately paranoid. That was a good thing. But this was not the general's first rodeo, and he was taking precautions. I took him at his word.

Half a mile of hiking through the piney woods wearing NVGs is not as easy as one might think. NVGs throw off depth perception and limit peripheral vision. You reach your hand out for a tree an arm's length away and nearly fall because, as it turns out, it was actually a few inches out of reach. Or, you jam your fingers because it was closer than it looked. Then there are roots, vines, and big rocks. It is best to high-step over obstacles just to be safe.

Gabe and Great Hawk agreed we were far enough away from the LZ to do a little land navigation. The Hawk took a ruggedized tablet from his pack and brought up our position on GPS, his poncho wrapped around him to block the light emitted by the screen. A minute or so went by before he emerged.

"We went a half mile in the wrong direction," he said. "Rendezvous is northeast of here."

Gabe leaned his head back and let out a sigh. "All right. How about we swing south half a klick, turn east until we're in line, and then head north to the rendezvous."

The Hawk nodded once. "A good plan."

Hicks also concurred. Nobody looked at me. Since my opinion clearly did not count for much, I adjusted my pack and said to Gabe, "Lead the way."

We fanned out at five meter intervals and got moving. Gabe set an easy pace. We had radios, but decided not to use them. With the NVGs, we could see each other just fine. The forest around us grew taller the farther we went, transitioning from saplings and brush to tall, old-growth pines, maples, elms, and cedars. The canopy overhead blocked sunlight to the ground, which prevented the formation of significant undergrowth. It made for easy travel, but if we saw someone, there would not be much to hide behind. Tree trunks only conceal from one angle. It takes foliage to provide camouflage. I thought about the ghillie suits we all carried and wished I had suggested putting them on before setting out.

Next time.

We reached the point where we were due south of the rendezvous and turned north. Three kilometers to go. Half the distance went by with no problem. Then, up ahead, Gabe stopped and held up a fist. When he saw we had halted, he lowered a palm toward the ground and walked his fingers a few steps. *Danger ahead. Approach my position low and quiet.*

The ground had been sloping upward for roughly the last hundred meters. Gabe was just down from the top of the rise. When I joined the others next to him, I saw what the holdup was.

A horde.

Not a big one. By its size, maybe thirty or forty ghouls. The horde may have been small, but it presented a big damn problem. The undead are more active at night than during the day, and if the fight got too loud, every walking corpse within a mile would be coming for us.

"We are too close," Great Hawk whispered. "If we back off and try to go around, they will hear us."

I noted the direction the horde was walking—due south. Which meant they were headed straight for us.

"Hawk, my man, I think they already have."

TWELVE

Fighting ghouls in the dark is, under most circumstances, suicidal. It is hard to fight what you cannot see. And since the undead have a tendency to go for the throat, many of them are unable to howl and groan like their less damaged counterparts. Furthermore, for some reason, at night, ghouls do not snarl until they are right on top of you. During the day, they'll holler at you from a mile away. At night, they wait until they are within lunging distance. To my knowledge, no one knows why.

If we had been fighting blind, our only option would have been to run for it and hope for the best. But we did not need to run. We had night vision. With NVGs, the ghouls' stealth became an advantage in our favor.

"Hicks, Eric, you two come with me," Great Hawk said. "Gabriel, stay up here on overwatch. Do not fire unless you have no other choice."

The set of Gabe's mouth said he didn't like it, but he nodded anyway. "Skirmish line," he said. "That's your best bet. Hold the high ground and make them come up the hill."

"Agreed."

The Hawk nodded to Hicks and me. We dropped our packs and rifles and drew our hand weapons. In Hicks' case, it was a spear with a short handle and a long, narrow blade. Spears are not the best tools for fighting the infected, but Hicks' skill with the weapon more than made up for any inherent disadvantages. I'd been tempted on more than one occasion to ask him where he learned to use it, but held back. One does not ask people about their lives before the Outbreak. It just isn't done.

97

My blade of choice was not actually a blade. The Europeans used to call it a small-sword. It looks sort of like a rapier, but the blade does not have sharp edges. It is triangular in design and has a needle sharp point. An ornate handguard winds from the crossguard down to the pommel. The crossguard itself is round, almost like that of a katana. The blade had originally been 27 inches, but I found this unwieldy after a while, and reduced it to eighteen inches with a pair of bolt cutters. Two hours with a steel file later, and the sharp point was restored. The shorter length worked very well; I no longer had to reach three counties behind me to stab something.

By itself, the small-sword is not very useful. The only practical way to kill a ghoul with it is to stab it through the eye—a difficult proposition most of the time. However, I had found a way to overcome this limitation. In my left hand, I held a short length of wood that split into a Y-shape six inches from the end. A handle protruded from its side like a policeman's night stick, and I had bolted a brace on the lower end that wrapped around the back of my forearm. The idea was to hold the ghoul's head steady with the Y-pole and stick them with the sword. I'd had plenty of practice. Most people, at first glance, did not believe my method would work. Invariably, this doubt went up in smoke the first time they saw me in action.

The three of us went halfway down the hill and stopped, put on goggles, and wrapped scarves around our mouths. I took a few deep breaths to steady myself. This was going to be a challenging fight; I was not used to battling ghouls at close range with impaired depth perception. I scanned the green-washed area around me and noted the locations of trees and anything I might trip over while walking backward. I took a fighting stance and shifted my weight forward for better balance. Balance is crucial when fighting the undead. Falling down in front of a horde is much akin to tying a steak around your neck and jumping into a pit of starving hyenas.

Great Hawk drew his knife and tomahawk and spun his arms like windmills to loosen them up. Hicks set his feet and held his spear at shoulder level, tip forward, both hands gripping tightly.

"Hold steady," Great Hawk said. "Let them come to us."

We waited. Great Hawk was in the center, me on his left, Hicks on his right. I rechecked the distance between us by raising an arm. My fingers just touched the hem of Great Hawk's shirt. He glanced over, saw what I was doing, and turned his attention back to the horde.

A minute went by. The horde struggled up the incline, which was much steeper on this side of the hill than the southward side. From where we stood, the ground tilted down toward the river a few hundred yards to our right. I put my weapons down, wiped my hands on my shirt to dry them, and resumed my stance. No one said anything. I searched the front rank of undead and picked my first target—a gray. I hate grays. Genderless, skinless, horrid things. A mockery of humanity. Something about them made me feel laughed at, like some powerful, malevolent force in the universe despised everything that was good about me. My hands tightened on my weapons.

Finally, they reached us. The gray I had picked moved a little faster than the infected behind it. Its arms were badly chewed up, but its legs were intact. I caught it by the throat with my Y-stick, raised my sword, and thrust the tip into its left eye socket. A little turn of the wrist, a quick pull backward, and I was ready for the next target. The gray shuddered twice and slumped to the ground.

Half a step back. Catch the throat, thrust, pull, release, repeat. To my right, Great Hawk used the spiked end of his tomahawk to crush skulls while his other hand stabbed infected through the eyes with his knife. When a weapon got stuck, he kicked the ghoul in the mid-section and ripped it free. I did not know many men strong enough to do that, and Gabe was one of them. That told me something.

I could not see Hicks, but I knew his fighting style. A quick thrust through the soft palate or the sinus cavity, a twist that traveled from his hips all the way to his hands, and out came the spear. Kick the dead body out of the way and look for the next one.

99

Behind my scarf, I kept my mouth open and took big, long breaths. Fighting hand to hand is exhausting, and one of the most fatal mistakes a person can make is to forget to breath. You kill two or three ghouls and think you're doing okay, and the next thing you know your arms feel like they're made of lead and your lungs are on fire. Good thing I stay in shape.

The hill made things easier. Holding the high ground gave us a reach advantage, and as we killed more and more infected, their dead bodies tripped the ghouls behind them and slowed their advance. The farther up we went, the more spread out the horde became. At the outset, I'd had to work fast. Now, I could take my time and be sure of my footing before attacking.

When we reached the crest of the hill, there were only eight left. I heard the distinctive *shing* of Gabe's sword leaving its scabbard just before I felt his presence beside me.

"Don't worry, buddy," I said, breathing a little faster than normal. "We saved a few for you."

"And I appreciate it." Gabe took two steps forward, swung his falcata, and half of a cranium spun away into the forest. Its former owner was still falling when Gabe slashed at the next closest ghoul. Sensing what he was doing, I backed off and told Great Hawk and Hicks to do the same.

There was a time when Gabe would have fought with two weapons—sword in the right hand, axe in the left. But a few months ago, someone took exception to his left ring finger and shot it off. He had been working on strengthening the remainder of his hand to compensate, but was not yet confident enough to start dual-wielding again.

While the rest of us watched, the big man went through the ghouls like a scythe, killing all but one of them with a single blow. The last one was nearly as tall as him, and had very long arms. Not wanting to risk it grabbing him, he spun his sword in a figure-eight and sent the arms flipping away into the darkness. An overhead chop completed the motion, splitting the walking corpse's head straight down the middle. The two halves yawned away from each other to reveal a grotesque cross-section of the human skull. Gabe pulled his sword free and the corpse went down.

"Come on," he said, turning back to us. "No time to waste."

We took a moment to clean our weapons with homemade disinfecting wipes—AKA rags soaked in nearly pure alcohol from Mike Stall's still—and headed northward. As we circumnavigated the horde, I looked at them through the grainy image of my goggles. No funeral for these folks. No mourners. Someone must have loved them, once. Someone had given them their first bath, their first dress, their first kiss. They must have had wives, husbands, siblings, children, friends. But none of that mattered now. The dead in this little patch of woodland would be attended by vultures and insects until their flesh was gone, and after, their bones would lay in this place until they turned to dust.

The last dead ghoul I passed was a gray. The grays were a recent phenomenon. At first they had been a rumor, something a friend of a friend had seen, but no one in Hollow Rock gave the stories much credence. Then, about four months ago, we started seeing them. Only a few at first, but lately in greater numbers. There was a lot of speculation as to what it meant, but no real answers. All anyone knew was the grays had all been dead a long time, probably more than a year, and they were ugly as hell.

Personally, I thought the answer to the mystery lay in the age factor. Was it something they all went through if they lived long enough, or only specific ones? In either case, there had to be some kind of catalyst that triggered the change. Which, to me, begged an obvious question:

Over time, would they change any further?

No, I told myself. *I'm sure there is some perfectly logical explanation why they change. Probably something to do with being dead and exposure to the elements.*

I wanted it to be a comforting thought. But as we cleared the horde, I could not help but stare, as if staring long enough would answer my questions. The gray looked so utterly alien, so completely inhuman, I could not help but wonder what its transformation meant.

And the wondering made me uneasy.

THIRTEEN

Gabe was the only one with optics.

It was a Leupold hunting scope, the kind thousands of people owned before the Outbreak. The accessories Gabe used to mount it to his AK could have been scavenged from virtually anywhere—very plausible if we ran into an Alliance or ROC patrol. He peered through it at the rendezvous point, looking for our contacts.

"Don't see anyone," he said.

He put the rifle down, dug around in his pack, and came out with an infrared scope. If the wrong people found that one, plausibility would no longer be a problem. Who could shoot fastest, however, would be.

Gabe peered through it for several long minutes. I sat and waited with Great Hawk and Hicks. Bugs swarmed around us, buzzed in our faces, and tried to climb in our ears. Mosquitoes had already raised several bumps on my neck and hands. Oddly, the normally stoic Great Hawk seemed the most irritated. He slapped, and gesticulated, and muttered something about missing the goddamn desert. I would have laughed if I was not sincerely worried he might cut my throat for doing so.

"Got 'em," Gabe said. "They're under a tarp near the waterline."

"Where?" Hicks asked.

Gabe pointed. "See that clearing just south of where the river starts bending east?"

103

"Yep."

"The treeline just north of it. Looks like they're waiting for us."

"Just to be safe," I said, "why don't we swing around and come up on them from behind. If they spook, we have the pre-arranged code word."

"Just thinking the same thing."

It took us most of an hour. The ground got softer and squishier the further down we hiked. There were fewer trees and more undergrowth, both a good thing and a bad thing. I had a feeling we were standing in a flood plain that had not flooded in a few months, and hoped it was not raining up north. If it did, things could get bad in a hurry.

We got to within fifty yards before Gabe held up a fist. He motioned to Great Hawk and pointed in front of him. The Apache nodded and went ahead. I tried to follow his progress, but he was too good. In seconds, he was just another shadow among the trees and bushes. A few minutes later, movement caught my eye. I couldn't hear it, but I had a feeling Great Hawk had just made contact. If he had, it meant he was looking at whoever was out there through the aperture of a gun sight.

There was a little more movement, but no gunshots rang out. So far, so good. A couple of minutes later, Great Hawk emerged from the undergrowth.

"It is them," he said.

"Great," Gabriel replied. "Let's get the fuck out of here. I'm starving."

We approached and gave the password. The voices ahead of us answered with the correct response and emerged from cover. I could not tell much about their appearance. One was a little taller than me, and the other was around five-foot eight. Both wore ghillie suits and NVGs, their faces painted so dark they disappeared beneath their hoods.

"Come on," the shorter one said. "Give us a hand."

He led us to a large lump a few yards away and pulled aside a few tarps to reveal a black boat. It was long, more than long enough for the six of us to fit comfortably, and had low bulkheads and a fiberglass hull. There was a blanket-wrapped bundle in the middle I assumed contained oars. At least I hoped it did, since there was no outboard motor.

We helped the two special-ops guys drag the boat out of the woods down to a narrow strip of muddy riverbank, and climbed in. Gabe stayed out to push the stern until we were afloat, then hopped in. One of the men in ghillie suits unwrapped the bundles and handed out oars.

"Head straight for the opposite shore," he said. The rest of us acknowledged and began paddling.

Rivers are deceptive, as are lakes and any kind of flat water in general. You look across to the opposite shore and it does not seem very far away. You tell yourself you could probably swim it. If you are smart, you do not try. It is always farther than it looks.

We paddled and paddled, but the other shore never seemed to get any closer. A few times, we had to make course corrections. The current beneath us was strong, but not too swift. I figured we must be on one of the wider parts of the river that could be over half a mile across. If I remembered correctly, there were places where it was a full mile or more. I hoped we were not on one of them.

I looked behind me after what felt like forever, and where we had left seemed equidistant to where we were going. A few minutes later, I thought the trees on the bank ahead looked taller. The more we paddled, the taller they got. At long last, we finally felt the hull bump against the muddy bank.

We jumped out into ankle deep water. There was a layer of sediment beneath me, but it was mercifully shallow. It only sucked at my boots a little until we finally hauled the boat ashore.

"Help us hide it," said the same guy who had spoken earlier. I figured he must be in charge. We dragged the boat behind the

105

treeline, then covered it with camouflage tarps. That done, the short guy addressed us again.

"Follow me," he said.

We went.

*****

The base of operations was a two-story house built far back from a winding country road. The driveway was white gravel and must have been over half a mile long. The windows were dark, the paint peeled, and the wide front porch had begun to sag in places. To me, it looked like the Ritz Carlton.

"We got nothing going on tonight," the short guy said. "We'll get you settled in and introduce you to everybody. Don't worry about standing watch tonight, we got it covered."

I thought I detected a trace of California in his speech. The taller one had yet to say anything. Up close, I noticed he had broad shoulders and looked to be about Great Hawk's size. Not a small man.

From the outside, it looked like there was no light in the house. But once we were through the door, I saw someone had nailed thick black blankets over the doors and windows. I had to push one out of the way to get inside.

The front door opened into a living room. The living room contained folding tables littered with guns, packs, ammunition canisters, LAW rockets, and a radio and satellite array. There were several plastic olive-drab crates stacked along one wall. The room was dimly illuminated by a couple of low-banked propane lanterns that did not quite reach the blackness to our left. If the island counter in that direction was any indication, I was looking at the kitchen.

I saw no furniture aside from a few green camping stools and some lawn chairs. We stood on dingy yellow carpeting that had probably been white a few years ago, but now was covered in

106

muddy boot prints, dirt, leaves, and other detritus. There was a large bloodstain to my right by the window, and rusty brown spatter on the walls. I breathed in through my nose. Yep. Someone died in here. The place smelled faintly of death and strongly of mildew. We were the only people in the room.

"Where is everybody?" I asked.

"Outside," Short Guy said. "They'll be back in a few minutes."

"What are they doing?"

"Watching."

I walked to the stairs and peered upward into darkness. "Yeah. Sure."

"Take a lantern and head upstairs," he said. "Second door on your right. The bedrooms are pretty big, so you'll have plenty of space for your bedrolls."

The two men pulled back the hoods of their ghillie suits and began stripping them off. The first thing that struck me was how young they were. The shorter one was the older of the two, and I would have been shocked if he was a day over twenty-five. Short guy had a medium build, brown hair and eyes, and a full, dark beard. The face was square and the eyes held a striking combination of strength and intelligence.

The taller one was blond, blue eyed, longish hair and beard like his counterpart, and had a distinctly Nordic look to him. Where the short one's expression was thoughtful and curious, the big one's was insolent and cocky. I sensed the potential for trouble there.

"I'm Anderson," Short Guy said. "He's Bjornson."

"Nice to meet you," I said. "Eric Riordan."

Anderson nodded politely. Bjornson snorted.

"Sergeant Caleb Hicks, First Reconnaissance Expeditionary."

107

"Heard of you guys," Anderson said. "New unit. Been through some shit."

"Indeed we have."

"Staff Sergeant Gabriel Garrett. Marines."

Both men nodded. Bjornson seemed less scornful of Gabe.

"Chief Petty Officer Lincoln Great Hawk."

"Great Hawk?" Bjornson said. "You Navajo?"

"*Mashgalende*. Or Apache, for the ignorant."

"I've heard of you. You're a SEAL."

"Not anymore."

Anderson said, "I've heard of you too. Good to have you on the team."

"I did not come to join your team." Great Hawk dropped his pack and removed a green metal tube from one of the pockets. He handed it to Anderson. "I came to lead it."

I had known this was coming, but had not thought much of it. From the look on Anderson's face, it was not welcome news.

"I wasn't told about this," Anderson said.

"I am telling you now. Read the orders. They are from General Jacobs himself."

Anderson unscrewed one side of the tube and pulled out a rolled sheaf of papers. There were three pages. He read them all carefully. When he was finished, he took a butane lighter from a vest pocket, carried the papers over to the fireplace, and burned them.

"A little dramatic, don't you think?" I said.

"It is procedure," Great Hawk said.

"Oh."

Bjornson snorted again and pointed at me. "Who the fuck is this guy? He a spook or somethin'?"

Southern accent. Deep South. I could practically smell the kudzu and humidity.

"He is a civilian contractor," Great Hawk said. "As for who he is, he gave you his name. And, technically, he outranks you. So play nice."

"I don't answer to fuckin' civilians."

"I am a civilian. As is Mister Garrett. So yes, you do answer to fucking civilians."

Bjornson clamped his mouth shut.

"To clarify," Anderson said, "It's Captain William Anderson. Loudmouth over there is Sergeant Hans Bjornson. He's annoying, but he does his job."

"Very Icelandic name you got there," I said. "First generation American, I'm guessing?" Bjornson did not answer, and did not look amused.

A strange pattern of knocks sounded at the door. Anderson walked over and knocked back. The door opened and four more men in ghillie suits filed in.

"LaGrange and Stewart take the watch?" Anderson asked one of them.

"Yes sir," came the reply.

The four men took off their ghillie suits. There was a round of introductions. May, Liddell, McGee, and Taylor. All of various ranks that meant little to me and did not seem to make much difference to the spec-ops guys either. Anderson appeared to be the only one who warranted a nod to the rank system. Taylor asked me if I was a technical consultant. I told him I was not. He asked if I was an intelligence operative. I said I could tell him, but I would have to kill him. He did not think this was funny.

The four men would have been tough to tell apart in a police lineup. Between the camouflage and the face paint, they all looked the same. Except for May, whose dark brown skin and

109

shiny bald head set him apart. They were friendly to me in a reserved way, and respectful to the other three.

Gabe once told me military guys can spot one another in a crowd, and most can tell if someone has never served. Something about a tension in the shoulders, a straightness to the posture, a certain look in the eyes. I don't know anything about it, but the men of Task Force Falcon could tell immediately I was not one of them.

Going to have to prove yourself, Riordan.

"It has been a long day," Great Hawk said, indicating Gabe, Hicks and me. "This will probably be our last chance for a full night's sleep for the next couple of weeks. We should take advantage of it."

We raised no argument. Great Hawk said he would give a briefing at 0900 hours. He wanted everyone there. Anderson said he would make it happen, and we all dispersed to our rooms.

Anderson had not been lying when he said the bedrooms were large. I had seen apartments smaller than ours. And like the downstairs area, there was no furniture. I wondered what had happened to it.

As I lay down in my bedroll, I thought I would have trouble sleeping. I still felt amped up from fighting the infected earlier. Turned out I was wrong. I closed my eyes, and roughly four seconds later, a hand grabbed my shoulder and shook it. When I opened my eyes, expecting to see darkness, I was greeted by dim light filtering through the blanket over the window. The hand belonged to Hicks.

"Rise and shine, amigo. It's 0830. Just enough time to get ready for the briefing."

"I feel like I just fell asleep."

"Yeah, that happens sometimes. See you down there."

As I sat up stiffly, body sore from the previous day's exertions, I began to wonder if I had made a mistake coming

110

here. Then I thought of Allison, and my baby, and I stood up and got moving.

FOURTEEN

The briefing went as briefings go.

Great Hawk did not repeat things the way General Jacobs had. He also did not rely on paper. With the windows and doors blacked out, it made sense to connect the ruggedized tablet to a projector Anderson retrieved from one of the green plastic crates. He set it on a table and squared the image on a bare white wall. The information was the same as the last time I heard it. There were a few questions, which Great Hawk answered clearly and succinctly.

A few times, I zoned out and found myself staring at the generator we used to power the projector and charge our radios. It was small, multi-fuel design, and about as loud as the little fan I kept at my desk when I used to work for one of the big banks in Charlotte. The inner workings were contained in a green box, about two square feet, gas and oil inlets on top, with an air intake on one side and an exhaust tube that snaked across the room and vented the waste fumes out the nearest window. A panel on the front showed the usual controls and outlets. I resolved to ask around when I got home and ascertain the cost to procure one.

"All right," Great Hawk said after just over an hour of lecture. "Any questions? Anything at all?"

No one spoke.

"Very well. If you think of anything, do not hesitate to ask. There are no dumb questions on this mission. It is too important."

There was little conversation afterward. We all knew what to do. We wasted no time. The mission started immediately.

Our first order of business was to conceal the things we were not bringing along. Using shovels and entrenchment tools, we dug holes, buried most of the crates, the radio and satellite array, and the weapons and ammunition we were not bringing with us. After we left, a recovery team would HALO drop in at night, retrieve the gear, and ride out on a stealth Blackhawk.

The house had a detached garage in which were hidden five hand-drawn carts. The carts contained the kinds of goods one would expect to find in an average trade caravan: guns and ammunition of varying types and calibers, dried fish packed in salt, last year's vegetables canned in mason jars, shovels, mattocks, axes, and rakes, clothes and shoes, and in lockboxes, feminine hygiene products, instant coffee, bags of tea, and the holy of holies, sugar. There were also a few bars of pre-Outbreak soap, laundry detergent, all-purpose cleaner, spray disinfectant, and ever-popular trash bags. Rounding things out were blankets, a box of diapers (which would go for a pretty penny, so to speak), coffee filters, cotton balls, a case of toothbrushes, and a few small boxes of razor blades.

The carts were heavily modified utility trailers, the kind people used to drag behind riding lawn mowers. They had been reinforced with steel re-bar, and each one had a crude rawhide harness clearly designed for human shoulders. Handles on the back allowed people to push from behind and lift the carts if the wheels got stuck. They reminded me of the cart Gabe and the Glover family and I had loaded our belongings into before heading east from the Appalachians over a year ago. The intention then had been to go to Colorado and start a new life. We made it as far as Hollow Rock. And if not for Allison, I would never have gone anywhere again because I would be dead. But that's another story.

The spec-ops guys ditched the fatigues and changed into traveling clothes. Lots of flannel and Carhartt, waterproof boots, head rags and ball caps, scarves and goggles. We armed ourselves with Chinese AK-47s and 9mm pistols Gabe told me

113

were Russian manufactured Makarovs. I accepted one, two spare magazines, three boxes of ammunition, and put it all in my pack. It was there if I needed it, but I preferred my Kel-Tec. And of course, Bjornson noticed my mostly plastic composite gun and could not resist the opportunity to sling a barb.

"The fuck is that toy on your hip?" he said. "Looks like a little girl gun."

I had my back to him, so I said, "You staring at my ass again, cupcake?"

"What? What the fuck did you just call me?"

I turned and enunciated slowly. "Cup. Cake. Idiot. That's your name from now on. Cupcake. As for the gun, it's a Kel-Tec PMR 30. Fires twenty-two magnum, magazine holds thirty rounds. Great for fighting hordes, and not bad against people if you know how to aim."

"You fucking call me cupcake again and I'll stomp your ass."

"Anytime you're ready, cupcake." I put down my pack, stepped forward, and set my feet.

"Hey," Anderson shouted, overhearing us. "Knock that shit off. We don't have time for a dick measuring contest. You're supposed to be professionals. Act like it."

Bjornson tried to bore a hole in me with narrowed eyes. He must have thought it made him look mean. I wondered if he practiced that look in the mirror when no one was around. For some reason, I just could not bring myself to be frightened. I looked at Anderson.

"Keep your ape on a leash, and I won't have to hurt him. He seems to have a problem minding his own business."

"You little shit, I'll-"

"Enough." Anderson's voice cut the air like a whip. Bjornson stiffened. "Hans, he didn't say a word to you. If you start acting like an idiot, I'll send you packing and you can walk

114

your ass home. This mission is too important to spare your fragile little ego. So grow up. Do I make myself clear?"

"Yes sir." Bjornson stomped away.

I returned my attention to the cart I was working on. The bottom layer of steel sheeting, when pulled in exactly the right way in exactly the right place, opened to reveal a four-inch depth of false bottom. Within this, I stowed the weapons General Jacobs had arranged for me:

-Body armor.

-M-6 carbine, sniper configuration, chambered in hard-hitting 6.8 SPC, adjustable stock.

-210 cartridges loaded in 30 round magazines and more in boxes, all match-grade stuff.

-Screw-on suppressor.

-Adjustable one-to-six power illuminated-reticle VCOG scope.

-MOLLE tactical vest and web belt.

-Night vision goggles and scope attachment.

Gabe's gear shared the same false bottom as mine, and would remain in the cart until needed.

We also stowed our hand weapons in the cart. Gabe's falcata and my small-sword/Y-stick combination were well known among the Alliance. We were both wanted men in this territory, and descriptions of us had been widely distributed. To mask our appearances, both of us had grown out our hair and beards. I hoped it would be enough. If not ... well, I was pretty good with the AK-47. Better than the competition, I was willing to bet.

Anderson and Great Hawk conducted a final inspection to make sure anyone who found this place would not know we had been here. When they were satisfied, Great Hawk checked his map and pointed northeast.

115

"It is still early, but we have many miles to cross. Stay alert for infected. Move out."

Gabe took up the reins of our cart and buckled them on. I walked behind the cart, ready to lend assistance when needed. Otherwise, I was responsible for watching the area around us for threats. I knew Gabe would do the same.

There were no rousing speeches, no fanfare, no muttered prayers or final instructions to comrades if we did not make it back. Great Hawk set off at a trot to scout ahead, Anderson took point, and, to a soundtrack of strained grunts and squeaking axles, the mission began.

*****

We went south through the forest for a mile or so, then followed an arrow straight path razed before the Outbreak to make room for high-tension wires and their associated towers. The path would lead us to Highway 13, the primary trade route into the Alliance capital.

Overhead spanned power, T1, and T3 lines, no longer humming with electricity and digital communications signals. The towers looked rusty. The cables and insulators looked to be in poor repair. I hoped none of them broke. I hoped there were no big battles ahead of or behind us. I once saw what happens when the big lines snap. The result had been a lethal whipsaw of heavy cable that traveled for miles and leveled everything in its path. Such an event would rip the lot of us to shreds without slowing the cables in the slightest. Great Hawk seemed aware of this, and had us stick close to the treeline.

Three hours in, it started raining.

Of course it's raining, I thought. *Drought last summer, a few feet of snow in the winter, and nothing since the spring thaw. But when I'm out here in the middle of nowhere, in enemy territory, pushing a heavy damn cart through the mud while carrying fifty pounds of gear,* now *it rains. Lovely. Just fucking lovely.*

The terrain did not help. Scramble up one hill, stop and catch my breath, try to keep the cart from sliding away on the downslope, repeat, repeat. The soldiers were having the same problems, but did not complain. So I kept my irritation to myself and trudged on in silence.

At least we had not seen any infected. Yet.

Our destination was Carbondale, Illinois, an unlikely place for the capital of an infant nation. But that was where the Alliance's president and council of representatives had set up shop. The town had been mostly abandoned during the Outbreak, making for easy cleanup for Alliance forces. There was a large lake near the town, providing a ready source of food and fresh water.

The people who had moved in and took over the place farmed, raised chickens and goats, and manufactured ethyl alcohol to power multi-fuel generators and vehicles provided by KPA forces now occupying Alliance territory. Carbondale was open to trade, as were most Alliance towns, but trade caravans were heavily extorted by the town guard. Which mattered not in the slightest to any of us. We didn't care about the goods we were transporting.

We made seven miles the first day, less than half the distance to Carbondale. The plan had been ten miles, but Great Hawk called us to a halt late in the afternoon when we came upon a road intersecting our path. According to the tablet, there were buildings two klicks away at the end of that road. Any shelter was better than nothing, so off we went.

Traveling on the road was easier until we came to a point where several trees had fallen across some time ago. Rather than go over them, we took the carts around one at a time. It took four men per cart to force them over the soft, wet forest earth. Down the road, we had to repeat the maneuver twice more until, finally, a clearing came into view. Great Hawk signaled a halt, turned, and gestured to Hicks and me.

When we reached him, he pointed toward the field. "Scout ahead. Look for infected, or anything else. Do not engage. Come back and report what you see."

"Can do."

Gabe helped me empty our cart so I could retrieve my ghillie suit and sniper carbine. There was enough daylight I did not bother with the night vision equipment. Caleb borrowed Gabe's ghillie suit and sniper carbine to save time.

"Don't mess up my gear," Gabe said, nudging Caleb on the arm.

The young soldier grinned. "No promises."

Hicks took the left side of the road while I went right. At the top of the rise, we melted into the forest and began our sweep.

FIFTEEN

We brought radios. Mine crackled in my ear while I was lying behind some brush and scanning the windows of a building for movement. I guessed I was looking at some kind of processing facility for a chicken farm.

"Got infected," Caleb said. "Over."

Shit. "Where? Over."

"There's a big production house behind the processing plant you're looking at. I'd say there's probably about sixty or seventy infected in there hibernating. Over."

Hibernating infected. The most dangerous kind. They don't eat for long enough, or see any food go by, and they shut down like killing the engine on a car. Later, you walk into a town, look around carefully, think the place is clear, think you're safe, so you bust a window to get into a house or a store or something, and the next thing you know ghouls start pouring out of doorways and around corners and migrating in from the woodlands. A very easy way to find yourself surrounded. And a very painful way to die.

I carry a snub-nosed .38 caliber revolver on the small of my back. Caleb sold it to me, said he took if off a guy who tried to mug him back in Colorado Springs. It has a five-round cylinder, two-inch barrel, and each bullet therein has my name on it.

I will not become one of the infected. Not if I can help it.

"Let's keep circling," I said. "See what else there is to see. When were done, we'll meet on the road down the hill a ways and head back. Over."

119

"Sounds good. Out."

I got up slowly and moved as silently as I could northward. The damp ground and wet leaves made my job easier, if not more comfortable. The rain had stopped, but my clothes were soaked and I could feel water seeping in through the tops of my boots.

As I walked, I kept my head turned left, only glancing in front of me to read the way ahead. I rounded the corner of the processing building and saw the clearing open up farther out. The grass was chest high, so I needed to get to higher ground to see across the field.

A maple tree near the treeline made a likely candidate. I jumped and grabbed a thick lower branch and hung there a few seconds. The tree shuddered a little. A bird took flight. No groans, no howls, no gun-wielding North Koreans screaming a language I did not speak. I did a pull-up, swung my legs over the next nearest branch, and levered myself into the tree.

It was not comfortable. The branch I sat on was strong, albeit narrow. But I could see clearly across the field. As I raised my rifle to look toward the large shed that thousands of doomed chickens had once called home, I saw movement in the grass a few feet in front of me.

A ghoul. Must have heard me.

It stood up and whipped its head around, the mannerism disturbingly birdlike. My right boot, which was bracing my weight against the trunk, chose that moment to slip an inch against the rough, wet bark.

Fuckity, fuck, fuck!

The head stopped moving. The white, red-rimmed, lifeless eyes stared straight at me. The mouth opened. It began to draw in a ragged breath, probably the first one it had taken in months. There was no choice. I raised the carbine, sighted in quickly, and squeezed the trigger.

Muted crack. Backwards snap of the infected head. Hiss of damp grass as it slumped to the ground. I saw another one raise its head, come up to its knees, and turn its head in the same odd manner as its predecessor. I remained absolutely still, not even daring to breathe. One minute passed. Two. Finally, with an almost human expression of disappointment, the ghoul lay back down. I waited another couple of minutes, then slipped carefully, ever so carefully, down from the tree. When I felt far enough away to be safe, I keyed my radio.

"How you doing, Hicks? Over."

"I think the field is littered with infected. Kind of like undead land mines. Over."

"I can confirm that. I woke one of them up. Over."

A pause. "You take care of it? Over."

"Affirmative. I think we should head back now. Over."

"Roger, on my way. Out."

I was the first one back to the road. I waited for Hicks, and right when I thought I should radio him to make sure he was all right, the limb of a sapling moved seemingly of its own volition and Hicks appeared from the trees as if conjured. I had not heard him, nor seen any indication of his approach. Although, admittedly, I wasn't really trying. Regardless, the kid had talent.

"You good?" I asked.

"Yep. Let's go talk to Great Hawk."

We walked back and found the big Apache in conference with Gabriel and Captain Anderson. They stopped talking at our approach and waited for our report.

"Might not be the best place to bed down for the night," Caleb said. "Place is crawling with infected. Maybe a hundred or more."

Great Hawk looked disappointed. It was the first time I had seen any expression from him other than mild amusement. "Too many bullets to kill them all. Too loud. We'll have to find another place."

"Wait," I said. "I have a better idea."

121

"No," Gabe said quickly, slashing the air with his hand. "I know what you're thinking, and it's too dangerous."

"What are you talking about? I've done it plenty of times."

"Yes, and it's a miracle you're still alive."

"What are you two talking about?" Anderson asked.

Gabe pointed at me. "He wants to lead the horde away on foot."

"On foot?" Anderson's eyes went wide as he looked at me. "Are you insane?"

I glared at them. "Y'all are a bunch of candy-asses, you know that? I've done this hundreds of times. I know what I'm doing. I lead the horde away, you guys come in when I'm out of sight, kill the walkers left behind, and sweep the field for crawlers. If you don't want to waste ammo, use hand weapons. As for me, an hour, maybe two at most, and I'm back in camp eating cold jerky and dried peas. What's the problem with that?"

Great Hawk looked to the western sky. The sun was low on the horizon, framed in clouds of purple and tarnished gold. "We have less than an hour before sunset."

"Exactly my point. Do you really think we have time to find another shelter? We do it my way, we only risk one person. If we stumble around in the dark trying to find another campsite, we'll all be in danger."

Great Hawk's face was immobile for a few seconds. "You have a point. We will follow your plan."

Gabe said something unpleasant and stomped away. Great Hawk let him go. "Your friend worries for you," he said.

"I know," I said. "Now are we going to stand around sharing our feelings all night, or are we going to get to work?"

"You shouldn't go alone," Anderson said. "I'll ask for a volunteer to go with you."

"And if no one wants to help?"

"Then I'll voluntell somebody."

"Voluntell. I like that. But I don't think it's a real word."

"Sure it is," Anderson said, grinning. "It's what happens when you're voluntold to do something. Kind of like how I was voluntold to take this mission."

"Right. Well, volunteer, voluntell, whatever it is you're going to do, do it fast. I need to get moving."

"On it."

Anderson went to talk to his men. I dug out my NVGs, put in fresh batteries, and attached them in a pouch to the back of my web belt. My intention was to return before nightfall, but it never hurts to have a contingency plan. I also put my sniper carbine back in the cart—it would slow me down if I had to run—and put the suppressor for my Kel-Tec on my belt. As with the NVGs, I hoped I would not need it. But if I had to shoot my way out of a bad spot, I wanted to do so quietly.

"I still think this is a bad idea," Gabe said as I prepared to leave.

"I'm not arguing with you, Gabe."

He pinched the bridge of his nose with his left hand, the motion making the nub of his reduced ring finger wiggle. "Be careful."

"Really? Damn, I *so* wanted to give a ghoul a piggy back ride. Or maybe slow dance with one. Why do you have to suck the joy out of everything, Gabe?"

He tried to frown, but could not quite manage it. "Fuck you."

"Sorry, you're not my type. But maybe with a blond wig, some mascara, a little lip gloss ..."

"I'm going to slap you."

"My cue to leave. See you in a little while, amigo." I hit him on the shoulder and set off at a jog.

123

*****

An hour later, just as I thought I was home free, I tripped over a goddamn crawler.

The little shit was dragging itself through the field with one arm. If I had been looking down like I should have been, I would have seen it, dispatched it, and been on my merry way. But I was hungry, and tired, and pondering how running a four mile round trip through woodland was a lot tougher at thirty than it had been at nineteen when I competed on my alma mater's cross-country team, and the next thing I knew I was skidding face first through five-foot grass.

For a moment, I thought I had tripped over a large rock, or a piece of debris, but then I felt a hand clamp down on my ankle. The grip was immensely strong, like five pieces of steel digging into my flesh. I knew there was only one creature with that kind of strength, and I knew I did not have much time.

I tried to roll over, but the hand pulled and sent me back down to my stomach. My heel bumped against something, and I kicked out instinctively. The grip did not slacken, but for an instant, the pulling stopped. The hesitation gave me the time I needed to roll over.

The crawler was old. Its skin was dry and cracked, clothes worn away long ago, the flesh on its face tight and hollow. In a flash of thought, I realized I was looking at a ghoul in the process of turning into a gray. I also realized I had approximately half a second before it tried to bite me again.

My pistol was almost underneath me. I clawed at it, but could not turn to my left enough to free it from its holster. If I planted my right foot and strained, the ghoul would have a clear shot at my ankle. As I thought this, the crawler recovered and tugged at me again. So again, I kicked it in the face.

I gave up on the pistol and reached for my fighting knife. As it cleared its sheath, a size thirteen boot stomped on the crawler's head, pinning it to the ground. The hand holding my

124

ankle released and tried to grab the leg holding it down, but could not reach.

I scrambled away and got to my feet. "Just a second," I said.

I screwed the suppressor onto my pistol and took aim. "Okay, on three. One, two, ..."

As I said 'three', Sergeant Seth McGee stepped back and circled out of the line of fire. I fired twice, both rounds punching neat little holes in the crawler's forehead. Black and red ichor oozed from exit wounds on the back of the skull.

"Thanks," I said.

I looked at McGee, who had not been voluntold to come with me, but had volunteered. He was tall, maybe six-four, and very lean. Dark hair, full beard, and eyes even grayer than Gabe's. His nose had been broken once or twice, and a scar ran under his hairline from his ear all the way to his forehead.

"No problem," McGee said. It was the most he had talked since we left the others.

I'd had my doubts about McGee at first. At his height, and with his build, I estimated him at close to two-hundred thirty pounds. I wondered if he would be able to keep pace with me, being that I am four inches shorter and over forty pounds lighter. I need not have worried. He had broken a sweat during the run, but did not look overly winded. And he had had no trouble keeping up. In fact, I think he could have outdistanced me if he had wanted to.

I was vigilant the rest of the way back. There were a few more crawlers, but someone had already busted their skulls. To my left, I heard a grunt of effort and a wet crunching sound. I headed toward it and saw Hicks' head and shoulders rise above the grass.

"Where is everybody?" I called to him.

He held up a finger, keyed his radio and said, "See any others?"

125

A few seconds passed, then Hicks said, "Roger. Yes. They look fine." He looked at me and said, "Either of you bit?"

"Nope. I'm good. McGee?"

The tall soldier shook his head.

Hicks said, "Yeah, they're all right. We're heading in. Out."

I looked toward the processing facility and saw Great Hawk scanning the field with Gabe's thermal scope. He moved slowly and patiently, like he did everything else, and finally nodded in satisfaction. The three of us arrived just as he lowered his legs over the edge of the roof and dropped lightly to the ground. He motioned to us, and we followed him inside.

Most of the plant's processing equipment was still in place. A layer of light gray dust covered everything so thickly our boots left prints on the floor. It was obvious by the condition of the machines that someone had come through a long time ago and stripped the building of anything useful. I did a mental calculation of the dimensions, and figured the space at fifty meters in length, twenty wide, and perhaps twelve feet from floor to ceiling. Pitched roof overhead, exposed wiring, pipes, and steel support beams, cinder block walls painted white, cement floor polished smooth. Empty offices at the far end of the building.

Anderson's men had covered the windows with blankets and black tarps. The windows were rectangular and set high, almost six feet off the ground, which was good. I pulled a blanket back, looked up, and saw the glass was the kind reinforced with wire. Even better. If a ghoul, by some miracle, somehow managed to climb high enough to pound on the glass—and I had never seen a ghoul climb anything more challenging than a car—it would have a hell of a time getting through. Same for a living human. And the noise would give us ample time to mount an appropriate response.

All in all, not a bad place to spend the night. In fact, with a few friends and plenty of ammo, a person could clear the field, buy some seed, and make a home out of this place. But no one had, and I knew for certain people had found this place before

126

us—the stripped machinery was clear evidence of that. So why did they leave?

Easy answer? Marauders.

Better have a talk with Great Hawk.

SIXTEEN

"I agree," Great Hawk said. "And I have already taken precautions."

As usual, the Hawk had seen the same things I saw and drew the same conclusions. I was not sure if this spoke well for me or poorly for him. "So what's the plan?"

"What would you do?"

"Strict noise and light discipline. Four men per watch rotation, two-hour rotations. NVGs and suppressed rifles all around. Two men on patrol, one on overwatch, and a watch captain here in the building. Check-in at five-minute intervals, but otherwise, radio silence. Anybody misses a check-in, the watch captain wakes everyone up and we go on full alert."

Great Hawk nodded twice. "Two hour rotations?"

"Yes. You want to make sure the guys on watch are sharp. The longer people walk around in boredom, the duller they get. Shorter watches makes for fewer mistakes. We have twelve guys, which makes three watch rotations. Doesn't give us a lot of down time, but we knew that would happen going in. Just have to push through and hope we get another chance to rest."

One corner of Great Hawk's mouth creased upward. "You are a cautious one, Irishman."

"Kept me alive so far."

"That is true. But I think you are too used to dealing with civilian guardsmen. These men are trained professionals, like me. However, your thinking is sound. The watches will be three hours, but everything else will be as you say."

"Three hours is taking a risk," I said. "People tend to get sloppy after two."

"We need to rest. Tomorrow will be no easier than today, and we have farther to travel."

"Rest won't do us a damn bit of good if we're dead."

"I have made my decision, Eric. I ask you to trust me. I know what I am doing."

I turned to walk away. "Don't have much of a choice, do I?"

*****

I awoke to someone kicking me in the feet. Hard. I looked up and saw Bjornson standing over me.

"Wake up, dipshit. You're on watch."

I uncovered myself, stood up, and looked Bjornson in the eye. "That is the last time you ever touch me, cupcake. Next time, I hurt you."

"Hurt me? The fuck you gonna do that, little man?"

"Kick me again and you'll find out."

"Whatever, pussy."

He turned and walked away. I followed silently in my stocking feet, timing his stride. When the moment was right, I reached up, clamped a hand over his mouth, and kicked his feet out from underneath him.

He landed with all my weight on him. In the brief moment he was stunned, I grabbed an arm, applied a wristlock, and used my thigh as a fulcrum to lock his arm out at the elbow. A little pressure one way, and I could break his wrist. A little pressure another way, and his elbow would snap ninety degrees in the wrong direction. He started to struggle, so I put pressure on

129

both wrist and elbow and pinned his head to the ground with a knee.

"See how easy that was, cupcake?" I casually slid my pistol from its holster and applied the barrel to his temple. He drew a breath to yell, so I put more pressure on the wrist and elbow. The shout died with a squeak.

"Now, now," I said. "No need to go waking up the others. You're necessary to the mission, for the moment, so I'm not going to hurt you too bad." I holstered the pistol. "But just between the two of us, this mission is not only important to the Union, it's important to me. I have my reasons for this. And if you do anything, anything at all, to endanger this mission with your high-school, egotistical, testosterone-fueled bullshit, I will kill you. I want you to understand that very clearly. Your life is not important to me. But there are people I care about back home, and I am not going to endanger them by allowing you to be a fuck-up. Do you understand?"

"Fuck you."

I sighed. "Some people just have to do things the hard way." I began to apply more pressure to the wrist, but stopped when I felt a very large hand on my shoulder.

"Eric, that's enough."

The voice sounded like its owner gargled kerosene and razor blades every morning. I only knew one man who sounded like that.

"Didn't know we were on watch together, Gabe."

"That's because you didn't check the watch bill."

"No, I didn't. Probably should from now on."

The hand released my shoulder. "Let him up, Eric."

I did. Bjornson rose slowly. Even in the dark I could see his face was a light shade of purple. He eyed Gabe, looked back to me, and said, "This isn't over, you little shit."

"You don't learn very fast, do you?"

130

"Your friend won't always be around to protect you. We'll settle up soon enough."

"Gabe, are you protecting me right now?"

"You don't need my protection. Especially not from this clown. But I can't let you two fight in here. Too much noise."

To Bjornson, Gabe said, "You can go now."

The big young soldier looked at Gabe, then back at me. His eyes were hot with anger, but he did as he was told. I walked back to my bedroll, bundled it up, lashed it to my pack, and put on my boots. Two minutes later, I was ready to go on watch.

"You made an enemy tonight," Gabe said in a low voice as we walked toward the exit.

"No. He did."

"What did he do?"

"Woke me up by kicking the hell out of my feet. Fucking hurt."

Gabe shook his head. "Rule number one. Never underestimate *anyone*."

"Evidently no one ever explained that to Bjornson."

"Oh, I'm sure someone did. He just didn't listen."

"I might have to remind him."

Gabe unlocked the door at the northern end of the building and we walked into the cool night air. I looked up at a pristine cloudless sky, a nearly full moon shining brightly upon the clearing. The long, glistening grass danced contentedly amid a gentle breeze. By noon, the morning sun would burn off the heavy dew, and the afternoon would be humid as a wet blanket.

"You really think that's going to help the mission?" Gabe said.

"Actually, I do. Stomping a mud hole in Bjornson's chest might teach him a little humility. Make him feel a little less invulnerable, less apt to do something rash and stupid."

131

"And you don't think training to be a Green Beret did that?"

"Not nearly enough, as demonstrated by his attitude. A real professional would never have antagonized me for no reason. You may have noticed he's the only guy on the task force I've had trouble with."

"Maybe he was testing you. Maybe he's following orders."

"You don't believe that, Gabe."

He let out a breath and adjusted his tactical sling. "No. I wish I did."

"I don't care if he's mad. He wants to settle things man to man, he knows where to find me."

"I think you scared him, Eric. Surprised him. I think you should avoid turning your back on him. He may attempt to respond in kind."

I smiled in the darkness. "Better men have tried, you among them. I doubt he has more sneak on him than you do."

"That was training. I wasn't really trying to kill you."

"But shy of killing me, you weren't holding back, were you?"

"No."

"And I stopped you. Consistently. Even got the drop on you a few times."

"Yes."

"Then I'm not worried."

"Either way, Eric, he's not going to forget. And he's not going to let it go."

"Good. I hope he tries to do something about it. Maybe then we can put this little junior-high feud behind us and focus on the mission."

"Speaking of …"

Gabe handed me his NVG/IR goggles. I accepted the eighty-five thousand pre-Outbreak dollars' worth of high-tech optics and asked, "What's the occasion?"

"Maybe I'm expecting trouble."

"You're always expecting trouble."

I activated the goggles. The world turned from shades of silver and black to high-definition gray and white. Unlike NVGs, the IR setting on Gabe's goggles did not hinder depth perception. The image was crisp and clear, allowing me to see farther than with my NVGs. Anything living showed up bright white against the darker ambience of colder objects. I could make out details of trees, grass, bushes, and a few nocturnal rodents searching for seeds along the treeline.

Gabe had obtained the goggles and his IR scope the night he and Great Hawk set out to rescue me from the Free Legion. My deceased friend, Captain Steve McCray, issued them personally. After Steve died, no one asked Gabe to return the equipment. So he didn't.

Gabe put on a pair of standard NVGs and activated the IR scope on his rifle. Like me, he carried a 6.8 SPC suppressor-equipped sniper carbine. Between the two of us, we were toting enough trade to set a man up very comfortably in Colorado Springs, along with several of his closest friends.

"Who's on overwatch?" I asked.

"Hicks. Great Hawk's our watch captain."

"The civilian quartet. I wonder what Anderson thinks of that. He's suspicious of us."

"I don't give a damn what Anderson thinks. Not as long as he does his job."

"He seems all right to me."

"Probably is. Doesn't mean I have to care about his opinion."

"You seem touchy tonight, Gabe."

133

His NVGs pointed in my direction. "Touchy? Didn't you just twist Bjornson up like a pretzel?"

"He earned it. You're being grumpy toward people who haven't wronged you."

The green circles of light were steady a few seconds, then looked away. "Yeah. I guess you're right."

"You miss Elizabeth."

A grunt.

"But that's not all of it."

Gabe flipped up his NVGs and peered through the IR scope. His rifle swept the length of the field to our right, finger over the trigger, feet braced to absorb recoil. Maybe he really was expecting trouble. When he finished, he looked at me and scratched his beard.

"I'm forty-one, and I'm not getting any younger."

I did my best Danny Glover *Lethal Weapon* impression. "I'm gettin' too old for this shit."

"That was terrible. Anyway, Elizabeth is thirty-nine. And she has no interest in having children."

I nodded in understanding. "And that's what broke up your first marriage."

"Among other things. And what do you mean, first marriage? It was my only marriage."

"So you and Liz ..."

"No. We haven't said the words."

The words. Hardly anyone has weddings anymore. Too loud. Too time consuming. Eats up too many resources. Not that weddings are unheard of, they still happen, but they are rare. Most people just sit down and have a talk. I love you, and I want us to be married. Okay. I love you too, and I want to be your wife. Or husband. Or whatever. And from then on, two become one.

134

I remembered when Allison and I took that step. I was recovering from a gunshot wound and had just seen Gabriel off as he left town to find and kill a man named Tanner. Little did Gabe know, I had planted a tracking device in his pack and hired people to follow him. But again, that is another story.

As Gabe left, he told me to take good care of my wife. I said Allison and I were not married. He smirked and asked me if I was sure.

It hit me like a hammer to the forehead.

I stumbled home in a daze. When I lurched through the front door, I was sweating, and tired, and the recently-healed .380 caliber orifice in my calf muscle was aching something terrible. I sat down on the couch, propped my injured leg on the coffee table, and listened to Allison making noise in the kitchen. After a short while, she joined me in the living room, handed me a glass of water, and asked about Gabe. I turned my head and stared.

"What?" Allison asked, pushing a stray lock of hair from my forehead.

The sunlight through the window lit her eyes and set the honey-colored irises ablaze. I saw my whole life in those amber depths. I saw who, and where, I wanted to be. I said, "I love you, Allison. More than anything in the world."

She smiled. "I love you too, knucklehead."

"I want to be your husband. I don't want anyone other than you. Ever."

The smile faded. The eyes went from amber to dark copper as she sat up, suddenly serious. "Are you asking me to marry you?"

"Yes."

Silence. No movement for an endless stretch of time that was only a few seconds. My heart beat so loud in my ears I wondered if the neighbors could hear it.

"Then say it."

"Will you marry me, Allison?"

"Get down on one knee and try again."

I sat up, pulled my throbbing leg down from the table, and had to bite down on a white hot flash of agony. There was not enough room to kneel, so I started pushing the table back. Allison caught my hands and laughed at me.

"I wasn't serious, dummy. Lay back before you pop your stitches."

She took my face in both hands and kissed me. When she pulled away, tears ran down her cheeks.

"Of course I'll marry you."

I grinned. "Get down on one knee and try again."

She slapped me, but not very hard. And that was it. From then on, I had a wife.

In the here and now, I asked Gabe, "Do you want to, you know ..."

Gabe flipped his NVGs back down. "Marry her? I don't know. My instincts say yes, but it's more complicated than that."

"How so?"

"Because she's already married to her job. And as for me, well ... I am what I am. And I always will be."

"You willing to take a word of advice from an old friend?"

"Sure. Know any I can talk to?"

I punched him in the shoulder. I may as well have punched a cannon ball. "Fuck you, dickhead."

"Fine. Dispense your advice, oh wise one."

"What you and Elizabeth have is special. Sure, her job takes up most of her time. And you can't give up the military life. Big deal. You're both self-sacrificing human beings; it's something you have in common. And I'm willing to bet it's a significant part of what makes you compatible. So I think you should trust your instincts."

"What if she says no, Eric? What then? What if I ruin what little we already have?"

"What if she says yes? And since when is what you and Elizabeth have *little*, Gabe? Listen, maybe it works out, maybe it doesn't. That's life. It's the risk you take to make being alive less intolerable. And the way the world is now, you don't exactly have a smorgasbord of eligible women to choose from. Like you said, you're not getting any younger. So here's the question you need to ask yourself: Will you let fear make your decision for you, and spend the rest of your life wondering what might have been, or do you grow a pair and go after what you really want?"

Gabe's steps slowed until he came to a halt. He flipped the NVGs up again and stared at his feet. I stopped as well. The gray eyes were hidden in shadow, but I knew what they looked like at times like this. They darted in tiny increments from left to right, the subtle brain behind them sorting data like a computer, the tremendous intellect skirmishing against repressed emotions. And the emotions were winning. I had seen it before. He looked up.

"You're right. As usual."

"Very big of you to acknowledge that."

The rare smile appeared. It made my old friend look younger. "Wasn't easy."

"What's most worth doing rarely is. Now come on, we're supposed to be on watch."

"Right."

Gabe flipped down his NVGs and started walking.

SEVENTEEN

Once, over drinks, my friend Ethan Thompson explained the rules of standing watch. I do not remember them all because we had just come back from a lucrative salvage run, were flush with trade, and had decided to blow some of our newly-acquired wealth on a large volume of potent adult beverages. I do, however, remember the first rule:

When the shit goes down, it will always happen at the end of your watch. Not the beginning, or the middle, but the end. Always the end.

At the one hour mark, Gabe and Hicks switched roles. The only place close by to get a good vantage point without being exposed was the forest, and sitting immobile in a tree for three hours is the definition of discomfort. Since all of us were competent snipers, we saw no reason to leave one guy on overwatch the whole time.

At the stroke of the third hour, I relieved Gabe and climbed to his roost. He took the IR goggles, gave me his NVGs, and we swapped rifles so I could have the IR scope.

And of course, with ten minutes left in our watch and me looking forward to a few hours' sleep, I spotted a line of gun-toting bodies coming over a rise to the south. They were spread out at ten meter intervals and moving at a light jog, probably trying to outrun infected.

I keyed my radio. "All stations, this is overwatch. Possible hostiles spotted approximately five hundred meters due south, headed for our position. Over."

"Overwatch, watch captain," Great Hawk said. "How many? Over."

"Watch captain, I see eighteen. Could be more behind. Might want to wake the others. Over."

"Overwatch, are you sure they are headed toward our position? Over."

"Looks that way. The processing plant is a good place to hide from the infected, and we know people have been here before. So we're probably looking at marauders, and they probably use this place as a hideout. Something tells me they won't be happy to see us. Over."

"Overwatch, what makes you think they are marauders? Over."

"Because other than idiots like us, no one moves around at night. Too dangerous. Decent folks seek shelter after nightfall. Marauders like to raid under cover of darkness. Oh, and they're all carrying rifles and moving with military precision. I can't guarantee they're hostiles, but considering the evidence, we should err on the side of caution. If I were in your place, I'd wake the others. Over."

A moment's pause. "Point taken. Patrol, what is your position? Over."

"North of your twenty," Hicks answered. "Hundred yards out, not far from overwatch. Where you want us? Over."

"One of you move west and take cover near the production house. The other, find a likely spot in the woods to the east. Between the three of you, you will have the newcomers in a cross fire. I will have three men conceal themselves in the field for fire support. The rest will set up in here. If possible, let the people approaching enter the building with us. Once they are in, we can attempt to engage without bloodshed. But be ready to fight if necessary. Overwatch, can you see through the windows? Over."

"Sure, if you take all those blankets down. Over."

139

"It will be done. All stations, prepare yourselves. Out."

"Wonderful," I muttered. "Just fucking wonderful."

The maple branch I sat on was flat and broad, easily supporting my weight. However, I had to sit sideways in order to monitor a 360 degree field of vision. The process was to turn one way, scan 180 degrees on my left, then shift to the other side and repeat. But now, with an imminent threat coming from the south, I needed to face them head on. The only way to do that was to hook my right leg over an adjacent branch and lean back, legs spread. I did not like it. The position made me feel exposed, like I was dangling my balls in the air for the whole world to shoot at. But it was the only position that allowed me to aim properly, so I clenched my jaw and told myself to stop being such a wimp.

Once settled, I dialed the IR scope down to 2x power and waited. Three of Anderson's men exited the processing building in stacked formation, fanned out, and concealed themselves in the long, wild grass. They all wore ghillie suits, which would conceal them from the naked eye and standard NVGs. But through Gabe's infrared scope, they stood out like candles in a dark room. No wonder Gabe loved this scope so much. The tactical advantage it afforded was tremendous.

I shifted the red-illuminated reticle back to the processing building. It ran from east to west, the windows on the north side facing me. Anderson's men had removed the dark coverings from the windows, allowing me to see inside. The soldiers within scrambled to erase evidence of their presence by hiding the gear and carts in one of the offices, brushing dusty footprints away with hastily gathered bundles of grass, and taking cover behind dilapidated factory equipment on both ends of the facility. Not perfect, but the best they could do on short notice.

Then came the waiting. I hate waiting before a firefight. Too much time to think. Too much time to imagine all the things that can go wrong. Too much time to remember the bullet to the lower ribcage that nearly killed me, or the .380 round that tore out a chunk of my calf muscle and left a permanently puckered indentation. The old scars began to throb faintly.

Remembered pain. It exists only in the mind, but it exists nonetheless.

As the shapes in the distance grew closer, I distracted myself by turning my mind to life before the Outbreak. Sports, specifically. I wondered if anyone from the Panthers had survived. I thought about the heartbreaking year they made it to the Super Bowl only to lose to New England. The Panthers' quarterback at the time, Jake Delhomme, never seemed the same after that.

I remembered a subsequent game against the Vikings when a Minnesota defensive player, whose name and position I could not recall, got around the Panther's line and levelled Delhomme with a blindside tackle that, for a few moments, I was reasonably sure had killed him. It did not, but he spent the next play on the sidelines, hands on his knees, grimacing in pain.

After the hit, he always seemed a little gun shy. Too unwilling to run the ball. Too quick to throw it away if a play started to break down. Not that I blamed him. A man can only take so many bad hits before suffering permanent damage to something important and irreplaceable. Like the brain, for instance.

Thinking about brain injuries reminded me of the infected, which reminded me why I try not to think about sports very often. The National Football League did not exist anymore, nor did any other athletic organization. Which meant no more Super Bowl, no more English Premier League, no more March Madness, no more Stanley Cup playoffs, no more FIFA, no more college football Saturdays, no more NCAA national championships, no more Charlotte Checkers games, no more destroying Gabe and my old college buddies at fantasy football, and certainly no more late summer afternoons at Knights Stadium washing down hot dogs and popcorn with cold beer.

The familiar, sinking sense of unbearable loss found me again. So many things I once loved, that I once took for granted,

141

were gone. And they were not coming back. Not tomorrow, not next year, not ever. And like most emotional pain, the feeling was not made less unpleasant by repetition. I wondered if there would ever come a day when I could think about my old life and not feel like someone had just kicked me in the stomach.

The white shapes moving through the forest ahead of me cleared the treeline, crouched low, and began working their way across the field toward the processing facility. I called it in. Great Hawk agreed there could be no further doubt as to their intentions. He told everyone to stay as low and silent as frightened animals, and to take no action until he gave the order. Everyone gave a brief affirmative. Great Hawk ordered radio silence until told otherwise. Out. There was no acknowledgement.

When the gunmen were within a hundred yards, I noticed four of them were wearing NVGs. I thought about calling it in, but decided against it. If things went south, tactical situation permitting, they would be my first targets. And since the soldiers of Task Force Falcon were undoubtedly wearing NVGs of their own, chances were good they would quickly notice the opposition's optics and respond appropriately.

Most of the marauders—and my instincts screamed at me that was what they were—stayed in the grass while the guys with NVGs walked a circle around the processing facility. Same for the production building. Hicks was over there, but they did not see him.

I could tell by the marauders body language and hushed conversation they noticed the flattening of grass where we had dragged the ghouls into the treeline. They also noticed the blood, chunks of skull and brain, and probably a few tracks as well. Two of them followed the trails into the trees, stopped to stare at the infected laid out in disorderly rows, and quickly hurried back.

All four of them knelt. They brought their heads close together and talked. Three seemed agitated, their heads bobbing with harshly spoken words, hands gesticulating, while the fourth remained calm. Everyone was talking to the fourth one,

142

which meant I was probably looking at the leader. I took careful note of the marauder's outline, and after a few seconds, realized it was a woman. No matter. Marauders are marauders, male or female.

Keep them in line, lady. You don't, you all die.

It occurred to me Hicks was in a position to shoot all four of them. If I had been in charge, I would have been sorely tempted to give the order while the soldiers positioned in the field—who had also avoided detection—took out the rest. From my perch, I would have a clear shot at any marauder the soldiers missed. None would survive. But I was not in charge, and despite my well-honed paranoia, I could not fire on them until they turned hostile.

More waiting. The four-person conference broke up and rejoined their comrades. I hoped they would decide the risk was too great and seek other accommodations. While they were talking, I took the chance to scan the horizon behind them. And sure enough, I saw dark, bluish gray blobs stumbling through the scope's infrared image. A lot of them.

Time to risk the wrath of Great Hawk. "Hawk, overwatch. Horde incoming at five hundred meters."

A few seconds, then a whisper, "Roger. Size? Over."

"Not sure. Big. Possibly more than a hundred. Over."

"Copy. Disposition on the intruders? Over."

"They know someone has been here. Found the infected and the tracks. Four have NVGs. I believe the leader is female. Currently talking among themselves. Over."

"Copy. Advise when they are on approach. Everyone else, maintain radio silence. Out."

I let out a small breath of relief. I had broken protocol by calling in, but thankfully, the Hawk agreed it was warranted. A sensible man, that inscrutable Apache.

My hope the marauders would leave died when the sole female of the group began pointing her fingers in a decidedly

143

authoritarian manner. Men broke off in twos and threes, heading where she ordered them to go. Four of them moved into position less than thirty yards in front of me, bellies on the ground. I smiled.

Proverbial sitting ducks.

That left fourteen. Six set up firing positions in the field across the building from me, ostensibly to cover the entrance. Unbeknownst to them, they were at the center of a three-way crossfire between Hicks, Gabe, and the three Green Berets to the south. More sitting ducks.

The remaining eight stacked up on both sides of the door and tried the handle. They found it unlocked, which was smart thinking on Great Hawk's part. An unlocked door might put the marauders at ease, and since they did not have to break it down, we could still lock it when the infected showed up after the fight. My esteem for the former SEAL went up a notch.

I called in what I saw using the briefest language possible. Great Hawk keyed his mike twice to let me know he heard me. Below my roost in the big maple tree, one of the four nearby marauders raised his head and whispered, "Did you guys hear something?"

Sharp ears on that one. I whispered as low as I could, but he still picked it up.

None of his fellows had a chance to answer. The eight marauders stacked by the door, including the leader, pushed through the entrance and filed inside. *Not bad*, I thought. *I've seen better, but they're not complete idiots.*

I watched intently through the windows, careful to make no sound. Glimpses of the marauders fanning out and working to clear the building flashed in the glass spaces between spans of cinder-block wall. The soldiers stayed hidden at the far ends, but it was only a matter of time before the marauders found them. Great Hawk elected to act first.

There were a few flashes, barely audible cracks, and the marauders dove for cover. Seconds ticked by. Ten. Twenty.

Nothing else happened. Then my radio buzzed and Great Hawk's voice whispered, "Prepare to engage."

Figures.

I loosed a spare magazine, held it in my left hand, and shifted the reticle back to the group of marauders lying on the ground closest to me. More flashes and dull cracks sounded from the processing facility. Rather than wait for the order to open fire, I angled for a head shot and pulled the trigger twice. The marauder on the far right released his rifle and went limp. Two more cracks, two more splashes from a ventilated skull, and another death-shudder before limp fingers released a Kalashnikov.

The third and fourth men down the line figured out what was happening and rolled over. Rifles came up to shoulders. My reticle was already on the third one. A flick of the thumb, and my carbine fired on full-auto. A six-round burst perforated his midsection. He forgot about his rifle and started screaming.

The fourth one saw my muzzle flash and shifted his aim. Before he could open fire, I sent another burst in his direction. Then another. On the third one, the chamber locked open on an empty magazine. Without coming off my point of aim, I let the empty mag fall, slapped in a new one, and released the bolt. Two head shots to the marauder still screaming, then silence. I shifted and peered through a window of the processing facility.

A man moved from one machine to another and opened fire. The rattle of his rifle was loud and distinctive—AK-47. I took in a breath, let out half of it, and squeezed the trigger. The bullet shattered glass as it punched through the window. The gunman's head jerked to one side, dark liquid painted the machine beside him, and he slumped to the floor.

I searched the other windows, but saw no targets.

While all this was happening, I dimly noted the crack of suppressed rifles from the production building and the field beyond. Perhaps thirty shots fired, then silence. Lacking a target, I kept my eyes moving and waited.

145

"All clear," Great Hawk said. "Overwatch?"

I let out a shaky breath and said, "All clear on my end. No hostiles in sight."

"How many did you get? Over."

"Got four of them out here, one in the building. Over."

"Perimeter?"

"Six hostiles down," Hicks said.

"There are seven dead in here, and one prisoner," Great Hawk said. "I need a casualty report. All stations, call in according to protocol."

"I'm good," I said. Protocol required the man on overwatch to report first.

"Same here," Gabe said.

"Fit as a fiddle," said Hicks.

"We're all good here." I recognized the voice as belonging to Sergeant May. There was a pause while the Hawk evaluated Anderson's men.

He said, "No casualties in here. Well done, gentlemen. All stations, remain in position until given clearance to approach. Watch captain out."

I stayed in the tree, but shifted to a more comfortable sitting position. The hands began their shaky dance. The heartbeat was too quick. Breathing too shallow. I told myself to take long, deep breaths. Focus on the shoulders. Relax them. Let the muscles go slack. Now the back. The arms. Midsection. Legs. All the way down to the toes.

The adrenalin dump ran its course and the shaking stopped. I wanted to eat, have a strong drink, and fuck something pretty—in that order. We may not be cavemen anymore, but something of the old ways still lives on in the dark crevices of the human psyche.

Most people like to think they are highly-evolved creatures, but in truth, we are not far removed from our flint-knapping

146

ancestors. Anatomically modern humans have been around for over 250,000 years, but we've only been out of the woods for about 10,000 of them. Put in perspective, that is 0.04% of human history. Which means the whole 'civilization' thing is a relatively new concept. Consequently, much like our ancient forebears, when we experience extreme stress—combat, natural disaster, the end of the world—a relay closes somewhere in our circuitry and the baser urges float to the surface: the desire to eat, to mate, to experience pleasure, all the things we have developed over countless millennia to ensure the propagation of the species.

And in my experience, there is nothing quite like a good old-fashioned firefight to remind a man that he is, whether he chooses to admit it or not, an animal. A smart animal, but an animal nonetheless. And like all animals, we have things hardwired into us that no amount of mental conditioning can erase. They have a name. They are called instincts. And right then, my instincts were telling me to feast and screw and revel in being alive. It was not the first time. I doubted it would be the last.

Despite the urgings of my lizard brain, I stayed focused on the task at hand. The IR scope was running low on power. If Great Hawk did not call me in soon, I would have to ask him to send a runner with more batteries.

A faint rustle sounded behind me. I turned to see what it was. A nimble little fox appeared, trotted over to the treeline, and tilted its curious nose upward. After sampling the air, the fox backed up a few steps, sniffed again, then turned tail and ran away.

I licked a finger and held it up. The wind was coming from the south, directly over the horde and straight toward me. I checked the distance again. Four-hundred meters and closing. The fastest ghouls outpaced their more damaged brethren, causing the horde to assume a now-familiar teardrop shape. A lightly damaged ghoul could shamble at roughly two miles an hour. Four hundred meters is a quarter of a mile. Which meant the closest of them would be on us in less than ten minutes.

147

"Watch captain, overwatch. The vanguard of the horde will make contact in about eight minutes. Just sayin'. Over."

"Acknowledged. All stations, return to the processing facility."

No need to tell me twice. I slung my carbine and scrambled down from the tree. The others reached the building ahead of me and went inside. Great Hawk waited for me at the door. When I was through, he locked it.

"Give me a hand," he said.

Together, we reinforced the door with a few old crates of scrap metal and rusty repair parts.

"Hope that holds," I said when we finished.

"We must remain silent," Great Hawk said.

I looked around the factory and saw several dead bodies in various poses. One of them died on his knees, face on the floor, his butt sticking comically up in the air. An ignominious way to check out.

"The ghouls will smell all this blood," I said. "How are we going to get rid of them?"

"The standard method."

"I'm a little tired, amigo."

"Taylor has already volunteered. He is looking for a place to hide as we speak. When the horde arrives, he will redirect their attention."

"What about all these dead bodies?"

The black eyes glittered in the moonlight. "What would you do with them?"

I glanced up and studied Great Hawk's face. As usual, it was as expressive as a slab of sandstone.

"The way you keep asking me things, I feel like I'm being tested."

No response.

I sighed. "Fine. What I would do is drag them outside, double tap them in the head, capture a few ghouls, and let them do their thing. Then kill the ghouls and hide the whole works with the ones we killed earlier. That way, if any Alliance types find them, they'll think they were infected."

"Will they not wonder who destroyed the horde?"

I shrugged. "Not much we can do about that. Just have to hope the forest takes care of them before anyone comes back this way."

"We could bury them."

I braced my hands on my hips. "You hiding a bucket loader in your underwear? Because if we try to bury all those bodies by hand, we're going to be here for the next two days. We don't have time for that, Lincoln."

A nod. "There is the matter of the bones."

"Like I said. Nothing we can do about it. Best we can do is haul ass to Carbondale, complete the mission, and get the hell out Alliance territory. If all goes well, they won't even know we were here."

Great Hawk headed toward the offices at the end of the building. "Then let us hope that all goes well."

EIGHTEEN

The leader may have been pretty, once. But three years of surviving in the wastelands had taken its toll.

She stared at us with hard brown eyes that held all the compassion of a starving crocodile. Her hands and feet were bound with zip ties, and she sat on a folding metal chair surrounded by Anderson's men. I counted three guns aimed at her head.

"So tell me," I said to Great Hawk. "What led to the shoot-out?"

"I asked this one to identify herself." He pointed at the prisoner. "One of her men pointed a weapon in my direction. I fired a few warning shots. They took cover. She told us to leave or die. I told her there was no need for bloodshed and asked if we could talk. She did not respond. I asked again. Still nothing. McGee spotted one of them moving toward me in a flanking maneuver. I decided enough was enough. You know the rest."

"Who the fuck are you?" the prisoner asked.

"Who we are isn't important," Anderson said. "What is important, to you at least, is how you answer our questions."

The reptilian stare shifted toward the captain. "Go fuck yourself, you little shit. Do whatever you want to me. I'm not telling you a damn thing."

Bjornson chuckled. "Don't be too sure about that. We can be very convincing."

150

Great Hawk shot him a look that wiped the smirk off his face. "Gag her," he said. "We will search her men for clues. Then we will proceed with the interrogation." He cast his gaze around the room, making eye contact with each man. "She is not to be harmed."

We had less than five minutes before the horde arrived. Anderson left May and Taylor to guard the prisoner while the rest of us dragged the marauder's bodies in from outside. The horde probably heard us, but made no sound. Not for the first time, I was grateful for the darkness.

The dead men wore sturdy clothes, some obviously homemade. They carried the usual assortment of tools and equipment common among nomadic survivors. The heavy objects like water, ammunition, crowbars, bolt cutters, and hooked rope ladders were distributed to lighten each man's load, which spoke of possible military experience. The men's faces and hands were dark and leathery from long days in the sun. Their weapons were standard Alliance AKs, pistols, and RGN grenades.

"Got a question," I said to Gabe as we dragged a body through the door. "Why didn't they use their grenades?"

"I'm guessing the grenades are too valuable. Good for trade. Probably didn't want to waste them."

"Yeah, but in a *firefight* ..."

"I'm kidding."

"Oh."

"The fight happened at close range. A grenade doesn't care who it kills. Or wounds."

"Good point. Didn't think of that." I thought a moment, then asked, "How the hell do these assholes have so much ordnance?"

Gabe gave me an amused look. "You ever been inside a Cold War era ammunition depot?"

"No."

151

"I have. There are warehouses, enormous warehouses, stacked floor to ceiling with nothing but bullets. Billions of them. If the Flotilla brought over even a fraction of just *one* of those warehouses, they could have over a hundred million rounds. Not to mention what they might scavenge from the countryside."

We dropped the body and went out to get another one. Hicks and Anderson passed us and told us they got the last one. We went back inside, locked the door, and pushed the crates back into place.

I thought about what Gabe had said. I thought about Cold War era warehouses and acres of stockpiled ammunition. I thought about my own hoard of ammunition and weapons, and remembered a few times when, in the course of salvage runs, I had stumbled across abandoned military convoys overrun during the Outbreak.

It is grim to say, considering that brave men and women died in these places defending others, but those lost convoys are treasure troves. Guns, ammo, rockets, mortars, grenade launchers, mines, helmets, body armor, MREs, clothes, boots, tactical gear, communications equipment, vehicles, … and that's just the beginning of the list. If a lucky salvage hunter can arrange transportation and safe storage, just *one* of those convoys can set him up in a secure community for life.

However, the treaty between Hollow Rock and Central Command stipulates that any US military property found in the course of salvage operations is to be turned over to the proper authorities. In my case, that would be Captain Harlow. And my feelings toward Captain Harlow are no secret.

While I am quick to quote the treaty when it suits my purposes, I gleefully ignore it when it does not. The men who accompany me on salvage expeditions—Delta Squad and some guys from the Ninth TVM—could not care less what the treaty says. They like trade. They like what it buys. They like feeling like they are getting away with something. Most importantly, they know how to keep their mouths shut. Because each man knows if he divulges something I said not to, he will never accompany me on a salvage run again. No exceptions.

Greed. It's a hell of a lever.

And so it was, when we found that first convoy of nearly incalculable value, we sat down and had a little chat. I told the men we did not have to bring anything back to the FOB. All we were required to do was report the convoy's location and let Echo Company take care of the rest. But that did not mean we couldn't charge a finder's fee. Especially considering no one would know about it but us. Thompson asked me what I was suggesting. I told him that while the convoy was government property, we were the ones who had found it, and despite what the treaty said, I felt we were entitled to fair compensation for our efforts. After all, salvaging is dangerous work. It was hardly fair to expect us to walk away empty handed.

There was some reluctance at first. So I told them I would double their regular percentage, effectively cutting my own profit in half. They happily agreed.

We were in possession of a large cargo transport the Phoenix Initiative had loaned the city of Hollow Rock. I gave the men a list and told them to stick to it. If there was room left in the transport, we could go back for more. The items on the list filled up the cargo trailer and most of the troop carrier.

I kept the transport running while we loaded it. Every few minutes, I put it in gear and watched the console. If the load came within five-hundred pounds of the transport's substantial towing capacity, a little red light would start blinking. When it finally came on, I told the men to unload some of the less valuable stuff so we could get up hills without having to push. On the way home, I trundled along at a sedate five miles an hour, the men following behind on foot.

At the main gate, I gave the guards their usual bribe and proceeded to my warehouse. After I had unloaded mine and Gabriel's share, we divvied up the rest and drove it to where the men kept their private fortunes—a public storage facility owned by none other than G&R Transport and Salvage. I held a final

153

meeting where I admonished the men not to tell anyone what we had done, and sent them on their way.

I then returned the transport to the sheriff's office, paid the fine for being three hours late, reported the location of the convoy to the officer on duty at Fort McCray, and went back to my warehouse to rub my hands together and titter over my good fortune.

Three large shelves sagged from the weight of it. They ran four feet across and twelve feet from floor to ceiling. My share was two dozen M-4 rifles in restorable condition, thirty thousand rounds of 5.56 ammunition (ten thousand belted), two-hundred fragmentation hand grenades, five boxes of MREs, seven LAW rockets, fifty claymore mines, eight M-203 grenade launchers (along with a hundred high explosive shells), a SAW, an M-240 machine gun, five thousand belted 7.62 rounds, ten serviceable vests of body armor (several in my size), and various tactical gear and assorted equipment. After counting it again, I looked around at the vast stores in the warehouse and marveled that half of it was mine. I had been a rich man before we found the convoy, but now I was *filthy, stinking* rich. The 7.62 ammo alone was enough to keep me warm, fed, and happy for several years.

Captain Harlow, of course, did not buy for a second that I had not taken anything. He showed up at my place of business and asked if he could inspect my warehouse and the storage units rented by his men. Just a precaution, you understand. I told him he was welcome to tour my warehouse and storage facility just as soon as he obtained a warrant. He said he had probable cause, and could go to the sheriff. I smiled and said, "Good luck with that. And by the way, you're welcome."

Harlow's eyes narrowed. "For what?"

"Finding the convoy."

"I think I'll go pay the sheriff a visit."

So he tried to get a warrant. The sheriff told Captain Harlow it was not going to happen. Not because he likes me—he despises me, actually, and I have no idea why—but because he would have to get approval from Mayor Stone. And without hard evidence of wrongdoing, she would never agree to allow military personnel to search civilian property.

This put Harlow in a bad spot. He was under orders to stay in the good graces of the civilian populace. He needed my salvage to keep his men happy. Without it, morale would deteriorate quickly. And he knew if he leaned on Delta Squad or the Ninth TVM, I would cease doing business with him. Further, even though his men were enlisted, he could not force them to open their storage units because they were not located on government property. Any attempt to do so would be met with armed, stone-faced guardsmen explaining to the good captain he was overstepping his legal authority.

It bears mentioning that every watch tower in Hollow Rock has a hot plate, a kettle, and a jar of instant coffee, all donated by G&R Transport and Salvage. The guardsmen love it, and they tend to be protective of their generous benefactors. Unlike Harlow, I never underestimate the power of goodwill.

Compounding the situation, unbeknownst to Captain Harlow, the mayor is a close personal friend of mine. She does not trust Captain Harlow any farther than she can throw him, and would want to see conclusive evidence of a violation before she would allow the sheriff to issue a warrant. The fact that Gabe and I give her whatever she needs, whenever she needs it, does not hurt.

And, lest I forget to mention, Gabe and Elizabeth have been romantically involved for over a year. Any damage done to our business would be damage done to him. Mayor Stone takes good care of her town, but she is not above favoritism toward those she deems deserving.

So I stood near the doorway and thought about green boxes with smaller cardboard boxes inside, each one containing twenty rounds of 65 grain 5.56 cartridges. I thought about how many I owned, and how much they could buy me if I ever had occasion to spend them. I thought about Mayor Stone walking through the warehouse, eyes wide, saying we had enough heat stockpiled to outfit a small army. I tried to imagine my

155

impressive armory in scale against what the Flotilla might have landed with at Humboldt Bay.

It felt like holding a firecracker up to a nuclear warhead.

Central Command is generous with weapons and ammunition to loyalist communities, but only to the extent needed for survival. The Alliance, from what I had seen thus far, put guns, bullets, and explosives in the hands of any yahoo with a grudge against the federal government. And they did not care how that ordnance was used. The Union military could hold its own against the best the Alliance had to offer. But what about civilians? The Alliance was already successfully displacing border communities. What would happen if they launched an all-out, scorched-earth offensive?

The thought made my stomach hurt.

*****

I do not like looking at dead bodies. They make me think of how many people I have killed since the Outbreak. I do not know the exact number, but I know not all of them deserved it. That said, when someone points a gun at me and pulls the trigger in earnest, all moral considerations become irrelevant. In combat, what someone deserves, or does not deserve, has no bearing on the equation. There is only one variable—you or me. And it ain't gonna be me.

Looking at the seventeen dead men lying in a row, I wondered which ones I had killed. When I shot them, I had been looking at them through an IR scope. They had been faceless shapes with no discerning details. But five of the bodies lined up on the floor were my doing.

A mental calculation told me I had done twenty-nine percent of the day's killing. What would Anderson's men think of that? Would they be jealous?

I looked at my hands. They were steady. Something was not right. The fluid shifts under the waking mind that bend and distort the tectonic plates of awareness should have been boiling like magma. The tremors should have started by now. I waited for the symptoms. The dull ache in the stomach, the weakness in the legs, the hollowness in the chest. But they did not come. There was only the ice that had begun spreading through me in my living room two days ago in Hollow Rock, and was still spreading. I felt no regret. I felt nothing at all.

Anderson's men had arranged the bodies in as dignified a manner as possible. The effect struck me as disingenuous, like a flirtatious smile on a prostitute. Dignity tends to depart a body along with its former owner, and what we leave at the crossing is a heavy, awkward meat-sack.

Anderson, Great Hawk, and Gabe searched the marauders' bodies and rucksacks. Since I had nothing else to do, I paired up with Stewart and helped him re-hang the window coverings. While we worked, he said, "So what's your story?"

I glanced at him. "*The Snows of Kilimanjaro* and *The Cold Equations* are tied for first."

"Huh?"

"Hemingway, Tom Godwin, ever heard of them?"

"The fuck are you talking about?"

I let out a sigh. "Never mind. Guess you're not the literary type."

He gave me a confused look and we worked in silence for a while. Halfway through the windows on the opposite wall, he tried again.

"So you're ex-military?"

"No."

"Could have fooled me."

He waited for me to respond. I did not. He said, "So what, CIA, FBI, ATF, one of the other acronyms?"

157

"None of the above."

"You a cop?"

"No."

He taped his side of the heavy blanket to the wall and turned to face me. "Look man, I'm not trying to give you a hard time. I just like to know who I'm working with."

I studied the young man. He was medium height and build, dark hair, eyes, and beard, and he had a narrow, unassuming face. The kind of man a person might pass on the street a hundred times without noticing. I would have said he was unremarkable, if not for the fact he was a member of the 10th Special Forces Group.

"I don't think the truth will make you feel any better."

"Try me."

"Fine." I pointed at Gabe. "You see that overgrown wad of scar tissue over there? The one with eyes like a Siberian husky?"

"The Marine, yeah. Garrett."

"He trained me, for the most part. A few others helped later on. But most of what I can do, I learned from him, or on the job."

"So you're ... what, a civvie?"

"Yes. I am a mere civvie."

He looked confused again. "Then what the fuck are you doing on this mission?"

"I've been asking myself that very same question lately."

"You're full of shit. No way would the head of ASOC send a civilian on a job like this."

"Listen, Stewart. I don't have a problem with you, but I sincerely do not give a shit if you believe me. I also don't feel obligated to prove or explain myself to you or anyone else. So if it's all the same, how about we hang these blankets before sunrise? I'd like to get a couple more hours' sleep."

He stared a moment longer, shaking his head. "Unbelievable."

"I told you the truth wouldn't help."

He spoke to me no more. We finished hanging the blankets. He gave me a last skeptical glance, and the darkness swallowed him as he walked away. I thought about the guys from Delta Squad, and how telling one soldier something was as good as telling his whole platoon.

Great, I thought. *By morning, they'll all distrust me.*

I looked back in the direction of the dead bodies. Small pools of ashen light slipped down from the slight gap between blankets and windows, illuminating the way only a few feet. The rest of the factory floor was smothered in inky blackness.

I withdrew a flashlight from my vest, slipped a red filter over the lens cover, and pressed the switch. A weak scarlet cone helped me find my way along without bruising a shin on something metal and unyielding. At the row of bodies, only Gabe remained. Great Hawk and Anderson had gone elsewhere.

"Learn anything?"

"Definitely marauders."

"How do you know?"

The big head swiveled. "Weren't you the one so sure of himself a little while ago?"

I stared at him blankly. When he did not get a rise out of me, Gabe said, "We found things in their packs."

"Like what?"

"Tampons, toilet paper, preserved food, a few guns in varying calibers. Typical salvage stuff."

"Doesn't exactly convict them of highway robbery."

"No. But the trophies do."

159

I closed my eyes and turned away. My stomach went heavy with soul-sickness. "Fingers? Ears?"

"And then some."

Gabe was right. There could be no doubt. Marauders liked to keep trophies from their victims and make necklaces out of them. The more bits and pieces on the string, and the fresher they were, the more respect marauders got from their fellow scumbags at the secret hell-pits where they gathered to trade.

"How many do you think they got?"

"Hard to tell. I'd say at least eight. Maybe more." Gabe turned away and began walking toward the offices.

"Women and children?"

"A few."

I looked at the dead bodies with renewed disgust. Their victims had probably been travelers, the kind of tough, gritty people who band together for safety and survive by hunting, scavenging, trading, and staying on the move. There are a lot of them out there. Far more than people living in secure communities. Often they are mixed family groups, the children hunting and fighting right alongside their parents.

There were a few such people living in Hollow Rock. When travelers' women get pregnant, they seek the safety of walled villages and towns to have their children. I knew three of them who shopped regularly at the general store. The women travelers in Hollow Rock had formed their own little community—or pack, as they called it—and their sincere intention was to teach their kids what they needed to know to survive out in the open, and then rejoin their original pack.

Sadly, these people often fell victim to large, well-armed groups of insurgents and marauders. And since the Alliance had thrown in with the ROC, things had been getting steadily worse. It did not pay to be a traveler anywhere east of the Appalachians or west of Kansas. Even Kentucky and Tennessee were no longer safe.

I followed Gabe to the office where Great Hawk was speaking to the prisoner. The door was closed and locked.

"What do you think is going on in there?" I asked.

"I don't hear any thuds or screaming," Gabe said. "He's probably just talking to her."

We waited. I retrieved a blanket from my bedroll, tucked it under my head, and lay down on the floor. Something scraped and thudded against the wall next to me. I heard the occasional croak and groan, the rustle and slap of bodies colliding. Muted scrapings and thuddings increased in frequency until the cinder blocks against my shoulder began to vibrate rhythmically from the impacts.

Infected. They had smelled the blood.

A few minutes later, from outside, a gunshot fractured the air. I remembered Great Hawk saying Taylor had volunteered to lead the horde away. I wished him luck and closed my eyes. I did not dream.

Voices close by woke me up. A few feet away, Gabe sat with his back against the wall, chin against his chest, breathing slowly. I nudged him on the arm.

"Hey, wake up."

He did, instantly. His eyes cleared and he looked toward Great Hawk. "Let's go see what he found out."

Before following, I reached a hand under one of the blankets and peered at the window. The curtain of night had withdrawn and given way to a pale gray dawn. I caught up with Gabe and said, "I knocked out at four in the morning."

"I wasn't far behind you."

"They been in there this whole time?"

"Looks like it."

When we reached the office, Great Hawk's skin was drawn tight against his face, there were dark circles under his eyes, and his upright posture looked forced and unsteady.

161

"Must have been a long conversation," I said, pointing the office door. "Learn anything useful from yon fair maiden?"

"Yon maiden," Great Hawk said, "is about as fair as a knife to the scrotum. Come on. We need to wake the others."

He started walking. Gabe and I looked at each other, shrugged, and followed.

NINETEEN

We gathered in the clear space in front of the entrance, and Great Hawk gave us the short version.

In the beginning, there were questions. The prisoner heard these questions, and saw that they were bad. Great Hawk persisted. He received no answers. And if looks could kill, he would have been impaled from anus to mouth on a thorny pole.

He told her we were federal agents working undercover to root out bands of marauders. He told her the Union was through messing around with marauders, sick of them raiding and slave-hunting in Union territory, and ours was a search and destroy mission. He told her he was not going to torture her. But if she did not talk, she would be taken to a detention camp where she would be. Still nothing.

Great Hawk asked more questions and received no response. An hour passed. He threw his hands in the air and told her, "Fine. Have it your way. But when they shove that feeding tube down your throat when you refuse to eat, and waterboard you to within an inch of your life, and lock you in a three-foot metal box in the blazing sun, remember this: you were warned. You had a chance to save yourself, and you blew it."

With that, he left the room.

But he did not go far. He waited outside the door for what he knew would eventually come. She held out half an hour. She called out to him. Great Hawk did not respond. Nor did he on the second, third, or any other attempt for fifteen minutes. It was necessary to make her desperate. To let her sit tied down and helpless awaiting a fate she probably took as a lie on its face. The longer she was alone, the more plausible the lie became.

I can only speculate as to what broke her. Maybe it was the darkness, or the silence, or the realization that this was really happening. Her men were dead, she was in federal custody, and she was about to be shipped off to some hellish Guantanamo-esque torture pit. Only now there was no news media, no congressional inquiries, no judicial oversight, and no outraged public to petition for clemency on her behalf. Just her and a lot of people who wanted to know what she knew and would pull no punches to get it. Literally.

The shouts became cries, and the cries became sobbing. Her throat grew ragged with desperation. Her voice broke. Great Hawk burst into the room and told her if she did not shut the fuck up he would shove a dirty sock in her mouth and duct tape it shut. People were trying to sleep.

Then came the begging. The bargaining. He knew he had her. He turned an old metal chair around backwards and folded his arms across the top.

"Fine. Spill, if it will stop your sniveling."

She spilled. What she told Great Hawk was something none of us were expecting. The silence was not shocked, but it was close. Perhaps unpleasantly surprised is more accurate.

She was a high-ranking member of a paramilitary wing of the Alliance government. Her squad, and others like it, had spent six months training with KPA special operations troops and a menagerie of defected Union operatives. Their job was to operate under the guise of marauders, raid Union communities, capture Union loyalists, and forge alliances with marauder groups.

"Sleepers," Gabe said. "They're trying to plant sleeper agents among the marauders."

Great Hawk waved toward me. "What do you infer from this?"

164

Another test. This was getting irritating. "I infer the Alliance is trying not to make enemies of the marauder groups the way the Union has. I infer they're planning an offensive against the Union and want to minimize the number of people raiding their supply lines. I infer these fake Alliance marauders are doing recon as much as anything, and looking for people they can use to carry coded messages during the offensive."

Gabe nodded. "Makes sense."

"I see a problem there," Anderson said. "What's to keep the marauders from keeping their word to the Alliance? It's not like they have a fucking sanctioning body. Supply lines are easy pickings; a marauder's wet dream."

"The Alliance is probably offering them something better," I said. "Something more lucrative, acquired with less risk."

"Like what?"

"First crack at conquered towns would be a good start. It's not like the Alliance needs the spoils. Not with the ROC helping them out."

Anderson scratched his cheek and crossed his arms. "Okay. But the part about messengers still seems shaky. A marauder's word is worth tits on a turtle."

"True. But for them it's still a low-risk venture. Think about it. They know the territory, they've been avoiding Union forces for a couple of years now, and if the messages are coded, the messengers can't tell anyone what they mean if they're captured. With no way to prove it's an Alliance message, the Union can't do much to the messenger except hold him on suspicion of conspiracy."

"They can do a hell of a lot more than that," Bjornson said. For once he sounded professional. "I've been to one of those detention centers. Wouldn't wish that shit on my worst enemy."

A few of the other Green Berets nodded along.

165

"Nevertheless," I said, "it won't do them much good. A man can't tell you something he doesn't know. The Alliance is counting on that."

"Then there's the ROC," Gabe said. "We need to remember how they fit into this whole thing."

"So far, supplying weapons and personnel," Great Hawk said. "Our intelligence sources believe the Alliance is supplying food and grain in return. It is likely when the attack comes, it will be coordinated from both sides."

Anderson said, "The ROC has aircraft. I bet they have fuel and they're saving it."

Great Hawk nodded. "You are probably right."

I stood up, stretched, and said, "Well, this is all very interesting, but it's academic. As soon as we complete this mission, the Alliance will fall apart and the ROC will be left twisting in the wind. Then the political dynamics will shift and we'll have a whole new set of problems to deal with. Nothing we can do about that from here. For now, we should focus on the job in front of us."

The Hawk agreed. The Green Berets nodded and looked at me like I was talking sense for once. It made me feel better. I was beginning to worry they had dismissed me out of hand.

I looked at Great Hawk. His face remained dark, lips pressed into a frown. The mohawk shook slowly from one side to the other, and he muttered so softly I had to read his lips to understand him.

This is not going to end well.

*****

We waited another day. The intelligence asset said that was fine, and to avoid the western gate when we arrived. At least that's what Great Hawk told us.

166

A stealth helicopter came in the night and whisked away Crocodile Lady. I never did learn her name. Gabe and I stood under the full moon, grass swaying around us in a warm breeze, and watched the silent aircraft disappear over the treeline. I wondered what the rest of her life would be like, and did not envy her. It occurred to me if our mission failed, and I was captured, my fate would likely be far worse.

Nope, I thought. *That's what the backup revolver is for.* Failing that, I had the cyanide pill. Put the little plastic canister in my mouth, bite down hard, and say *sayonara*.

"Get some sleep," Great Hawk said to everyone not going on watch. He turned to walk back into the building. "Tomorrow, we make for Carbondale."

Lying in my bunk that night, I thought about Allison. I wondered what she was doing. Was she still at the clinic? At home? Having dinner with coworkers? Prosaic things. Things that didn't involve guns, and politics, and dodging hordes of undead. It did not seem possible I had left home only three days ago. My life, and everything in it, felt light years away. I thought about the way perception can bend time and wondered if distance is subject to the same mental warping.

It was very warm in the processing facility, but I bundled up anyway. The coldness inside me was getting worse.

TWENTY

The human power of accumulation never ceases to amaze me.

Take water, for example. Under accommodating circumstances, a human being drinks an average of two liters a day. If that person lives to be seventy-five, they will drink a whopping 54,750 liters of water in their lifetime.

Looking at the wall surrounding Carbondale, I bore witness to what nearly eight thousand people could accomplish in three months when they all worked together.

Carbondale was far larger than Hollow Rock, and the perimeter wall seemed to stretch for miles even though I knew it was not that far. The north and east gates were built mostly of concrete with rolling steel doors to restrict the flow of traffic. Long sections elsewhere were made of concrete as well, others masonry, and some of shipping containers welded together and weighed down with ballast. Unlike Hollow Rock, however, none of the wall consisted of double-layered wooden palisades.

Steel and stone. Exclusively.

It made me acutely aware of how vulnerable Hollow Rock really was. Our wall was great for keeping out the infected, but one insurgent with a napalm Molotov could reduce nearly two-thirds of our outer defenses to ashes. If that happened, the dirt sandwiched by the layers of palisade would crumble into the trench below, exposing a second line of timbers. If they went down, Hollow Rock would be wide open.

We followed a four-lane stretch of crumbling asphalt surrounded by artificially short grass. Highway dividers lined the road the last half mile into town, forcing us poor, straggling pedestrians into a semblance of a line. There had once been woodland all the way up to the city's edge, but the locals had cut it back to provide a field of fire for the city's defenses.

Rotting tree stumps and the burnt, crumbling remnants of buildings were visible in the field, slowly sinking into the earth. To my right, in the distance, I saw tiny figures swinging blades at ankle level. Other figures armed with rifles followed along. The people doing the work appeared to be chained together, but I could not be sure without a closer look. I wondered if the gunmen were there to protect them or keep them in line. Maybe both.

"Look alive," Gabe whispered. "We're getting close."

We trudged along, pushing our cart with hundreds of other tired, filthy people. There were mutters of sullen conversation, grunted curses as carts jolted over potholes, and the snort and bray and stench of horses, mules, goats, sheep, and pigs.

Ahead of us, a woman pulled a small wooden cart loaded with chickens. Rather than transport them in cages, the woman had bound the chickens with lengths of vine and stacked them like cord wood. Their little heads gyrated and clucked, eyes bulging in desperation. An efficient method of transport, if not terribly humane.

Despite the multitude, I heard no laughter, no singing, no calling of friend to friend. Surely, I thought, these people must know each other. Walk the same path to work long enough, and you get to know everybody. At least that's the way it was in Hollow Rock. The morning commute—which is to say, foot traffic—was a jovial time. Back home there would have been conversation, jokes, people sharing gossip, and everyone complaining about their husbands and wives and lazy kids. Here, there was a feeling of dull drudgery and a heavy sense of muted foreboding. It reminded me of driving to work when I used to crunch numbers for the hated, long-dead mega bank. I still shudder when I think about that place.

169

A bell sounded ahead. One hour until lockdown. Our intel was the gates were only open twice a day: two hours after sunrise, and two hours before sunset. We would make it. I hoped the others entering through separate gates would as well. As per the intelligence asset, we avoided the west gate. It would have been nice to know why.

I called to mind the city data for this place. There were close to eight thousand souls living inside the wall, and another ten to fifteen thousand in the surrounding area. Three quarters of the population within the wall were free citizens and one quarter were slaves. More than half the slaves were owned by the government. They swept the streets, cleaned up garbage, maintained the landscaping, collected buckets of piss and shit for fertilizer production, distributed daily water rations, conducted repairs and routine maintenance, and did just about everything else that made life livable for the people enslaving them.

The slaves' every movement was watched over by the city guard. Any guardsman could punish a slave for even the slightest infraction, real or otherwise. The only restrictions were the guards could not inflict mechanical injury, impregnate a slave (without authorization), or kill them. The city wanted its slaves functional. Beyond that, they did not care.

The rest of the slaves were privately owned and performed a variety of tasks according to their abilities. Treatment varied from owner to owner. Sexual abuse was epidemic. Disobedience was punished harshly. Attempting to escape could result in anything from flogging to execution; it was up to the owner. Slaves had no rights of any kind, meaning a slave owner could do with a slave as he or she pleased. They were, in the truest sense of the phrase, nothing more than property.

I looked again at the people walking toward the gate with me. Many of them had been up since before dawn and had walked hours to get here. When their work was done for the day, they would walk those same weary miles back, and tomorrow, do it all again. I wondered what they thought of the slave trade. In its absence, many of them would have been

170

employed by the city or by citizens that owned slaves privately. They could have lived within the wall, their families protected, and enjoyed a decent, dignified living. Instead, they had … whatever the hell this was.

The line bottlenecked at the gate. There was no order. The guards picked someone out of the crowd, pointed at them, and ordered them forward. Then came a quick inspection for bites and signs of infection, a pat down, and on they went.

"They might not like that we're armed," I said.

Great Hawk spoke without turning his head. "It will be fine."

We waited in the midst of a grumpy, sweaty, stinking press and slowly inched toward the entrance. The gates were wide enough to allow a cart through, but no more. Two guards with scoped rifles looked down from watchtowers while four others conducted inspections. Half the guards were short, wiry, and quite obviously Asian. They wore combat fatigues, old-fashioned load bearing harnesses, and carried their AK-47s with practiced ease. They spoke only among themselves, and only in their native language. The American guards ignored them, but I noticed the looks sent their way by passing civilians. Hostility, fear, and naked hatred. It seemed pretty clear the North Koreans were not well liked. By the evil glares on the foreign troops' faces, I surmised the feeling was mutual.

A watch captain—non-North Korean—stood atop a raised platform observing the morning indignities with bored eyes and a dispassionate bearing. The proceedings beneath his boots held as much interest for him as a slug crawling across a rock. Overhead, the sky was cloudless and bleak, the hot sun beating down without mercy. I was glad I had remembered to wear a hat. It was straw, and it was ugly, but it was better than nothing.

Ahead of us, the woman with the chickens approached at a signal from the guards. They searched her, groping as they did. If the treatment affected her, she gave no sign. Her expression did not change throughout the process.

Good for you. Don't give them the satisfaction.

171

The guards then sorted through her cart, took one of her chickens, and sent her through. She walked out of sight and the guards turned their attention to us.

"You four," one of them said. "Park it over there." He walked through a gap in the highway dividers and beckoned us closer. We obeyed. He told us to stop and eyed us up and down.

"You're armed."

"Yes, we are." Great Hawk said.

"You the one in charge?"

"Something like that."

"Let me see your rifle." Great Hawk handed it to him. He looked it over, compared it to his own, and said, "Where'd you get this?"

"Traded for it at Dead Crow Station. Municipal auction, same as all our weapons."

The guard asked to inspect them. We let him. He said, "First time here?"

"Yes."

"Where you coming from?"

"Missouri. Trading salvage from outside Jefferson City."

"You got balls to be salvaging out there. Heard the place is crawling with Rot."

"There are many infected, but we know how to handle them."

The guard handed Caleb his rifle back, his manner now relaxed. "Yeah. You shoot the fuckers in the head."

The guard gestured for Gabe to peel back the tarp covering our cart. We watched as he dug around, pulled items out of boxes, and generally made a mess of things. He took a bag of dried fish, an ancient box of condoms, and a jar of homemade peach jam.

"All right," he called to his fellow guards. "They're good."

172

As we turned to leave, he said, "You can keep your ammo, but you'll have to turn your guns in at the armory. You'll get a voucher for them in case you want to trade or gamble them or whatever. Guns aren't allowed in town, so don't get let a guard find you with one. It's worth ten lashes in the city square and a month's hard labor."

Gabe pointed to the stag-horn handle of his bowie knife. "What about these?"

"Knives are fine, just don't kill anybody with it. And if you do, don't make a fucking mess, get rid of the fucking body, and don't leave any fucking witnesses. Too much goddamn paperwork."

With that, the guard walked back to his post. The way opened and we walked into Carbondale, capital city of the Midwestern Alliance.

*****

"I hope he uses those condoms," Caleb said. "And I hope he catches the clap."

We had rented a room two blocks away from the restaurant where we planned to meet the intelligence asset after nightfall. The building had once been mixed-use office space, but had been converted into what passed for a luxury hotel. Some attempt had been made to improve the décor—scarlet curtains on the windows, single beds with clean mattresses and laundered sheets, a highboy with a wash basin, soap, and a large pitcher of water, and a complimentary bottle of moonshine—but the carpet was the same cheap, shitty crud all office buildings seem to have.

"Why do you care?" I said. "It's not like that stuff is worth anything to us. We're leaving it all behind."

Our room was large. By its shape and dimensions, it had probably once been a conference room. Two beds on one wall, two on the other, and a narrow walkway between. Small tables next to each bed with large beeswax candles in brass holders. Dressers and wardrobes in the middle, one of each per bed. At the far end by the door stood the highboy. I walked over to it and poured some water in the basin, washed my face and hands, and dried off with a small white towel.

"It's the principle of it," Caleb said. He had taken off his boots and was lying on a bed with his hat over his eyes. "Folks getting robbed just going to work in the morning."

There were four expensive crystal tumblers on a shelf above the washbasin. I took one down and opened the bottle of moonshine. By the smell, it was of post-Outbreak vintage. I tasted it. It wasn't bad.

"You want a drink?"

"That shit any good?"

"It won't kill you. Other than that, no promises."

"Sure. Got nothing better to do."

I poured two and handed Caleb his. "To victory."

"To victory."

We clinked tumblers and drank. I walked over to the two large windows facing the street and opened them. The windows were new, probably placed there by whoever owned the hotel. If the building had been like most office buildings, the windows on the upper floors probably did not open when the proprietor bought this place. Not a problem in the winter, but damned hot and stuffy in the summer. Hard to run a luxury hotel if your guests keep dying of heat stroke. Hence the windows.

The breeze felt good. It did not smell good, but the movement of air against my skin cooled me a bit. The windows looked down on the front entrance of the hotel, so I leaned my palms on the sill, stuck my head outside, and took in the scene.

People bustled by in both directions while scantily clad whores worked the corners with bored eyes and empty smiles. A kid wearing a poster board sign advertising a casino walked by shouting invitations and puffery to an indifferent audience. The bar across the street was doing brisk business. A food vendor rounded the corner with a steaming cart. I smelled charcoal. The old vendor stopped under my window and sold a man some kind of meat and vegetable matter folded in a large piece of bread. The man paid with coins.

Currency? Interesting.

The scent of roasted pork, onions, and peppers wafted up to me. My mouth watered and my stomach rumbled. I took a sip of the moonshine and wished like hell I had some ice.

"See the others anywhere?"

I shook my head. "No. Might not be back for a while."

Gabe and Great Hawk had gone to put the cart in storage, make contact with the rest of the team, and buy us all something to eat. We still had rations left over, but fresh food beats preserved road food any day of the week.

I took off my boots and lay down on one of the beds. My vest and other equipment rested against the wall within arm's reach. Upon arriving at the hotel, Great Hawk had distracted the manager and his staff with questions and requests while the rest of us unloaded the government-issue weapons and equipment and smuggled it all up to the room in overnight bags. Once behind a locked door, we cleaned and reassembled the weapons and stowed them in bureau drawers. A suppressor-equipped Berretta waited under my pillow in case we had any uninvited guests. Caleb had one as well. My beloved Kel-Tec resided in my rucksack, along with its ammo. The .22 magnum was great for dealing with the undead, but there is no substitute for stopping power when fighting the living. Ergo, the Beretta.

I still had the backup revolver. The guards had not found it when they searched me. Amateurs.

My fighting dagger lay on the table. I picked it up, unsheathed it, and thumbed the edge. Still sharp enough to shave with. No blood stains. Vague scent of alcohol from when

I had cleaned it the night before after plunging it into several ghouls' eye sockets.

I thought about Stewart. I wondered what would happen to his body, how long it would take his corpse to decay. I wondered how his fellow soldiers were taking his death. I searched myself and tried to find a scrap of feeling for the lost man, but found only coldness.

I stared at the ceiling, thumb flicking along the blade of my knife, and wondered how long it would be until I lay on the ground as Stewart had, torn and bleeding and breathing my last. I hoped, on that day, I would not be alone. I hoped I would not lay abandoned where I fell, dead eyes staring like dull glass into that final, unending night. I remembered Anderson's hand slowly pressing Stewart's eyes shut. I remembered the somber voices speaking in low tones as they stripped his gear. I remembered calloused hands wiping away tears on the way back to camp.

At least Stewart died among friends. Not that such things mattered to him anymore.

*****

After leaving the abandoned chicken farm the previous day, we had set a hard pace to reach Carbondale. Unfortunately, by the time we arrived, the gate was closed for the night. Tired and dejected, we'd backtracked a couple of miles until we found a suitable clearing next to the road. We circled the carts, ate a cold meal, set a watch, and bedded down for the night. No fire. Too warm for it, and we did not want to attract attention.

Stewart and Taylor took the first watch. I unrolled my bed in the grass and was out in seconds.

I dreamed of my childhood, my mother and father sitting in lawn chairs on the shores of the Outer Banks. Ocracoke, I think it was. I played in the sand and collected seashells in a bucket. My mother's blond hair blew in the breeze, her sky-colored eyes hidden behind a pair of Chanel sunglasses. A man with my face but dark hair and eyes sat next to her, tall, handsome, a dimpled smile. His white teeth flashed below a pair of Ray Bans while he watched me.

The sun was warm overhead and the sea breeze whipped against my skin. I splashed in the shallows and let the balmy Atlantic water pull my ankles as spent waves rolled under the breakers. There was a sense of disorientation while I watched the tide roll out, as though the retreating foam wanted me to follow it. Maybe it did. Maybe it wanted to feed me to its sea creatures.

Outgoing waves suctioned sand from under my feet, making it coarser until I stood upon the shattered fragments of seashells. A new wave came in, buried me to my shins, and tried to knock me over. I kicked free and ran laughing up the beach.

A voice called behind me in a pleasant tenor. I turned and saw my father waving a tanned arm for me to return. I sprinted back, anxious to show him my bucket and its bounty. But when I arrived, my father was no longer smiling. The face so much like mine was different. The straight nose was not straight anymore. It had a bend in the middle, like a small knuckle. I stared at it; my father's nose had never been broken, not like mine. Where did that bend come from?

"What will you do now?" he asked.

"What?" My voice was not the voice of a child. Too harsh. Too grating. Too damaged from shouting over gunfire and explosions.

Mom looked over and removed the sunglasses. My own irises stared at me, skin the same golden pallor I obtained when I spent too much time in the sun. "You've made it this far, Eric. What will you do now?"

"I don't know. What should I do?"

"Only you can answer that," Dad said. Michael. His name was Michael.

"Any suggestions?"

177

"We can't do that, baby," Mom said. Julia. Never forget. Julia Marie Boisseau Riordan. Born in Baton Rouge, Louisiana, July 12th 1960. Died November 22nd 20-

"Your uncle is still alive." Dad said.

I shook my head to clear it. "Roger?"

"Yes."

"I barely know him."

"He remembers you. Go to him."

"Where is he?"

"You'll find him. Just look."

"How …"

"Honey." My mother. I looked at her.

"Yes?"

"Does Allison know your middle name?"

I shook my head. "No. I haven't told her."

"Where you went to college? Grad school?"

"No."

"Does she know our names?"

I shook my head again.

"What about her parents?"

Another shake.

"You know her father." A statement, not a question.

"What?"

"You heard me."

"Okay."

"Ask her. Tell her the things she doesn't know."

A change in the light made me look up. The afternoon shifted quickly, the sun plummeting and giving way to harshly glaring stars. The light of the moon was absent in the empty sky. I struggled to make out the figures of my parents in the oppressive darkness.

"That's what you live for now," Dad said. "Go back to Allison. Do as your mother and I say. It will start you on the path."

I heard a pop and listened as fireworks boomed and red lights lit up the ink-colored beach. More pops. More flashes. My father's face alternated red and black. I said, "What path?"

"The only one that matters."

More pops. I was being pulled away, pulled upward and downward at the same time. The world spun, the waves took me under, I struggled to breathe, felt water pour down my throat and then …

"Riordan!"

I awoke. Gunfire. Moans. *Infected.*

"Riordan, you awake?"

"Yeah, yeah. I'm awake." The hand on my shoulder stopped shaking me. "We under attack?"

The voice above me belonged to Anderson. "Yes. Grab your rifle and follow me."

I sat up. Unlike my dream, the moon above was just past full, still plenty bright. Now that my night vision had kicked in, I could see well enough to move around. I grabbed my rifle and sprinted after Anderson.

The fight raged on all sides of the cart barrier. Stewart and Taylor ran back toward camp in a low crouch as Hicks and Bjornson fired over their heads, taking out pursuing infected. The two fleeing soldiers leapt over the barrier and tumbled to a halt a few feet past the firing line. In an instant, they were back on their feet, reloading and joining the fight.

I took position where Anderson told me to. The only person there was Liddell, and he was hard pressed to keep the infected back. The closest of them were only a few feet away. I let the

179

AK dangle from its sling and drew my pistol. The Makarov felt strange in my hands, but the sights lined up just fine. I focused on a pallid face and fired. The forehead erupted red and the face disappeared. I repeated the process as fast as I could until the mag was empty, only missing once. Now we had some breathing room.

"Thanks," Liddell said as he reloaded. He was my height, shaved head scorched brown in the sun, long red beard, strong build. "Nice shooting."

"Kind of my thing." I aimed the AK and fired. Better. Much more accurate than the pistol at this range. The thirty-round mag was nice too.

I went to work. The old hypnotic feeling came over me the same as it always did. I could almost swear I heard a metronome at work in the back of my head, and with each tick of the striker, each second, my finger twitched and a ghoul dropped. I no longer took note of their features. My eyes were motion detectors. My brain became little more than facial recognition software. Was it alive? No? Shoot it.

The chamber locked back on an empty mag. Reload. A little different process with the AK. I had to move the weapon off my point of aim, depress a lever, sweep the mag free, and then lock in a new one. With an M-4 configuration rifle, I could have just let the mag drop without shifting my aim. Much faster that way.

More bloody faces. More gunfire. The ghouls just kept coming, and coming, and coming. I knew what the problem was. It was the noise. All these guns firing, firing, firing, but we had no choice. We were surrounded. So I kept shooting, and eventually, I heard the shouts begin behind me.

"I'm out!"

"Last mag!"

"Going to my sidearm!"

"Get ready to draw hand weapons!" It was the first time I ever heard Great Hawk raise his voice.

Worry began to pierce the fog. I had my sword and stick, but would they be enough? No time to worry. It didn't matter. If things did not work out, there was always the backup revolver. I reached to the small of my back and felt its comforting weight there. The cyanide pill was in its place as well. No worries.

I emptied the last magazine on my vest. The barrel of my rifle glowed a dull, muted red in the darkness. Probably a good thing I was out of ammo, wouldn't want a cookoff with a round in the chamber. I dropped the rifle and handed Liddell my Makarov and two spare mags.

"Hold them off."

"Wait! Where are you-"

I did not hear the rest because Liddell started shooting.

I shouted, "Gabe! Gabe, you with me?"

"Over here!"

I stopped at my bedroll, grabbed my sword and stick, and ran toward the sound of his voice. When I reached him, he was emptying his own pistol, each shot sending an infected to its final rest.

"Got your sword?"

He reached a diminished left hand under his vest, grunted, tugged, and produced the blade. His right hand kept firing, each round finding its mark.

"Let's jump the carts. Hit 'em on the move."

He fired his last two rounds and dropped the pistol. "On me."

The big man did a flat-footed leap over the cart in front of him and hit the ground swinging. I lifted the handles, stepped past, and let the cart fall. No need for dramatics on my part.

I dug an Army surplus L-shaped flashlight with a red lens cover from my web belt, clipped it to my vest, and hit the switch. A dim cone of red light shone in front of me, lighting up the pale, wasted faces of ghouls. There were dozens of them. Piles of dead bodies littered the ground in a wide circle beyond the line of carts, making hard going for the undead. Good. I braced my Y-stick, brought my sword up to shoulder level, and went to work.

I allowed myself no more than two seconds per ghoul. Hit the neck with the stick, lift a little, touch the sword point to the top of the cheekbone, and thrust. A quick rotation of the wrist, then withdraw. I did not wait to watch them fall. It would have been a waste of time.

Ahead of me, Gabe's sword flashed in the moonlight, the polished blade growing dark with accumulated gore. The gunshots behind me stopped, and I heard Anderson shout for two of his men to collect magazines, grab a box of ammo from a cart, and get to work reloading. Everyone else drew hand weapons—axes, crowbars, and a couple of homemade warhammers—and started busting skulls.

"What are you two doing?" Great Hawk shouted. He sounded angry. "You are going to get yourselves killed!"

"Trust us," I called back. "We've done this before."

The others stood behind the carts and used them as a buffer, swinging their weapons from a distance. This technique worked fine so long as only one or two undead pushed against the barriers. Three or more, and their forward pressure would be enough to shove the carts out of the way. It was better not to rely on them, and instead utilize humanity's best weapon against the walking dead—agility.

We ran hard, killing only enough ghouls to clear the path until, finally, we were clear of the horde. Gabe and I paused a moment, hands on knees, and drew in deep breaths. We were not winded, but the work ahead would be difficult. Best to flood our muscles with oxygen while we had the chance. Back at camp, somebody shouted something unintelligible and I heard the unmistakable bark of an AK.

"Looks like they're reloading fast," Gabe said.

"Not fast enough. Come on."

182

We started shouting as loud as we could and clanging our weapons against our knives. Slowly, one by one, the ghouls turned in our direction. But others closer to the sound of gunfire did not notice us. Gabe indicated he was going right, so I took off to my left.

As I ran, I darted in from time to time and dropped a ghoul. I kept my mind carefully blank. Running half-blind through the darkness while surrounded by God only knows how many infected is the kind of thing best done with as little thought as possible. Think too much and you start to panic. Better to keep moving.

A minute or two passed. I ran into the forest, got disoriented, backtracked, killed four more infected, and found my way back to the clearing. Great Hawk must have figured out what we were doing because he and the others stood back-to-back in a tight, silent circle, weapons at the ready. Gabe's booming voice sounded directly across from me and perhaps a hundred yards away. The way back to camp was clear, so I ran to the barrier.

"Don't shoot, it's Riordan," I hissed as I drew close. No one fired.

"What's going on?" Great Hawk asked. It occurred to me this was the first time I had ever heard him use a contraction.

"We've got them split up into two groups. Gabe is straight that way. What we should do is fan out at double-arm intervals and start rolling them up from one of their flanks."

Bjornson lowered his weapon. "Are you out of your fucking mind? There must be hundreds of those things out there."

"Yes, but they're spread out, probably not more than one or two per hundred square feet. Easy pickings."

Bjornson shook his head. "No fucking way."

Anderson started to say something, but I interrupted him. "Fine. Stay here and be cowards. I'm going to help Gabe."

With that, I sprang over a cart and ran toward the sound of Gabe's voice. Great Hawk said something in his native

183

language I did not understand, but I got the impression it translated into something vile and very likely four-lettered. I heard a grunt, then more grunts, and then the sounds of boots pounding after me.

As I had asked, the men spread out roughly six feet apart and followed my lead. "Only kill the ones that get in your way," I called out. "Avoid them if you can."

We got bogged down a couple of times at some of the thicker knots of ghouls, but eventually we made it through and found Gabe standing in the bed of an abandoned pickup truck.

I had to give the man credit for quick thinking. He had let two layers of undead gather around the walls of the truck and lopped their arms off at the shoulder. Unable to grab him, they formed an impenetrable, if still dangerous, buffer zone from the rest of the horde. Rather than continue killing, he simply stood still in the middle, well out of reach and relatively safe. When he heard us coming, he started stomping his feet, clashing his weapons, and shouting as loud as he could. The ghouls surged at him with renewed frenzy, to no avail.

Great Hawk hissed and motioned for everyone to approach slowly and quietly. The only sounds we made as we closed in on the pickup truck were the soft crunch of boots over leaves and our own ragged breathing. We were in woodland now, emerging onto a narrow dirt road. A few ghouls turned at our arrival, but most stayed focused on Gabe.

Bjornson was the closest soldier to my position. He stood a few feet to my right, his hands clasping the haft of a hammer made from cast iron pipes. The hammer had a screw-on cap at the bottom, a T-intersection at the top, and a short, thick bolt held in place with silicone tape and a huge lug nut. It looked heavy, but Bjornson handled it with no problem.

A ghoul emerged in front of him from behind a tree. Without breaking stride, he pushed its arms out of the way, sidestepped, and nailed it on the back of the skull with a powerful overhand bash. The ghoul's skull shattered, chunks of bone and brain tissue spattering the surrounding trees more than ten feet from where it stood. The corpse went limp and slumped to the ground. Before it was down, Bjornson had already moved on.

Impressive weapon.

I moved to the pickup and started killing. The ghouls trying to reach Gabe had their backs to me, forcing me to tap them on the shoulder and wait for them to turn around before killing them. Four lay permanently dead at my feet before the rest figured out what was happening. By then, Great Hawk and the others had surrounded the truck and were hacking away at undead skulls.

My sword got stuck in a ghoul's skull. Unable to free it quickly, I let it drop, switched to my fighting knife, and kept on killing. It was the work of less than five minutes to dispatch them all. There was no conversation, just the moans of infected and the grunts of men swinging weapons.

As usually happens when exterminating ghouls in the dark, I pushed a dead body away from me, turned to find the next target, and saw only living people equally as frenzied and tired as I was. I let my arms fall but held on to my weapons.

An ear-piercing scream sounded from the front of the truck. I sprinted around the tailgate and saw Stewart on the ground with two ghouls attached to his back. The screams grew louder and shriller as the undead sank relentless teeth into his shoulders, each bite ripping away gobs of bleeding flesh.

No, no, no ...

Great Hawk made it before I did and buried his tomahawk in the back of a skull. Without thinking, I drew my revolver, aimed on the run, and when the last ghoul raised its head with a mouthful of gore, I fired. The bulled punched a neat hole through its eye, and a burst of skull fragments flew from the exit wound. The ghoul went limp.

"Ah shit," Anderson said as he rolled Stewart over, his voice anguished. "Goddammit, Stewart, you forgot to check behind you."

I don't know if Stewart heard him or not. He was in shock, face pale, eyes wide and vacant. My flashlight still shone, lighting his face in deep crimson. The blood covering his torso looked black in the sullen glow. I looked away long enough to turn a circle and check for other ghouls we may have missed. I saw none.

Gabe stepped beside me and we both stared as Anderson knelt beside Stewart. He looked at me and then at the revolver in my hand. "Mind if I borrow that?"

I handed it to him. He opened the cylinder, saw four rounds remaining, and nodded slowly. "No one needs to stay. I'll take care of it."

No one moved. Stewart whispered something. I could not make out the words, and decided I would not ask Anderson what he had heard.

Less than a minute later, Stewart died. Anderson closed the fallen soldier's eyes with a gentle hand, put the pistol to his head, and looked away. "Goodbye, brother."

The shot echoed into the night.

TWENTY-ONE

Gabe and Great Hawk returned shortly before sundown with a basket of food.

The basket was woven from vines and obviously not meant to last more than a few days. The food itself was wrapped in some kind of thick, inedible bread. To access our meal of roasted meat, potatoes, and grilled vegetables, we first had to break away the bread substance with hard taps from the hilts of our knives. The Frisbee-shaped bread broke easily around the edges, and the two halves made serviceable plates. Clever.

We ate with our fingers while Great Hawk laid out the plan. The rendezvous was set, all we had to do was wait and show up at the appointed time. He wanted me, Caleb, and McGee on overwatch. We would have radios, and if anything looked out of place, we were to notify Gabriel. I expressed to Great Hawk I did not like being left out of the briefing. I wanted to see the intelligence asset for myself before risking my life on his or her say so.

"You do not trust Gabriel and me to handle it?"

"It's not a question of whether or not I trust *you*. It's a question of whether or not I trust *them*."

"We have risked much, and this person has never been wrong."

"Fine. Great. Two points for them. I still don't like it."

"Eric, please. I need a competent sniper with sharp eyes to make sure we are not interrupted. And I have noticed that your eyesight is exceptional."

"Don't fucking patronize me, Hawk."

"I am not. I am stating a fact."

Gabe washed down a bite of carrots and squash. "What is it, 20-10 or something like that?"

"Yes. I have 20-10 vision. The doctor who did my Lasik surgery was an overachiever. Now can we focus on the topic at hand?"

"Lasik surgery?" It was the most Hicks had said in hours.

"Yes. My eyesight was shitty until I was 21."

"How shitty?"

"Coke-bottle glasses shitty."

"Really?"

I let out a sigh. "Yes, really. My old man paid for the surgery. Twenty-first birthday present. Had 20-10 vision ever since. Now, again, about this intelligence asset …"

"If I see something I don't like," Gabe said, "I'll tell you. I need to be in the room for that briefing and we both know why."

I could not disagree. There was no substitute for Gabe's perfect recall. He would be the mission coordinator, and I knew beyond doubt he would get everyone where they needed to be to do their jobs, and then get them out safely to the extraction site.

"The only other snipers on my level are you, Hicks, and McGee. You three are our best chance at stopping any trouble before it becomes a problem. Be practical, Eric."

I nodded reluctantly. As much as I hated to be out of the loop, even briefly, I had to admit the big man had a point. "All right. Fine. Just don't be in there all fucking night. I don't want to piss my pants before going into a fight."

I was not kidding. On sniper duty, one must remain as still as possible. Which meant if I had to urinate, and could not hold it, leaving my station was not an option. That left but one course of action.

Gabe chuckled. "I doubt it will take very long."

*****

"Lying bastard."

Gabe ignored me. He could hear me through his earpiece, but did not respond. Great Hawk elected to remain silent as well. Three hours had passed since I had circled the block, spotted a conveniently located rooftop, and set up my hide. Gabe, Anderson, the Hawk, and a couple of others had been in the basement of the restaurant all night. I could not hear what they were talking about, but no one had sent a duress signal. I could only assume all was well for the moment.

My radio buzzed, letting me know someone was trying to contact me on another channel. I looked at the readout and switched over. "Yeah?"

"You're breaking protocol. Radio silence."

"Chill out, McGee."

"Don't tell me to chill out."

"How 'bout I tell you to fuck off, then?"

"Enough," Caleb cut in. "We don't have time for this shit. Switch back over to the command net."

"Yes, mommy." I switched back over.

Another twenty minutes rolled by. The pressure in my bladder did not abate. I was beginning to seriously consider the option of last resort when I heard my earpiece buzz.

"Coming out." It was Great Hawk.

May emerged first, followed by Bjornson, Liddell, Great Hawk, Anderson, and bringing up the rear, Gabriel. I thought at first the asset had remained behind, but then the Hawk took a step to his right and I saw the person we were all risking our lives for.

189

She was petite, dark red hair hanging straight down to her shoulders, and stood maybe five-foot-two. The night vision scope did not reveal much of her facial features, but I got the impression she was attractive. Her age was indeterminate at this range.

"Overwatch, break off and meet at the mission rendezvous."

I keyed my mike. "Station one, copy."

McGee and Hicks acknowledged as well. I checked the streets. No late pedestrians, no guardsmen afoot. I disassembled my rifle, stowed it in my rucksack, and climbed down to street level.

The alleyway reeked of old garbage, urine, and something dead. It was almost completely dark. The night sky above was clear, allowing a small amount of starlight to filter down past the walls and rooftops. It would have been nice to have Gabe's IR goggles right then.

A shapeless bundle moved somewhere to my left, concealed in darkness. I heard a groan. My hand went to the suppressor equipped pistol under my Army surplus bush jacket. It was too warm for the jacket, but I had to hide the gun somehow.

The shape groaned again. I wondered if it was a trap. Had I been followed? Was someone launching a pre-emptive attack? Had we been compromised? My heart thudded in my ears as I crept closer, rolling my steps to keep them quiet. I drew the pistol and held it at the low-ready position, the glow-in-the-dark sights seeming to line up on their own. The bundle was now only a few feet in front of me. It rolled over, and I was damned glad I did not have my finger on the trigger.

An old man with a matted beard looked around blearily. He saw me, blinked, and did not move. I did not want to shoot him, but if he started to shout, he was a dead man. He looked at the gun.

"You here to rob me?"

"No."

190

"Good. I ain't got nothin' no way."

We stared at each other. I said, "Just passing through. My business is elsewhere."

"Then pass. Don't need to pay me any mind. No one else does."

I lowered the pistol a few inches. "You going to run for the guard as soon as I'm out of sight?"

He made a wet, phlegmy sound. His body shook, and his lips pulled back from nearly toothless gums. I realized he was laughing. "The guard? Those sons of bitches? Hell, son, my ribs still ain't healed from the last stompin' they gave me. You kill any of the bastards, and I'll buy you a drink."

I put away the gun. "Got a name?"

"Used to."

"You still do."

Something stirred in the old man's gaze. "Larry. Larry Bridges."

"I wasn't here, Larry."

"Fine by me."

I turned to leave, then stopped and went back over. I took a couple of rare and precious sugar packets from a vest pouch and handed them to Larry Bridges. "Here. A token of gratitude for your discretion."

The old man slowly took the packets and shook them. "This real sugar?"

"It is."

"Where'd you get it?"

I smiled. "A long way from here."

"Well, thank you. Thanks a bunch."

"Have a drink for me, Larry. Enjoy it in good company and good health."

Ragged laughter followed me out of the alley. I walked a few dozen yards, then doubled back and waited at the corner. Nothing stirred. I risked a peek beyond the wall and saw Larry under a pile of rags. He was snoring.

"Good luck, Larry." I turned north on the cross street and headed for the rendezvous.

*****

The others were already there.

The rendezvous was the storeroom of an abandoned gas station. The place smelled like mildew and dead rats, and it looked like vagrants had been squatting there until very recently. There were empty bottles, old vomit, and moldering feces along the walls and in every corner. I felt like I needed a shower just walking into the room.

"What took you so long?" McGee asked.

"Had to take a piss." It was true. And I had, shortly after leaving Larry Bridges to his fate.

"Must have been an epic piss."

"It was. People will write songs about it someday."

"Are you two finished?" Anderson asked.

I shrugged. McGee shook his head but said nothing. I looked at the intelligence asset. My impression had been right; she was very attractive.

"What's your name?" I said.

She blinked. "What's yours?"

"I asked you first."

"Why do you want to know?"

"So I can call you something other than Intelligence Asset. Makes me feel misogynistic."

To my surprise, I got a smile. "Lena Smith. Just call me Lena."

The name rang a bell, but I couldn't quite place it. "Works for me. Okay, Chief," I looked to Great Hawk. "What's the plan?"

He laid it out. There were a lot of moving parts, but mine was fairly simple. Hicks and I were to proceed to a building near the town square. Inside this building was the residence of one Bailey Sandoval, the Alliance's equivalent of a secretary of defense. He was a powerful man in these parts, and possessed far more knowledge of Union resources, methods, and plans of action than the shot-callers in Colorado were comfortable with. They knew who his informant was, and had him under twenty-four hour surveillance, thanks to Lena, but did not want to make a move until Sandoval was no longer a threat. Hicks and I were to separate him from his mortal coil, thus removing one of many thorns from the Union's beleaguered side.

I studied the map on the ruggedized tablet. I compared it to what I had memorized of the street layout of Carbondale, and said I should be able to find Sandoval's place without difficulty. Caleb said the same. Great Hawk gave a satisfied nod.

"Looks like we won't be working together on this one," I said to Gabe. There was more regret in my voice than I intended.

"You'll be fine. Hicks won't let you fuck up too badly."

"Thanks for the vote of confidence, good buddy."

"Anytime." He punched me on the arm. I put a middle finger a few inches from his face.

"Gabriel and I will storm the president's mansion along with McGee and May," Great Hawk said. "Anderson, you and Liddell will go after the speaker of the council. He is here, at this casino near the east wall. Plant your charges on the second level so as to collapse the roof above the gaming floor. This will give you the distraction you need to escape."

Anderson gave a short nod. "No problem."

"Bjornson, LaGrange, Taylor, the three of you will take out General Samson. He will be in his room in this building here, close to the north gate." Great Hawk's eyes shifted to Lena Smith. "Did you arrange for what we need?"

She pointed to a dark corner. "Two crates over there under the black tarp. You'll find everything I promised you."

Great Hawk turned back to Bjornson and his team. "Do not forget your armbands. General Samson will be surrounded by his militia. Do not doubt that they are fanatics. They will stop at nothing to protect their general. Yours is perhaps the most dangerous job of all. It is also the lowest value as far as our targets go. If things look insurmountable, do not hesitate to abort."

Bjornson shook his head. "No way. We kill him or die trying."

LaGrange and Taylor nodded but did not look quite as resolved to their task as Bjornson. I did not blame them. I had heard stories about General Randolph Samson and his militia. Samson's Silencers, they called themselves. Or the SS to Alliance citizens. The general and his men understood the historical significance of this label and the reputation for brutality that went along with it. Consequently, they did nothing to dissuade the widespread perception they were equally as merciless and sadistic as their Nazi forbears. If Bjornson and his team were captured, their deaths would be neither quick nor pleasant.

"Do not be a hero, Bjornson. Your lives are more valuable to your country than Samson's death."

Bjornson said nothing.

"You should check the crates," Lena said. "Make sure I didn't forget anything."

"Very well." Great Hawk motioned toward the lump of plastic in the corner. Lena walked over, pulled it away, and shined a small LED flashlight on two large crates. They looked like the big composite containers I often saw the Army using to transport ammo and equipment. Lena unlocked them with a key around her neck, opened them, and stepped back. The Hawk motioned Bjornson and his people to approach first.

Lena dug out three red armbands with the black SS symbol embroidered on each one. Looking closer, I saw each S was actually a slithering snake, and below the letters was a phrase in Latin: *Haud Misericordia pro Proditor.* If my high school Latin was accurate, it meant something to the effect of 'No Mercy for the Traitor'.

Sounds like a real pleasant bunch.

Also within the crates were RPG launchers, rockets, Russian grenades, flashbangs, explosive charges that looked suspiciously like C-4, remote detonators, claymore mines, and ten large black duffel bags.

"Take whatever you think you will need," Great Hawk said. "But do not allow any guards to search you. If they try, kill them quietly."

I deferred to Hicks. He grabbed six flashbangs, eight grenades, an RPG launcher, four rockets, four claymores, and one of the duffel bags. I put three of the flashbangs in an empty pouch and added three grenades to loops on my chest. Caleb did the same, then put the rest in the duffel bag.

"You're carrying that," I said, pointing.

"Yeah, I figured, me being bigger than you and all." He grinned as he said it. I let it go. When a man agrees to carry more than his share of the gear, it is bad form to give him shit about it. One simply takes whatever ribbing comes one's way with good humor and a sense of gratitude.

"Everyone put your radios on the command net," Great Hawk said. "Mr. Garrett will give the order when all stations are in position. Remember, this is a coordinated attack. Do not jump the gun."

We all nodded. Lena swallowed and took a deep breath.

195

"Good luck to all of you," Gabe said. "I'll be on the radio if you get lost. Remember, this is not a land-nav contest. If you're not sure of exactly where you are, *do not* hesitate to ask for help. It's what I'm here for."

Muttered acknowledgement.

"Before we leave," I said, "who's going to watch her?" I pointed to Lena.

"None of us," Great Hawk said. "She will proceed to the east gate to arrange transportation to the extraction point."

I shot her a hard glare. "Really."

She was unperturbed. "Yes. Really."

I stepped closer until we were less than a foot apart. "Maybe you can answer a couple of questions then."

He gaze was clear and steady. "Sure."

"Why did you tell us to avoid the west gate?"

"Protests."

"Protests?"

"Yes."

"Protesting what?"

"Foreign occupation. The North Koreans are extremely unpopular. There have been similar protests in other Alliance city-states that ended in bloodshed. To avoid it happening here, the president authorized the demonstration with the caveat it be peaceful. Nevertheless, I did not want any of you walking into a powder keg. Your job is dangerous enough as it is."

I tilted my head and nodded twice. "Okay, I'll buy that. Next question. How do you know so much about the Alliance's command structure?"

She waved her hands to indicate her outfit, a sensible charcoal-colored pants suit. "The clothes aren't a clue?"

"They're nice. The color definitely brings out the green in your eyes, and there's just enough hug in the hips to show off how fit you are. I'm guessing you work out a lot. Other than that, I'm clueless."

She surprised me again by blushing and pushing a strand of hair behind her ear. "Who still wears clothes like this?"

"I don't know. A few businesspeople I've met. Politicians."

"Precisely."

"So you're ..." I held out a hand.

"You really don't know who I am?"

"Would I be asking if I did?"

She signed and stood up straight. "I know as much about the Alliance's leadership as I do because I am *one of them.*"

A photograph from that first mission briefing with General Jacobs surfaced from the murky waters of memory, and it dawned on me why her name sounded so familiar. I could have kicked myself for not figuring it out sooner.

"Shit. You're *that* Lena Smith."

A sad smile. "Yes. I am the vice president of the Midwest Alliance."

*****

"That was nice back there."

I looked at Hicks. We were on our way to the town's central square and the residence of one Bailey Sandoval. "What?"

"Flirting with the vice president of an enemy country."

"I wasn't flirting."

"She seemed to have a different idea. I think she was sweet on you."

197

"*Sweet on me*? Who the hell says shit like that? What are you, an old west cattle rancher? Did I put a hitch in her giddyup, pardner?"

"Don't try to change the subject."

I sighed. "It was not my intention to flirt with her. I was trying to get information. I can't help it if the ladies love me."

Hicks snorted. "Did they love you back in your Coke-bottle glasses days?"

"Especially then. I was so hot they couldn't stand to talk to me. Just walked away or asked me to leave them alone. I didn't hold it against them. There's only so much chiseled manliness a woman can handle."

"I'm beginning to wish I brought my entrenching tool."

"For what?"

"To shovel my way out of your bullshit."

There was movement a few blocks ahead. Dark shapes ghosted through the shadows in a walking crouch. I saw hand signals pass back and forth, and the figures were clearly armed. I stopped and grabbed Hicks' shoulder.

"Stop."

Hicks froze and peered into the darkness. He had long ago learned to trust my eyesight. "You see something?"

"Yeah. Let's get off this street."

We moved to an alley two blocks over and waited next to an overflowing dumpster. "What did you see?" Hicks asked.

"North Korean special forces, unless I miss my guess."

"Shit. What are they doing out here?"

I shook my head.

We stayed still and quiet. Every second that ticked by grated against my nerves. We did not have all night.

"Okay," I whispered. "You take that end of the alley, I'll take this one. Use your night vision scope. Look for movement. You see hostiles, take them out."

Hicks checked his suppressor was firmly attached, made sure his scope was activated, and tapped me on the shoulder. He was gone in an instant, no noise, no wasted movement. I stared after him and wondered what secrets his past held. No infantry grunt I ever met had half his abilities.

Questions for another day.

I crept to the edge of the building and peeked around the bricks. The black shapes were still moving toward me, closer now. My instincts told me to hide, but the corner where I hid was dark. The short, fatigue-sporting soldiers seemed not to notice me. So I stayed, and watched, and whispered into my radio.

"Incoming on my side."

The radio crackled, and Gabe spoke up. "Everything all right?"

"Tell you in a minute. Stay off the net."

"Copy." Gabe's voice was strained, but he understood the necessity. Hicks chimed in. "Clear on my side."

"You sure?"

"Affirmative."

"Get back over here."

I did not hear him approach. One second I was alone, and the next I felt a tap on my shoulder. "Stacked up behind you."

"Stand by. I'm going to leapfrog the alley. Be ready to engage."

"Roger that." Not for the first time, I detected a note of excitement in his voice. I looked back.

"You like this shit, don't you?"

A grin. "I do. I really do."

"Sometimes I worry about you, Caleb."

"Worry about crossing the alley."

"Right. Okay, here goes."

There is nothing a man can do to prepare for the maneuver I executed. You just go as fast as you can and hope for the best. In my case, it worked out. I flung myself from cover, stayed low, ran on the edges of my boots to minimize noise, and stacked up at the corner of the next alley over. No shots fired. No shouts. No explosions. I keyed my radio.

"Hicks, see anything?"

He had pied out the corner with his night vision scope. I checked mine, found it dark, and activated it. "They don't seem agitated, but they're still moving in our direction."

"Tactical movement?"

"I suppose so. Their version of it, anyway."

"Prepare to engage. Leave no survivors."

"You sure about this? Maybe we ought to slip out of here."

I stuck my scope around a narrow sliver of corner. "No time. They're almost on us. On my mark."

"Standing by."

I called to mind everything Gabe and Captain Steve McCray taught me about close quarters combat. Accuracy. Speed. Violence of movement. Silence.

The shapes grew closer. Thirty meters. Twenty. Ten.

"Three, two, one, mark."

I slipped enough of my torso from cover to aim from a stable shooting platform. By the time I lined up on my first target, Caleb had already loosed three rounds. A dark black head snapped back, and the figure attached to it collapsed without a sound. In the same instant as I mentally praised Caleb for his marksmanship, my finger squeezed down on the trigger. Another head snapped back. I made a follow up shot and resisted the urge for a third one. I was firing 6.8 SPC after all, not standard 5.56 NATO rounds. Which meant I did not have to shoot a man five times to make sure he was dead. Twice to the head was enough.

As often happens in combat, my training took over and I was firing again before I knew what was happening. Another dark shape dropped. Caleb's rifle coughed twice and a fourth man died. Only two left now.

The one closest to me noticed something amiss, or maybe caught a dim muzzle flash, and started to shout something. He got out half a syllable before two rounds from my rifle tore his throat to shreds. Blood flew from his lips as I ended his misery with a third shot between the eyes. He went stiff, shuddered, and toppled like a felled tree.

Caleb let loose a final salvo of four shots. Two hit center of mass, and two blew holes in the diminutive commando's upper sinus cavity. He died without a sound. Caleb and I looked at each other, nodded, and waited. No more sounds. No movement. I let a minute go by. It appeared the high-quality suppressors had done their job.

Static. "All clear."

I gave Caleb a thumbs up by way of acknowledgement. Then I remembered Gabe was listening in and keyed my radio. "All clear. Let's move out."

"How many tangos?" Gabe asked over the net.

"Six. All down."

"You compromised?"

"No. Proceeding on mission."

"Roger." Gabe sounded relieved. Hicks gave a 'move forward' hand signal, to which I nodded, hid my rifle beneath my bush jacket, and followed.

I spotted another patrol shortly before arriving near the town square. They were not North Koreans, but were nonetheless heavily armed. One even carried an RPK light machine gun with a bipod and drum magazine. I grabbed Hicks' arm and led him down a side street. We stopped under an awning and stood in near total darkness. One of the guards carried a small oil lamp that let us see their outline as they passed.

"These fellas ain't messin' around," Caleb said. "Think they know something's up?"

"Could be. Doesn't change anything. Let's go."

We approached the building from the rear. It had once been a hotel, but had been repurposed to house government officials. Sandoval's residence took up three rooms, all connected by open doorways. He was on the second floor at the easternmost corner. There were two entrances, both manned by a pair of armed guards. If Lena Smith's intel was correct, there would be four more guards posted inside, also heavily armed.

"Mission lead, alpha team," Hicks told his radio. "We are in position, standing by."

"Roger alpha team. Stand by, will advise when it's time to start the party."

"Roger. Alpha out."

I checked my weapons for the tenth or eleventh time. Good to go. "So now we wait."

"I'll move to the corner of that building over there." Hicks pointed. "Have a better shot at the guards on that side."

"All right."

Hicks moved. I waited. And waited. Ten minutes passed. I saw no patrols, no citizens conducting late night business, no voices, no music from the bars or taverns, no sign at all anyone was alive in Carbondale. The streets so busy earlier were now empty and silent.

I thought once again how the silence was the hardest thing to get used to in a post-apocalyptic world. No drone of planes overhead, no Doppler hum of cars on the highways, no news or traffic helicopters, no buzz of air conditioners or power lines or street lights. Over three years had passed since the Outbreak, and it still bothered me. I was beginning to think it always would.

Static. "Mission lead, Bravo team in position."

"Copy. Stand by."

"Roger. Bravo out."

More time passed. Charlie team checked in. Gabe and Great Hawk's group were still en route to the president's mansion. I closed my eyes and visualized a map of Carbondale in my head. I traced imaginary lines from where I was to the east gate. There were several possible routes I could take. Hicks and I planned to split up and proceed separately. That way, if one of us was caught or pinned down, the other could attempt rescue. Failing that, it minimized the risk we would both be caught. Better for the Union to lose one operator than two.

The radio stayed silent. I thought about the target, visualized his face. There had been several photos in his dossier. He was tall, approximately six foot four, bald head, goatee, narrow features, a casual arrogance in the eyes that screamed 'hatchet-faced prick'.

It would have been a lie to say I was entirely comfortable with the idea of carrying out an assassination. I had killed before, but always in self-defense or defense of others. Reminding myself of the danger this man posed to untold thousands if he lived lessened the dread, but only marginally.

All the other times I had killed—the Free Legion, raiders and marauders, Alliance insurgents, etc.—I had made it a point not to look the enemy in the eye. Better to focus on hitting center of mass, or making a quick head shot. I rarely dialed a scope to more than four power, and that only at very long range. I did not like it when I could discern a man's facial features, his expression, and watch the shock and disbelief and pain overwhelm him in the moment before he died. The few faces I had observed in those final seconds still visited me in the quiet hours of the night when sleep refused to come. And when I finally did sleep, I saw them in my dreams—bloody, angry, accusing.

203

On the nights when they woke me from slumber, I disconnected my mp3 player from the solar charger, put in the earbuds, and poured myself a drink. Al Green, Jimmy Cliff, Buddy Guy, and Johann Sebastian Bach did a pretty good job of keeping the demons at bay. Mike Stall's finest moonshine didn't hurt either.

The earpiece crackled. "All stations are in position. Everybody ready to go?"

The teams responded in order, Hicks speaking up for the two of us. All stations were as ready as they were going to be.

"Very well. Good luck and Godspeed, gentlemen. If it all goes south, it's been an honor. Engage on my mark."

I eased out from cover and peered around the corner. Raised my rifle. Sighted in. The guard in my crosshairs looked bored. *They're not expecting trouble.*

Static. "Task Force Falcon, Wolfman. Hit hard, hit fast, show no mercy. Take 'em out."

The coldness inside me rose to a burning crescendo as icy heat coursed through my blood. The fire lent strength to my limbs, firmed my resolve, and burned away the last tremblings of fear. I went still inside. My hands were sure and steady. My mind and my conscience were clear.

I let out half a breath and fired.

TWENTY-TWO

Two shots. The head snapped back. Pivot right. Two more shots. Down they go.

I heard five dull cracks from Caleb's side, and then a fleeting shadow as he moved toward the west entrance. My feet pounded over cracked and broken pavement, eyes scanning quickly to avoid tripping over dislodged asphalt or small, struggling plants.

I reached the two dead guards, slung my rifle around to my back, grabbed the first one, and dragged him behind a couple of large, rusted air conditioners. Then the second guard. Heavy bastards both. Last, I stashed my rucksack and bush jacket in the same space as the dead bodies, donned my NVG's, and waited at the south entrance.

"Irish, Tex, in position." Caleb was referring to us by our call signs. Everyone had chosen one before the final phase of the mission, as call signs were the easiest way to avoid confusion once the assault began.

"Copy, Tex. I'm in position."

"Breaching now."

"Copy."

I tried the door and found it locked. Not unexpected. From my web belt, I produced a funny looking little gun with a needle instead of a barrel. I did not know exactly how it worked, but Gabe had given it to me a long time ago and told me it would open most conventional locks. I put it in the keyhole, depressed the handle a couple of times, and gently turned. The lock rolled over and the bolt snicked back into the door.

"Tex, Irish. I'm in."

"Wait one ..."

I waited. Looked around. No movement.

Static. "Irish, Tex. I'm in."

"On my mark. Two, one, mark."

I opened the door slightly and scanned for tripwires or other traps. A slight reflection flashed at ankle level a few feet beyond the opening. Tripwire. Never would have seen it without the NVGs or a flashlight, and a flashlight was out of the question; I couldn't risk drawing a guard's attention.

I stepped over it and proceeded inside, rifle up, barrel following my line of sight. I did not see the green line of the PEQ-15 laser sight, visible only with NVGs. I turned it on. The precise little beam was oddly comforting.

I found myself in a darkened hallway, beige walls, cheap trim and wainscoting, ugly paisley carpet, heavy doors, and the boxy metal key readers of modern hotels. No lights. No sound. No movement. The stairs were at the end of the hall if I remembered correctly. I moved toward them, ears straining in case any doors opened behind me. A vicious little picture show in the back of my mind envisioned armed men leaping from doorways and letting loose a volley of unavoidable high-velocity lead. No such thing came to pass.

I opened the doorway to the stairs and again checked for traps. There were none. I moved up, taking my time. The first set of stairs passed beneath me. On the landing, I stayed low and led with my rifle. Halfway around, I froze. The door at the top of the stairs was open and a guard lounged in a chair, his left side facing me, head leaned against the wall, feet crossed in front of him, rifle resting comfortably in his lap. The green image of the NVGs flared brightly where an oil lamp hung from a wall nearby.

Awake or asleep?

Doesn't matter.

I raised my rifle and put the green dot on his temple. *Clack.* I heard a wet splash of skull and brains hitting the wall, along with the muted thump of the projectile impacting the door beyond. I crouched and listened. The damn bullet hitting the door had been louder than the shot.

I waited, heart pounding, not daring to breath. Ten seconds passed. Nothing. I walked up the stairs and cut the pie around the corner. Another guard sat at the opposite stairway, looking around blearily as though just waking up.

"Ron. Hey Ron, you hear that?"

Shit. I shifted to sight in on him. Before I could, his head snapped to the left and he tumbled out of his chair. A green beam of light cut the darkness as Caleb ascended to the second floor. I flipped my laser sight on and off three times to let him know where I was. He gave a thumbs up and waved me forward.

We met in front of the easternmost door. I helped him pick the guard up, put him back in the chair, and compose his limbs as if he was asleep. Caleb extinguished the lantern next to the guard's chair.

There was still a fourth guard somewhere, and if he happened to come up the eastern stairs, the sight of a comrade sleeping in a chair would look less suspicious than if he was laying on the ground. At least for a few seconds.

"You ready for this," Caleb whispered.

"Yep. Let's get it done."

He tried the door. Locked. I tried the next two down the line. Same result.

Caleb cursed softly and produced his set of custom-made picks. "Watch my back."

207

I divided my attention between the two doors and wished we had a third man with us. Half a minute passed. It was the longest half minute of my life.

"We don't have all night, Caleb."

"Ssshhh."

More waiting. A sound caught the edge of my hearing and I went still. The sound became a steady rhythm that grew louder and closer with each beat.

Footsteps.

I turned toward the eastern staircase and sighted in on the door. The steps increased in volume and then stopped. "Mark?"

The guard stayed dead. More footsteps.

"Goddammit, Mark, wake the fuck-"

He never finished the sentence. The moment his head appeared beyond the doorframe, I fired three times. The effect was like cutting the strings on a marionette. His legs went limp and he crumpled to his side in a boneless heap. I waited. No movement, no sounds of pain, no gurgling breaths, just the utter stillness of death. I shot him in the center of his back anyway just to be on the safe side. I may as well have shot a lump of raw beef.

Glancing behind me, I saw Caleb still working on the door. *This is taking too long.*

I walked over to the fourth guard, searched him, and in his right hip pocket was an industrial looking key.

"Hey, try this."

Caleb took the key and slipped it into the lock. A twist, and the handle turned under his hand. He motioned for me to stack up behind him and slowly, ever so slowly, opened the door. No shouting. No alarm claxons. No legions of black-clad insurgents with chattering machine guns. Caleb counted down, and we moved.

The room we walked into was well appointed with antique furniture, a wet bar, and a small refrigerator connected to a panel on the wall. Solar power and a bank of batteries. Nothing but the best for this guy.

We cleared the room and stacked up beside the door leading into the next compartment. It was unlocked. We checked for traps and found none. Another countdown, another entry.

This room looked more personal. Maroon drapes, tapestries on the walls, thick carpets, dark wooden bookcases filled with leather-bound tomes, an expensive-looking globe by the window, and a painting on the wall next to me I was reasonably sure was an original Rembrandt.

At least he had good taste.

I realized I was already thinking of him in the past tense and shoved the thought away. The last thing I wanted to do was convince myself this mission was a done deal. Counting a victory prematurely is the kind of thinking that makes a man lazy. Gabe once told me 'lazy' (his fingers crooked in air quotes) was Swahili for 'dead'. He meant it as a joke, but the message stuck.

A quick sweep, and the room was clear. Last door. Caleb checked it. The door handle did not budge. He motioned for me to cover him and tried the guard's key. Again, it worked. I motioned for him to wait, extracted a small can of WD-40 from my belt, and gave each of the hinges a spritz. Finished, I put away the can and nodded to Caleb.

Three fingers, two, one. He opened the door slowly, leading with his pistol. The door opened silently. A bedroom, king sized bed, dresser and wardrobe on each wall, two nightstands, and two shapes asleep under a thin blanket, both snoring.

A light breeze tugged at the curtains, the cool night air making the room less stuffy than the two we had just searched. Caleb pointed at the larger of the two figures, and then at himself. I nodded, relieved not to be doing the dirty work.

Caleb walked around the bed and looked closely at the sleeping man, nodded a few times, and gave me a thumbs up. I stepped out of the room and keyed my radio.

"Wolfman, Irish. Target identified."

"Irish, Wolfman." Gabe sounded slightly winded. I heard the pop and clack of suppressed rifles in the background. "Positive ID?"

"Affirmative."

"Do it."

I turned to Caleb and nodded. He motioned for me to cover the other person in the bed. When I was in position, he aimed his pistol at the sleeping head of Bailey Sandoval. For a moment, Caleb stood still, not breathing, not a twitch of muscle. He looked like a dark, looming statue with NVGs and a suppressed pistol. Then he let out a breath, mumbled something I could not hear, and fired four times—two to the head, then two to the chest. The other sleeping figure sat up in bed, startled by the noise.

"Wha-"

It was a woman, probably Sandoval's wife or mistress. Or whatever. I did not bother to ask. The butt of my rifle hit her brain stem and she collapsed. For a moment I thought I had killed her, so I checked her pulse. It was steady. She let out a little moan, and I whispered, "Caleb, give me a hand."

He shook his head to clear it and took a small roll of duct tape from his vest. I grabbed a couple of zip ties from my belt, bound the woman at the wrists, ankles, and knees, and kept a rifle on her while Caleb cut a few strips of bedsheet, balled it up, and shoved it in the woman's mouth. That done, he wrapped it in place with duct tape. She would live, but getting that duct tape off was going to hurt like hell. We placed her on the floor so she would not have to lie in bed staring at a bleeding corpse when she awoke.

"Wolfman, Irish. Bingo hotel, I repeat, bingo hotel."

210

"Irish, Wolfman, Roger bingo. Repeat, roger bingo. Proceed to rendezvous and stand by."

"On our way." I turned to Caleb. "Let's get the hell out of here."

"Best idea I've heard all day."

*****

I got lost twice.

Both times, Gabe set me straight. How he did it while engaged in a firefight was beyond me, but that was Gabe for you. Cool under pressure.

It turned out Caleb and I were the first to complete our assignment, which explained the lack of radio chatter earlier and the profusion of it now. I was halfway to the rendezvous and thinking about how heavy my rucksack was when I heard a thump and a rumble shortly before I felt a shockwave through my boots.

I stopped and looked behind me. A flash of orange lit the night briefly from the direction of the casino Anderson and Liddell were to hit. From somewhere, a siren began to wail. I hoped they got their man. I hoped they got out alive. I hoped I could reach the rendezvous before the guards and the North Koreans turned out in force. Most of all, I hoped Gabe and Great Hawk were still alive.

Windows and doors opened around me and sleepy townsfolk with alarmed faces began filling the streets.

Did you hear that?

...do you think is going on?

Was that an explosion?

Keep the kids inside, Darcy. I need to get to the armory. Lock the doors and don't answer for anyone but me.

211

My rifle was under my bush jacket. Its barrel was shortened for close quarters work, but the suppressor was long enough to be seen if anyone looked too closely. I slowly wandered along with the growing throng of worried onlookers, worked my way toward a shadowy area between two apartment buildings, and ducked inside. Once hidden, I removed the suppressor and stashed it in my rucksack. The temptation to leave the heavy pack behind was strong, but I couldn't bring myself to do it. I would drop it if things came to a firefight, but not before.

I followed the street I was on until it intersected with the wall. This was not a good place to be. The catwalks and guard towers were abuzz with activity. I backed off a few blocks and proceeded along an area of town that had once been semi-industrial, but now looked abandoned.

Static. "Wolfman, Irish. Got a minute? I need directions."

"Where are you?"

I looked around and spotted a bent and faded street sign. I gave Gabriel the name written on it.

"Go straight. You'll reach the rendezvous in half a klick."

"Thanks. See you there."

No answer. It must have been a busy night at the president's mansion.

At the halfway point to the rendezvous, I felt a prickling sensation between my shoulder blades. My eyes began searching shadows, windows, doorways, any place where a man might hide. I don't claim to have prescient abilities, nothing supernatural, but I have spent enough time living like an animal to develop the baser instincts most people ignore. And my instincts were telling me I was being watched.

"Tex, Irish. What's your twenty?"

"En route to the rendezvous. Two mikes. Everything okay?"

"I think I'm being followed."

"Where are you?"

212

I told him.

"On my way," he said.

If he was two minutes from the east gate, then he was five minutes from me. I picked up my pace.

The farther and faster I walked, the more sure I became there was trouble in my road. Fleeting shadows detached from walls and disappeared in the warren of buildings and dilapidated equipment. I wished I was still wearing my NVGs.

A rock bounced off a rusty dumpster ahead of me. A bird call sounded in a place no bird would dare roost. Like most post-Outbreak towns, anything that walked, swam, crawled, slithered, or flew was a part of the food chain. And that included birds. Feathered creatures may not be as smart as humans, but they know enough to stay away from places where they are hunted.

If only I were as wise as a pigeon.

I headed toward a crumbling warehouse ahead on my right. The change of direction was the signal my pursuers had been waiting for. They emerged from the darkness like a pack of hyenas, slinking and wary, knees bent, weapons held low.

I had my rifle close to hand, but did not want to fire it if at all possible. The noise would attract the attention of the guards, which I did not want. I stopped, reached under my left shoulder, and put my hand on the butt of my pistol. It had a suppressor and a full magazine, much better suited for this kind of work.

"Stop right there." The voice was low, laced with authority, and sounded young. I kept walking.

"I said stop."

I drew my pistol and aimed in the general direction of the voice. The ring of dark shapes kept pace with me and began to close in.

"The first one of you within ten feet gets a bullet to the face." They still tracked me, but moved no closer.

"Just drop the pack," the voice said. I could almost make out his face. He was shorter than me, lean as a stick, and in his right hand, I saw a flash of metal reflect the dim starlight. "We want your trade, not your life."

"You're not taking either one. Leave, or I start shooting."

A vile little laugh. "No you won't. That'll attract the guards. Besides, there's a lot more of us than there are of you. You might get some of us, but not all. And if you want to shoot, you'll have to stop walking. We'll be on you in a second. Now drop the pack. Last warning."

I did not have time for this. Rather than slow down, I sped up to a run, aimed, and fired. There was a dull crack and the clang of the slide going back and forth. The source of the voice dropped without a sound, the bullet taking him through the head. The rest shouted in dismay and closed in.

I fired three more times, and three more shapes fell. A knife found my right side but deflected off the upper receiver of my rifle. I bumped the attacker with my shoulder, and as he fell, I aimed backwards and let off two more rounds. A shocked scream of agony told me at least one shot had found its mark.

Three more closed in from my right. There were pounding footsteps behind me. I stopped short, waited half a heartbeat, and lashed backward with an elbow. The three on my right skidded to a halt, my elbow met flesh and bone, and I felt teeth shatter against the thick cloth of my bush jacket.

"Grraaaghh!"

A piece of metal clattered to the ground. The other three pursuers had shifted direction and were coming in fast. Decision time. I could focus on the three incoming targets, but that meant the one behind me could grab me and throw off my aim. If I went down, I was done. So even though he was probably unarmed, the owner of the broken teeth was too much of a risk to let live. I put the suppressor to his chest and fired once. He made a choked sound, staggered backward, and fell.

The other three faltered when I aimed at them. I could see their faces now. They were young, no more than teenagers. Greasy, pimpled faces, scraggly facial hair, torn and ragged clothes, and malnourished cheekbones standing out sharply under wide eyes. Before I could stop myself, I fired twice.

The closest kid took two in the chest. His face scrunched in pain and surprise, he stepped back once, and went down. The other two looked at him, then at me.

"I told you the answer was no. You can't have my property. Leave now and I'll let you keep your lives."

There were no words, no begging, no apologies. They simply turned and ran like animals at a fresh kill when the bigger predators show up. For a moment, I thought about turning around and seeing if the others I shot were as young as the dead kid in front of me, but decided against it. I had seen enough tonight, and knew I would be seeing it for a long, long time.

They were just kids.

I felt hollow inside. "So what? They'd have done the same to me. They left me no choice."

They were just kids.

"Doesn't matter. Gotta move."

I set out at a jog. My feet pounded the road faster and faster until my lungs burned and my back hurt from the weight of my pack, but still I pushed for more speed. I was making too much noise, might be drawing attention to myself. I did not care. Running was all that mattered. But even as I ran, I was aware there are some things a man can never escape. They become part of you, a wire in the blood, and they never leave. I knew. I had plenty of them.

The east gate loomed up out of the half-burned buildings and empty houses and the stink of hopelessness. Finally, I slowed and holstered my pistol. I wondered how long it would take the others to arrive. I wondered how many people would die tonight. I wondered if Caleb had seen me and assumed his help was no longer needed and proceeded to the gate.

Mostly, though, I wondered how young those dead kids were, if anyone would miss them, and how many demons a man can harbor before they tear him apart.

TWENTY-THREE

Lena Smith waited at the gate with two men in black fatigues.

Caleb saw me coming and let out a low whistle. I followed the sound and saw him motioning to me from a ditch next to a scorched, collapsed cinder-block structure. Ducking low to avoid spears of rebar, I crouch-walked until I was close, then belly crawled next to him.

"She didn't say she was bringing anyone."

Caleb shook his head. "No way to know if they're friendly. How do you want to play it?"

I thought a moment. We did not have much of a choice. By now, the guard captains must have figured out Carbondale was under attack. We had to get through that gate. "Stash the rifles and packs here. We'll approach with just our pistols."

Caleb pointed up. "Snipers in the towers. Four guards close enough to see us."

"Nothing we can do about that."

We backed off, emerged onto the street leading to the gate, and did our best to look like frightened townsfolk fleeing the violence. We ran at first, then slowed as we approached the armed guards. Lena recognized us and, while the two troops had their backs turned, placed a finger over her lips.

"Stop right there." One of the guards raised his rifle.

We put up our hands. "I think we're under attack," I said.

217

Lena glanced up at the guard towers and made a cutting signal with one hand. At the same time, her other hand reached beneath her blazer.

"This gate is closed. No one in or-"

The man's sentence was cut off by the report of a small pistol. As his legs went limp, Lena shifted aim to the other guard and shot him twice in the back of the head. Both men fell dead at her feet.

Shit.

My heart tried to climb into my mouth. Caleb and I produced our pistols at the same time and aimed at the guard towers. The snipers had just recovered from surprise and were bringing their rifles to bear. They never got a chance. Two simultaneous reports split the air from maybe a hundred yards away, high caliber rifles by the sound. The guard in my sights jerked, dropped his weapon, and fell out of sight. I shifted to the other tower. The guard there was already down.

I glanced at Lena. "Friends of yours?"

She nodded, her face stricken. "We have to go. Now."

"Not without the others."

"There's no time."

Her eyes went flat and she pointed her pistol at me. For a moment, I stared in shock, then felt anger boil up like hot steam. "What the fuck are you doing, Lena?"

"I'm sorry, but we have to leave. Now."

"Not gonna happen, lady."

She took a two handed grip on the pistol. "It's not a request."

In my peripheral vision, I saw Caleb aim his Beretta at Lena's head. "Drop the gun," he said.

"No."

"Do it now, Smith. You shoot him, you die."

I put my hands in the air. It took every ounce of will I had not to dive sideways and put two bullets in her chest. "You're making a mistake, Lena. He *will* kill you."

She shook her head emphatically. "We don't have ti-"

Crack-clang. Lena shrieked and dropped the pistol from nerveless fingers. Her other hand came up to clutch her shoulder.

"You shot me!"

Caleb scanned the catwalk and noticed the other guards along the wall were looking in our direction.

"All I did was graze your upper arm. You'll be fine."

Lena let out a stream of curses and glanced around, obviously weighing her options. I leveled my gun at her.

"You call the guards," I told her, "and the sentence won't make it out of your mouth."

"They know!"

"No, they don't. They just know you're the vice president and a few guards are dead. You're a sharp lady. Think of something."

"But ..."

"Your friends with the high-powered rifles still out there?"

Her eyes shifted westward along the line of rooftops, the calculating mind spinning quickly behind the pretty green irises. She gestured for us to come close and put our weapons away. The guards closed in and leveled their weapons. A tall, grizzled man wearing the yellow arm band of the SS held up a hand to the others.

"Hold it, fellas. Madam Vice President, is everything all right?"

I almost laughed. Four men lay dead, Smith was bleeding from her arm, and the two men who had just assassinated the Alliance's secretary of defense stood helpless before them. Everything was most definitely *not* all right.

219

"Everything is fine," Lena said, waving her good arm three times over her head. "These men are with the secret police."

The SS trooper looked skeptical. "Please remain where you are, ma'am. I need to call General Samson."

As he keyed his radio and began to speak, two more reports rang out within a fraction of a second of one another, both from the same direction as the shots that killed the snipers. The top half of the SS trooper's head disintegrated while the guard behind him looked down with wide eyes at a gaping hole where his heart used to be. They both fell dead while the others stared in dumbfounded shock. A split second passed before they leveled their rifles and fired.

Caleb and I were already moving.

I did not grab Lena Smith. Caleb did. If he had consulted with me beforehand, I would have told him not to bother. Lena may have been a big help to the Union, but when things started looking hairy, she had tried to back out of her end of the deal by leaving without the rest of Task Force Falcon. I had no sympathy for her.

Above me, the two gunmen focused their fire on Caleb, as he was the one dragging their vice president by the arm toward a dark alcove. They managed three short bursts before two more high-powered shots thundered from the west and dropped them where they stood. I skidded to a halt behind the brick wall of a burned out furniture shop.

"Caleb, you alive?"

"Yep."

"Smith?"

"Yep."

We emerged slowly. We saw no more guards, but it was only a matter of time. If they had not heard the gunfire, which was a big 'if', sooner or later it would be time for the gate crew to check in. When they didn't, reinforcements would come running. We did not want to be here when that happened.

I marched over to Lena Smith and leaned down into her pale, frightened face. I did not put my pistol to her temple, but it was a near thing. "Where is the transportation you promised us?"

Before she could answer, my radio crackled. "Irish, Wolfman. Bingo Magnum. Repeat, Bingo Magnum."

Lena began to speak, but I held a finger up to her face and keyed my radio. "Damn good to hear, Wolfman. What's your twenty?"

"En route. Five mikes. Me, Hawk, and Gator. Red is Delta Foxtrot."

Goddammit. Delta Foxtrot. D and F respectively in the military phonetic alphabet—an acronym for *Died Fighting.* McGee had been killed.

"Any word from Shorty or Viking?" (Anderson and Bjornson's teams.)

"Shorty is en route. Bingo Eagle on his end. Ghost isn't coming. Delta Foxtrot."

Which meant Liddell was dead, but so was the speaker of the council. I cursed again, out loud this time, and then keyed the mic. "Viking?"

"No word."

Caleb waved a hand to get my attention. "Sitrep?"

"The president and speaker of the council are dead. We took out Sandoval, so Samson is next in line, if he's still alive."

"What do you mean 'if he's still alive'? Any word from Bjornson's team?"

I shook my head. "MIA. And McGee and Liddell didn't make it."

"Shit."

"Correctamundo."

"How long until the others get here?"

221

"Gabe and his crew need five mikes. Not sure about the others."

Lena grabbed my arm. "We don't have five minutes. The guards will be here any second."

I looked to the top of the wall and thought I saw movement in the distance. "We have to take cover. I'll find a rooftop on this side of the street and brief the others." I jabbed a finger at the vice president of the Alliance. "You keep quiet and out of sight."

Caleb gripped Smith's uninjured arm and turned to lead her away.

"Wait!" Smith tried to pull away from Caleb with no success.

"What?"

"We need to leave. You don't understand, there will be too many of them. We-"

I made a cutting motion in front of her face. "Enough. I know you're scared. In your place, I would be too. Hell, I'm not in your place and I'm scared. But I'm not leaving without the others, and nothing you say is going to change that. So if you want to live, do as you're told."

I looked around for signs of movement on the streets, but saw none. "Oh, and before I forget, where the hell are those transports you promised?"

"Horses. They're outside the gate just past the treeline."

"*Outside* the gate?"

She nodded quickly.

I groaned. "For Christ's sake, lady, you didn't think this through too well did you?"

"I ..."

I waved her to silence. "Forget it. Nothing we can do about it now. Listen, just go with Hicks and stay quiet. He'll keep you safe until we can find a way out of here."

"But-"

I put a hand over her mouth. "I hear boots running on concrete. They're getting close." A glance up to Hicks. "Move."

They went. I faded back into the nearest alley and worked my way to where we had stashed our packs. Caleb had retrieved his already. Mine was still there. I slipped it on, backed off two blocks, and used a dumpster to climb atop the roof of a long-abandoned strip mall. There was a three-foot false front facing the east gate, perfect for a sniper hide.

My NVGs were in the rucksack where I left them. I put them on and flipped up the lenses; best to keep them out of the way and save the batteries until I needed them. Next, I activated the night vision scope on my rifle, reattached the suppressor, and radioed Gabe. A few seconds passed with no answer. I started to worry. When the earpiece finally crackled, I let out the breath I had been holding.

"Irish, Wolfman. Got a sitrep?"

I checked my rifle to make sure a round was chambered. "Situation normal, all fucked up."

"I don't like the sound of that."

I filled him in. He asked if Hicks still had his black duffel bag. I said I believed he did. Gabe said he had a plan.

"Glad someone around here does."

"Hang tight, partner. We'll be there soon."

"Copy. Irish out."

I looked through the scope toward the gate. So close, but it may as well have been on the surface of Mars. More guards had discovered the dead bodies and were chatting excitedly into radios. Not a good sign.

Whatever Gabe's plan was, I had a feeling it was going to involve gunfire, screaming, and lots of explosions. Which, for him, was pretty much par for the course.

I forced myself to relax, waited, and felt the reality of the situation begin to sink in. We had done it. We had accomplished the mission. Three out of four officials dead, and the most important targets at that. General Samson could be dealt with later, assuming he survived the fallout from the collapse of the Alliance's command structure. To say he was not popular amongst his countrymen would be a profound understatement. If Samson did not want be hanging by his feet a la Benito Mussolini come morning, he would do well to get out of town.

Whatever else happened this night, the mission had been a success. The Alliance was done for, they just didn't know it yet. It was beyond surreal to know I was a part of it, a part of history, for good or ill.

Now I just had to get out of Carbondale alive.

TWENTY-FOUR

"This won't be easy."

I keyed my radio. "Never is. Why should today be any different?"

Through the slightly grainy resolution of the night vision scope, Gabe looked like a greenish gargoyle crouched behind a brick smokestack. He sat motionless, rifle aimed toward the guards at the gate, finger no doubt taking up the slack on the trigger. I shifted back to the task at hand and did the same.

Static. "All stations, Tex. In position."

"Tex, Wolfman. Copy. Stand by."

The plan was not complicated. Gabe, Great Hawk, Hicks, and those of Anderson's men not killed or missing fanned out and took position a block away from the gate. I stayed where I was to provide close sniper support. Same story for Gabe. Hicks and May moved in with big bags of nasty explodey stuff and the deliberate intent to do mayhem in the name of God and country.

More static. "All stations, Wolfman. Engage on my mark."

A pause. Deep breath, held it a moment, and let it out slowly.

"Three, two, one, *mark*."

The next sound I heard was the tremendous *hiss-BANG* of two RPGs hitting the gate simultaneously. I flinched as the shockwaves rolled over me, creating a terrible, familiar hollowness in my chest and stomach.

The gate disappeared in a cloud of smoke and flying debris. Seconds later, two more RPG's hit, making more smoke and sending up more debris. I heard screaming, shouted orders, the panicked sounds of confusion. At the same moment, from rooftops all around me, the chatter of automatic gunfire filled the night.

A breeze that had picked up while Hicks and I waited for Gabe's crew to arrive carried the worst of the smoke away, revealing the remnants of the gate. The guards closest had been blown to pieces, limbs and weapons and twisted fractions of torsos littering the ground in a semicircle around where two large steel doors once stood. The doors and their support columns had collapsed, spilling a few wounded Alliance troops to the ground. Gunfire from Task Force Falcon ripped into them, creating terrified disarray.

I added my own rifle to the chorus. The reticle centered on a downed figure firing his weapon randomly in the general direction of the lead hailstorm ripping his comrades apart. I aimed a little high to compensate for the drop of the projectile, let out a breath, and fired. A plume of dark liquid painted the crumbled concrete behind the doomed insurgent's head.

Next target. Not a person, not an enemy, just a target. This one was on his feet, gesticulating, shouting, others looking to him and going where he pointed.

Leader.

I hit him three times, center of mass. Opened my left eye to take in the overall picture. Guards were fleeing the gate. Confusion, panic, fear, surprise, the dawning knowledge they were facing overwhelming firepower.

Now, Gabe.

Just as I thought it, the radio crackled. "All stations, *move now.*"

I didn't need to be told twice. My feet carried me to the edge of the roof, I sat down, pushed away, caught the edge of the dumpster with one hand to slow my descent, bent my knees with the impact, rolled sideways once, felt something jab painfully into my side, then was up and running.

Buildings and crumbled ruins zipped by on either side. I was in full stride, arms swinging, head down, legs pumping, mouth wide open to take in as much air as possible, big deep breaths, barrel shroud of my carbine clutched tightly in one hand. I stayed to the edge of the street where the shadows were deepest. Ahead of me, a grenade exploded. I ducked instinctively, realized I was out of its range, and kept running.

One second I was alone, the next someone ran next to me. I almost raised my rifle, but then realized it was Gabe. Great Hawk followed behind, gaining ground quickly. A few seconds later he passed us, long legs covering ground swift as an antelope. I'm not slow and neither is Gabe, but Great Hawk outclassed us both.

As he closed in on the gate, I saw the Hawk had a pistol in one hand and his ancient tomahawk in the other. A guard emerged from cover and tried to sight in on him. The pistol in Great Hawk's hand barked twice. The guard fired, missed, and screamed in fear and pain as razor sharp steel bit into the side of his neck. The big Apache jerked his weapon free without breaking stride and kept on trucking.

I leapt over the dying guard's body on the way by. Did not look at his face.

Push, push, push, digdigdigdigdig, get there!

More people joined me on the way, some in front, some behind. I knew them, recognized them. Kept running. Voices to my left. Looked. Bjornson and LaGrange emerging from a side street, no sign of Taylor. Waved my arm for them to hurry up.

GOGOGOGOGO!

Sprinted up and over fallen concrete. Slipped once, recovered, kept moving. Dodged sharp blooms of metal, fallen doors, steel twisted and blackened from the blasts, smell of chemicals and thick dust.

227

Now across grass. No more gunfire. Kept running, running, running. Breathing hurt. Legs hurt. Kept moving. Voice shouting.

"This way!" Lena.

The fog in my head cleared a little. Lena ran in front of Hicks in her stocking feet, the dress shoes discarded so she could run faster. I turned in the direction she pointed. The treeline loomed larger and larger until it towered over and enveloped me. I slowed down and moved gratefully into its concealing darkness. There may have been infected nearby, but they were a far less daunting threat than what lay behind me.

I smelled the horses before I saw them. Two nervous looking men moved among the animals speaking in whispers, trying to keep the horses calm. I approached one of them and took the reins from his hand.

"Got it from here, chief."

He backed away, eyes wide. "Okay."

I swung into the saddle. He horse nickered a little, but did not try to throw me. A good sign. The others were climbing onto horses of their own. Most handled the reins with competence, if not tremendous enthusiasm. I wondered if horsemanship had become part of ongoing training for Green Berets.

Great Hawk took the time to unstrap his pack, dig out his ruggedized tablet, and fire it up before climbing atop his mount one-handed.

"Follow me," he said simply. A swift backwards kick, and his horse trotted into the woods.

"Eric."

I looked to my right. It was Hicks. He pointed to my forehead. "Might want to turn those on."

"Shit." I flipped down the NVGs I had forgotten about and activated them. The pitch dark night became a buzzing sea of motes and shadows the color of spring grass. Not perfect, depth perception a little off, but I could see. The others had already taken Great Hawk's lead and were riding away. My horse, probably as a result of herd mentality, followed without any prompting.

I leaned over the saddle and kept my head low to avoid branches. The horse sped up to a trot, the sound of shod hooves pounding the earth ahead of me. It was a joyful noise to my ears. With each beat of the fifteen-hundred pound living drums, Carbondale grew farther and farther away.

We covered what I figured must have been close to two miles before we emerged into a clearing. Great Hawk sat calmly astride his horse, Lena Smith in close conversation next to him. I could not hear them, but I saw the Hawk point to the sky. I looked where he pointed, but saw nothing. Heard nothing. Perhaps a minute passed. Some men dismounted and held reins in nervous hands, eyes casting impatient glances back the way we came.

"The fuck are they," I heard Gabe mutter next to me. "Should have been waiting for us."

Another minute. Anderson said something about riding back to Union territory. Great Hawk shook his head once and said, "Everyone shut up. Listen."

Silence. Straining ears. And then I heard it. *Thumpthumpthumpthumpthump*, growing louder. Trees swayed in the distance from the force of rotor wash as two stealth Blackhawks drifted into view. My face split into a grin and I hit Gabe on the shoulder. He was smiling as well.

"Never been so happy to see a helicopter in my life," I said.

Gabe grabbed me by the shoulder and gave me a shake. "Makes two of us."

The choppers landed in the clearing, sending a wave of dust and plant detritus into our faces. I dismounted and let my horse gallop away and ran toward the closest helicopter. Gabe, Great Hawk, Hicks, and May did the same. Anderson took Lena

229

Smith by the arm and led her to the Blackhawk farther away. LaGrange and Bjornson went with them.

A crewman with a painted face, NVGs, and black fatigues waved me into the cargo hold. It was dark inside, hot, and redolent of exhaust. It was the best thing I had ever smelled. I moved to the back, sat down, and began buckling my harness. A dark figure handed me a helmet and told me to put it on. I thanked him and obeyed.

The others were inside within moments, the helicopter lifting off before we were all strapped in. As we gained altitude, I lay my head back and felt the adrenaline begin to subside. I was tired. Everything hurt. There was a gouge and a large streak of blood on my right arm. I tested it with my fingers and found a shallow groove coagulated with blood. Must have took a grazing shot somewhere along the line. I had not felt it then, but I certainly felt it now.

I remember leaning toward Gabe sitting across from me. I remember reaching out and clasping hands with him, a half-hysterical laugh bubbling from my chest. I remember the relief on my friend's face, the whiteness of his smile in the dark, and the welcome thrum of rotors vibrating the metal beneath my feet.

The next thing I remember is waking up.

TWENTY-FIVE

The world was blurry and green.

Sounds came to me from a far, far distance, muted and unintelligible. Voices shouting. I was sleepy, wanted to drift down into the dark, wanted to rest. Something shook me, had been shaking me for a while now. Stinging pain hit the side of my face.

"Wake up, amigo. We gotta move."

My vision cleared. I was still wearing my NVGs, still strapped to my seat. Gabe was standing over me, boots on either side of my chest. A blade appeared in his hand and cut the harness away. I realized I was lying on my back and the helicopter was on the ground sideways. That wasn't right. We were supposed to be in the air.

Strong hands hauled me upward and propped me on trembling legs. Turned me around. An arm gripped me around the waist and I took three steps. At the front of the chopper, I saw a tree trunk where the windshield used to be. The pilot and co-pilot were motionless, pressed against their seats, chests crushed almost flat. I looked away. Stepped on something yielding. It was the crewman who had handed me the helmet I still wore. He lay inverted, legs bent at strange angles, head twisted unnaturally to one side. I mumbled something about helping him.

"He's gone," Gabe said. "No use. Now come on, we have to get out of here."

231

Then I was being lifted up. Hands grabbed me from above and pulled. I saw Great Hawk, May, and Hicks. Fell into their arms, tried to help, was dragged to a tree and sat down. Someone shined a light in my eyes and told me to follow it around.

"How bad?" Gabe.

"He will live." Great Hawk. "He should not sleep tonight."

"I don't think any of us will be sleeping tonight." Footsteps walking away.

I looked toward the chopper and wondered how it was my NVGs still worked. The helmet was uncomfortable. My fingers felt like poorly connected sausages as I fumbled at the clasp along my jaw. Opened it. Let the helmet fall away.

Christ my head hurts.

I felt for lumps and cuts. A big sore spot on the back of the precious, one-of-a-kind skull, but no damage otherwise. The helmet had done its job. Probably saved my life. I felt bad for thinking ill of it a moment ago.

At the chopper, Hicks and May had climbed in and were tossing rucksacks out the cargo door. Gabe grabbed his and mine and walked over to me. Helped me stand up.

"Come on, don't go all limp noodle on me. It was just a little bump on the head."

I managed to get the straps over my back and buckle the clasps at chest and waist level. The ruck was heavier than I remembered.

"Everybody ready?" Great Hawk said. Heads with protruding NVGs nodded in unison. I muttered something I don't remember.

"Hicks, Garrett, make sure Riordan does not die. I will take point. Does anyone have a working radio?"

I fumbled at mine and turned it on. "Check, check."

"Got you."

232

Caleb and Gabe's radios worked. May's did not. Caleb took mine from my belt, disconnected the earpiece, and handed it to May.

"Won't do you much good right now anyway," he said.

I had neither the energy nor the inclination to argue.

The next part is hazy. There was a lot of running, and, in my case, a lot of falling down. Every step was torture. My head was a pulsating ball of agony. My shaky, traitor legs couldn't seem to find any kind of rhythm. The path a .380 round had taken through my calf muscle a few months ago felt like it was trying to rip itself free. The shallow graze wound on my arm burned and itched. Every muscle, tendon, and joint felt battered and inflamed. I ran anyway.

An explosion lit up the night behind us. Great Hawk stopped, looked back, nodded to himself, and started running again. I vaguely remembered someone mentioning something about where to place the charges. Made sense. Wouldn't want any insurgent types to get their hands on a stealth helicopter.

I remembered the pilots and the crewman. McGee. Liddell. Stewart. All dead, and all to thwart the ambitions of a few small-minded, power-mad little men. And what had anyone gained? Deaths on both sides, and a larger conflict prevented. That was all.

I pitied the people of Carbondale. Nuclear winter, even a fading one, makes for short summers. The cold season would be a long one this year.

*****

I remembered a line from a poem I read a long time ago. Lord Byron, I think:

Morn came and went and came, and brought no day / And men forgot their passions in the dread of this, their desolation.

233

Morn came. But in our case, it brought day with it. The light did little to ignite my passions, and nothing at all to decrease the dread of my desolation.

"We are eight miles south of Carbondale." Great Hawk swiped the cracked screen of his ruggedized tablet. Images moved sluggishly under his finger, indicating the battery was almost dead.

"No problem." Gabe produced a compass and tapped the side of his head. "Got everything we need to get home right here."

A warning light flashed on the tablet and the screen went blank. Great Hawk closed the cover flap and stashed it in his pack. He had a folding solar charger, but the forest canopy blotted out too much of the sun and we were short on time.

"It will have to do."

Eight miles. How I had run that far in my condition was beyond comprehension. But I had done it. And I had much, much farther to go before I could stop looking over my shoulder. I thought of the horse I had set free before boarding the crashed Blackhawk and cursed my shitty luck.

"Any word from Anderson?" Hicks asked.

Great Hawk shook his head. "No. I think they were hit as well. Probably went down somewhere ahead of us."

"Speaking of," I said, teeth clenched against the pounding in my head, "what the hell happened? Why did we go down?"

"Enemy aircraft," Gabe said. I looked at him.

"Are you kidding me?"

A shake of the head. "Nope. Alliance must have had one on standby. Outfitted with an M-240, unless I miss my guess. Chewed up our tail rotor, and I think they got a piece of Anderson's ride as well. Good thing we were skimming the tree tops. Didn't have far to fall."

"I saw LaGrange hanging out the cargo bay," May said. He looked to be in good condition save for a nasty cut on the side of his head. Someone had bandaged it, the white of the gauze standing out sharply against the sheen of his dark brown scalp. "Had an RPG. The other helo blew up a few seconds later."

Hicks popped some kind of pill and washed it down. "Saw it too."

"Then at least we know that particular threat is gone." Great Hawk tucked his tomahawk into his belt and stood up. "I realize we are all tired, but we have to keep moving."

No one complained.

*****

More walking. A breeze began blowing from the north and the sky darkened overhead. Trees swayed and branches rustled like static white noise, the dull roar masking the sound of our passing. From overhead, sticks and leaves and loose bark fell and whipped about, all of it seeming to aim for the five of us. Birdsong and bugs and the skittering of small mammals stopped. The forest sensed a storm coming.

My head was beginning to clear. I still had no memory of the crash, but my steps were steadier and I did not feel like I was going to pass out anymore. Which was the only good news in a day otherwise filled with abject misery. My head still hurt. I needed to answer the call of nature and dreaded using leaves in lieu of the washable damp cloths most people wiped themselves with these days. Something was seriously wrong with my right knee. I was hungry and sleep deprived and the water purification tablets did nothing to improve the flavor of the stream runoff in my canteen. I took a long drink to alleviate the burning in my throat and felt a fresh coat of silt settle over my teeth. I definitely had seen better days.

A chirping sound cut through the increasingly loud roar of leaves blowing in the strong wind. Great Hawk stopped and fished a satellite phone from his vest, pressed a button, and held it to his ear. He gave an authorization code and the earpiece buzzed, but I could not make out the voice on the other end.

"Copy. Aircrew KIA on our end. Bird was not compromised. What is your twenty?"

Great Hawk motioned to Gabe and repeated a set of coordinates. The big man closed his eyes, concentrated a few seconds, then looked at the Apache and gave a thumbs up.

"Proceed on mission, Falcon Lead. Great Hawk out."

"Anderson?" May asked.

"Yes. His chopper lost hydraulic pressure and landed three klicks south of where we stand."

"They frag it?" I asked.

"Yes. We must have been too far away last night to see the explosion."

"Lose anybody?"

"The crewman and co-pilot were both hit by fire from the enemy helicopter. They did not make it. The pilot is fine. Anderson's sat-phone needed time to charge, which is why it took so long for him to check in." Great Hawk passed a hand over his forehead and looked southward. "They have already started moving toward Union territory. Anderson, Bjornson, LaGrange, and the pilot will focus their efforts on getting Lena Smith to safety. It will be roughly forty-eight hours before another chopper can make it out to pick her up. In the meantime … we have problems to deal with."

Gabe stepped closer. "Like what?"

"Bjornson's team was not successful in assassinating General Samson. Taylor was killed in the fighting, and General Samson was wounded, but not seriously. He has rallied his troops, some hundred and fifty of them, and has begun a widespread search for Lena Smith."

"Light cavalry?" Gabe asked.

A nod. "Forty of them. The rest are light infantry."

"Shit," I said. "Eleven of us against forty mounted troops and a hundred-ten infantry. I don't like those odds."

"It is worse than that, Eric," Great Hawk said. "It will be only the five of us. We are to hold off Samson's forces until Lena Smith is safe. Anderson and his team will not be able to help us until she is out of danger. Their orders are to keep Smith away from the fighting."

"Lena fucking Smith." I shook my head. "Whatever she knows better be worth all this shit. If it's not, I'll kill her myself."

Great Hawk shot me a warning look. "She is the reason we were able to complete our mission, Eric. Do not forget that."

"Right. Sure. Be nice to the traitor. Got it."

The obsidian eyes flashed and darkened. "You have no idea what you are talking about. You know nothing about Lena Smith or her reasons for doing what she did. Until you do, you should shut your ignorant mouth."

His tone bristled the Irish devil in me. "That supposed to scare me, Hawk?"

"Enough." Gabe's voice cut the air like a blade. "We don't have time for this. Hawk, what kind of support can we expect?"

The dark eyes continued to stare at me. "A transport plane will fly over and drop supplies. Anderson will call in the landing coordinates once it is down. There will be ammunition, explosives, food, clean water, batteries, weapons and optics. Everything we need to mount an offensive."

"I got a better idea," I said. "How about Anderson debriefs Smith, calls in her intel to Central, and we hide like fucking rats until the choppers get here. Seems like the more survivable option to me."

The Hawk shook his head. "No. Lena will speak only to the President and Joint Chiefs."

"She'll damn well talk if we let Bjornson do some convincing."

237

Another head shake. "No. I will not permit that. Not when there is a better way."

"Like all of us getting our asses shot off because one enemy politician wants to be stubborn?"

"First of all, Eric, Lena is not our enemy. Second, I will not condone torture. I have done it before, and the weight of my actions weighs heavy on my conscience. Third, and most importantly, it is vital to national security that only a select few people know what it is Lena wishes to disclose. If word gets out, it could compromise our efforts to defeat the ROC and liberate the people they have subjugated."

I walked toward Great Hawk until we were a foot apart. "What makes you so sure? What do you know that you're not telling the rest of us?"

No answer for a few seconds, then he put the sat-phone back in its pouch and started walking. "Need to know, Irishman."

"Fuck that. I did my part, Hawk. If I'm going to risk my life for this woman, I deserve to know why."

"As you said, Eric, you did your part. The mission succeeded, and on behalf of a grateful nation, I thank you. Your responsibility has been discharged. General Jacobs has been notified and will arrange for your payment. Feel free to take your leave whenever you wish."

He kept walking and did not look back. Lacking any better options, I followed.

TWENTY-SIX

Rain began falling in sheets. The canopy overhead did little to shield us. Large branches thrashed and broke from powerful storm-gales. Limbs big enough to kill a man—widow-makers, my father used to call them—fell around us with nearly the same frequency as raindrops, forcing us to fan out to avoid losing everyone in case one of the heavy missiles found its mark. Twice, I heard cracking above my head, looked up, and barely managed to dive out of the way before being crushed.

As if I didn't have enough problems.

Great Hawk shouted above the wind for everyone to stop, pressed the sat-phone to his ear, and listened. The dark eyes closed and, for once, I actually saw weariness on the Apache's inscrutable face.

"What is it this time?" Gabe called out.

Great Hawk put the phone away. "Infected. Anderson's group is surrounded. They have taken to the trees."

I looked upward to the twisting sea of branches and howling wind. It was a better option than being eaten by infected, but not by much.

"How many?" I asked.

A shake of the head. "Legion."

I leaned back and laughed. It was either that or scream. "That's great. Just fucking wonderful. What's next? Bombs? Fire? Bears with assault rifles and goddamn laser beams coming out of their eyes?"

239

I earned myself a glare. "We will lead the infected away so they can escape."

May cursed softly, wiped his brow, and flung a stream of rainwater to the ground. Hicks was silent and expressionless, hands on his rifle. Gabe nodded grimly and drew his falcata. I reached over my shoulder and realized I did not have my sword. Must have lost it at the crash site. The loss of the weapon hit me sharply, like waking up and finding a limb missing. I had carried the sword since the Outbreak, and it had saved my life many times. Being without it gave me an uncomfortable sense of vulnerability. If my ammo ran out, I was down to just my knife. Not a good feeling.

"Sure," I said. "What the hell. Got nothing better to do."

The storm lessened as we covered the remaining ground to Anderson's location, which meant the widow-makers stopped falling and the torrential downpour settled into the kind of slow, soaking rain that makes the ground muddy for days after it ceases. I did not mind. It covered the sound of our footsteps.

We approached from the east because Anderson said there was a natural rise in that direction which would give us the high ground. Near the top, Great Hawk signaled for everyone to drop and belly-crawl to the ridge. I obeyed, silently cursing the whole way. By the time I reached the top, in addition to being soaking wet, I was now streaked with mud from neck to nuts.

Great Hawk pointed at me, made a remarkably natural sounding bird call, and motioned me closer. I crawled slowly to his position and gave him a look that said, *what do you want?*

He handed me a small pair of binoculars. "Tell me what you see."

The vision thing again. At least the Hawk appreciated my talents.

I adjusted the lenses and scanned the area in front of me. At the base of the hill, I saw the burned out remnants of a house slowly being consumed by bugs, rot, and creeping vines. A barn disintegrated in comfortable silence a short distance beyond,

240

several rusty vehicles were sinking into the earth next to a collapsed garage, and where the treeline ended, grass, shrubs, and saplings created a tangle of crud that stood six feet at its lowest and far taller at its highest. The grass swayed and the saplings trembled, but not like they would in a wind. Looking more carefully, I saw glimpses of wasted gray and white flesh, and the occasional hand bent into a claw.

Infected, and a hell of a lot of them.

There was no sign of Anderson or his party. I told Great Hawk what I saw. He grunted and said, "Search the trees."

So I did. It took a while, but I finally spotted a mote of fiery red among the greenery that turned out to be Lena Smith's wet, tangled hair. I switched to my rifle, dialed up the magnification on the scope, and looked again.

Her clothes were torn and ragged and not at all appropriate for running around in the wilderness. She wore no shoes and her feet bled from myriad cuts and scrapes. By comparison, the soldiers and pilot looked well put together, if not exactly comfortable.

Again, I filled in Great Hawk. He nodded slowly, thought for a few seconds, and said, "You and I will draw the infected east. The others will follow along the flanks until we have led the horde two klicks away. Then the others will lead the horde north a klick and draw them west before doubling back. That will put a wall of infected between us and Samson's men."

I mulled it over. Aside from the obvious dangers, it was a good plan. "Let's test our weapons. See if they were damaged in the crash."

Great Hawk leveled his rifle and let off two shots. "Sounds good to me."

I did the same, and the rifle worked just fine. Then I produced my pistol. As soon as I drew it, I knew it was a lost cause. The suppressor must have gotten wedged between me and the bulkhead of the helicopter when it went down. There was a plainly visible bend where the can connected to the barrel threads, rendering the gun inoperable.

"Well that fucking sucks." I removed the magazine, which did not appear damaged, and hurled the useless hunk of metal into the clearing. Great Hawk's pistol worked fine.

Figures. At least I still have my Kel-Tec.

The .22 magnum pistol was fine against the undead, but if I was going to be fighting the living, I wanted something with more stopping power. Oh well. Beggars can't be choosers.

The others conducted their own tests. No problems. I should have figured I would be the only one with a damaged weapon the way my luck was going lately. Hopefully the airdrop would yield another sidearm. Preferably a suppressor-equipped Beretta M-9, but I would take whatever I could get.

Great Hawk called Anderson, told him the plan, and then radioed the rest of the team. "It is time to move out," he told me. "Are you ready?"

I slid my rifle around to my back and did a few stretches. "Just another day at the office, chief."

*****

Five long hours later, it was midafternoon, the horde was scattered nearly half a mile north of us, I had expended eighteen 6.8 SPC rounds shooting infected I could not avoid, and had experienced the unique pleasure of having to shoot two grays while taking a crap.

Not when I was finished, or cleaning up, or on my way back to where Great Hawk waited. Oh no, that would have been too dignified. As per my usual luck, they attacked right smack in the middle of the really emotional part.

At least I'd remembered to keep my rifle close at hand.

242

As soon as Great Hawk gave Anderson the all-clear, his party descended from their perches and headed south. We caught up with them near nightfall taking a rest on the edge of a riverbank. At least I think it was a river. Maybe just a big stream. I don't know. My grasp of Southern Illinois geography is not that great.

We rested, boiled some water, filtered it as best we could, and spent half an hour trying to catch fish with lines and hooks from our little survival kits baited with worms we dug out of the ground. No such luck.

Hungry, dejected, and damn near dead on my feet, I plopped down near the little smokeless Dakota fire Gabe had dug and ate the cookie bar from the lone MRE in my rucksack. We all had one, but most of the others were saving theirs. I could go a few weeks without food if it came down to it, but since Gabe, Hicks, Great Hawk, May and I would be venturing forth in less than an hour to retrieve the air drop, I wanted some quick energy.

"Maybe you should stay behind," Gabe said. "You look like shit."

"Thanks, old buddy. You always know just what to say. And for the record, I feel like shit."

"So take a pass on this one. No one will blame you."

I shook my head. "Nope. I want first dibs on the gear. Besides, you'll need help carrying it all back."

Gabe shrugged and let it go.

After nightfall, we put the last of our fresh batteries into our NVGs, I borrowed Anderson's pistol with a solemn promise to bring it back or die trying, and off we went. We did not make it more than a few hundred meters before I heard a limb snap, looked, and saw a knot of twelve infected approaching. The others noticed at the same time.

"Got 'em," I said.

The ghouls were only fifty or so meters away. A quick ammo inventory revealed I had a full mag in my rifle, four more

243

full ones on my vest, and an orphan with only eight rounds in it. One-hundred and fifty-eight rounds all together. I could spare a dozen.

"I'll go with you," May said and drew a long-handled hatchet from his belt. "Save some ammo."

"Fine by me. Just stay to my right, and if you get in trouble, fall back."

"Got it."

I evaluated the young soldier as we walked. He was a little taller than me, broad through the shoulders, narrow at the waist, and very long of limb. There was an athletic spring to his step and he gripped his hatchet with casual familiarity, giving me confidence he was well experienced with the weapon. Looking closer, I figured his age at somewhere in his mid-twenties. I wondered if he had already been enlisted in the Army when the Outbreak hit, or had signed on afterward.

"Let me get the first two," May said. "Make it easier to take out the rest."

Before I could respond, the young soldier took three running steps and buried his hatchet in an undead woman's skull. She looked like one of the older ones, pre-Outbreak clothes in tatters, shoes gone, most of her face and the flesh covering her stomach missing, long ropes of intestine dangling to her knees, the ends torn away by sharp brush or her own feet. There was a dark, maggot-ridden cavity where her digestive organs had once dwelled. I did not want to look, but found my eyes drawn there anyway.

May pulled her sideways so she made a trip hazard for the ghouls behind her, ripped his hatchet free, and hit the next one. A man this time, dressed in durable post-Outbreak clothes, the shoes still intact, obviously not dead for very long. *A victim of one of the Alliance's border incursions? Marauders?*

It did not matter. I raised my rifle, fired three times, and three undead fell across their fellows to form a small pile. The rest neither noticed nor cared. Hands reached, faces contorted, milky eyes stared wide and fevered, mouths opened to expose blackened teeth, animal moans and hisses and some kind of creepy yipping sound. Typical ghoul behavior.

May stepped to the side and cracked another ghoul on the back of the head, a professional blow, the brain destroyed on impact and the blade aimed so it passed through flesh and bone and exited the base of the neck smoothly. Another kill on the backswing, and a few bouncing steps to get out of the way. I took it as a cue and fired twice more. Two less ghouls in the world.

"Nice shooting."

"Thanks."

May stepped in and swung again. Like all of his kills thus far, he was careful not to attack head on, but rather from the side. It was a good strategy for an axe wielder, being that the front of the skull is the strongest, densest part. It is much easier to smash the big spherical bone at the thinner parts on the sides and back where it is less difficult to break. Additionally, attacking from an outside angle keeps one free of a ghoul's grasping hands.

I have been grabbed by the walking dead before. Their tireless strength is nothing short of terrifying.

Of the last two undead, one fell to May's axe and the other to my rifle. May cleaned his weapon with wet leaves and slid it back into its harness. I led the way back to the others.

"Feel better now?" Gabe asked, smirking.

"Actually I do." And I did. Nothing chases away the blues like doling out a few high-velocity lead injections to the undead.

"We must be careful and silent from here on out," Great Hawk said. His voice was like an ice bath, shattering the levity of the moment. "There may be more infected, and some of Samson's outriders could be nearby."

"That could be a good thing," Caleb said.

We all gave him a look.

245

"Horses."

"Ah," I said. "Still, I think we'd be better off following the Hawk's advice."

As we began walking again, I heard Caleb mutter, "Speak for yourself. My damn feet hurt."

TWENTY-SEVEN

The pickup went fine.

The rest of the night did not.

We found the dropped crates with no trouble—two small olive drab containers dangling from parachutes caught in high branches. Hicks climbed up, slithered out on a limb like a tree snake, and cut them free. A short drop, two thumps, and we were in business.

One of the crates yielded several new Beretta M-9 pistols equipped with suppressors. I made a little *yessss* sound, stashed Anderson's gun in my pack, and slipped a replacement into the empty holster under my arm. Next, I filled the empty slots on my vest with freshly loaded P-mags for my rifle, and, on my leg, fifteen-round standard metal magazines for my pistol. I thought about ditching the orphan with only eight rounds in it, but decided not to. What good was a cargo pocket if I never used it?

Okay. Primary weapon. 270 rounds of 6.8 SPC for the carbine and a last-chance eight rounds in my pocket. Another hundred cartridges still in the cardboard boxes in my pack. Standard 5.56 NATO would have been lighter, but was not available. I didn't mind. The extra stopping power was worth the back strain.

Sidearm. Fifteen rounds in the weapon, four spare mags with fifteen rounds each on the drop harness, and a box of fifty spares in the ruck. Sounded like a lot, but really wasn't. Not with the infected around. I would have to use the pistol sparingly.

Food. Three MREs. I could easily stretch the rations out to six days, and planned to do so.

The little revolver was fully loaded and there were twenty spare rounds in the rucksack. I hoped I would not need them. If I did, I doubted I would have time to load more than one. Which, considering the gun's intended purpose, would be all I needed.

Grenades. Four of them. There were other explosives—LAW rockets, claymores, breaching charges, etc.—but I left those to the professionals. Grenades scare me badly enough. No need to weigh myself down with implements of destruction I have neither the experience nor the inclination to use.

Now my ruck was full and the weight was beginning to grow uncomfortable. I ignored it. The pain was a much easier problem to deal with than being low on ammo in ghoul-infested wilderness. Such things are not conducive to longevity and good health. Besides, ammo is like water. The more you use, the lighter it gets. And the closer you are to dying.

Within the second crate were several of the Army's newly-developed MK 9 Anti-Revenant Personal Defense Tools. The MK was pronounced 'mark' for some reason. No one ever accused the military of being good at spelling.

I stared at the ugly black-coated blades for a moment, reminded myself my sword had been lost and I needed another ghoul-killer, and removed one. It was lighter than it looked. I guessed the blade length at twenty-two inches, which meant this was a second generation weapon. The originals had only been twenty inches.

The blade widened along the length of a distal taper and was sharp enough to shave with. The profile was similar to that of a Chinese war sword; Da Dao pattern, if memory served me. Looking closely at the edge under the light of a headlamp, I saw dark whorls in the metal that indicated folded and layered steel that had been differentially hardened. Which meant the spine was tempered to be softer for flexibility, and the outer lining harder so the steel could hold an edge. All good things.

248

The handle was a foot long with hardwood scales, full tang construction, and a round lanyard pommel twice as big around as my thumb. Simple steel bolster welded to the tang. Belt sheath made of hard plastic and woven nylon. Fit and finish were tight and functional. It would do.

A few practice swings felt pretty good, although the sword was a bit front heavy. I added the sheath to my web belt and tried a few practice draws. Not exactly smooth, but not completely terrible either.

"Think you can use that thing?" Gabe asked.

I shrugged. "If eighteen-year-old conscripts can do it, so can I."

"I'll get you another pig-sticker for your birthday."

"If we live that long."

The wolf grin flashed in the darkness.

The most important items in the arsenal were our real weapons: radios. And plenty of batteries. I grabbed one of the former and several of the latter. More than I needed, probably, but I am a firm believer it is better to have and not need than need and not have.

Great Hawk smiled a little at the discovery of a new tablet and a ruggedized laptop. Flipped it open. Powered it up. Found our location on GPS. Stuffed a cylindrical black thing in his vest. I asked him what it was, and he told me it was a backup power supply. Gabe deemed it a wise addition. I agreed.

The next part involved stuffing things into duffel bags and carrying them back for the others to root through. I doubted they would be disappointed with the pickings.

*****

When one is flush with ammo, replacement weapons, food, explosives, and in the company of trained killers friendly to

249

your cause, it is easy to grow complacent. But complacency is bad. It is lethal. It kills smart, capable people every day. In these moments, when I have been through some disaster or another and survived when most people would not, and I think I've made it through the worst and things will get better soon, I always try to be extra cautious. Because, in my experience, the hammer always falls when I think I am farthest from the anvil.

We were halfway back to the others when we heard gunshots. I wondered briefly what idiot was firing an unsuppressed weapon and then realized it was not an M-4. The Kalashnikov rifle has a very distinctive chatter. I would know it in my sleep. And it was very close.

"Down!" Great Hawk hissed.

I dropped the duffel bag I was carrying and hit the dirt. The ground was wet and muddy and smelled of rotting vegetation. The rain had stopped, but water dripped from soaked leaves and branches with steady cadence. A drop fell and landed on the rear aperture of the back-up iron sights that sprang up in front of me. I do not remember raising the rifle or even thinking it was something I should do. It just happened. Kind of like breathing.

My hands moved and my eyes scanned while my brain struggled to process the rapid influx of new information. The NVG lenses got in the way, so I flipped them up and activated the night vision on my scope. No green beam from the PEQ-15. I thought about turning it on, but saw the others had not done so, and decided against it. Made sense. We did not know if the enemy had night vision capabilities, and until we did, discretion was the best policy.

"Got anything, Riordan?" Great Hawk again.

"Not yet. Hang on."

Another burst of fire thundered through the trees. *Fucking moron is ringing a goddamn ghoul dinner bell.* My teeth clenched as I shifted to scan in the direction of the shots. At first I saw nothing, then I caught movement. Increased the scope magnification and looked again.

250

"Got him."

"How many?"

I watched and waited. About a hundred yards away, a lone, armed horseman rode slowly through the trees. Two dead ghouls lay to his right. Seconds passed, and nothing else happened. No other riders approached.

"I only see one, but I guarantee there are others nearby."

"Take him out."

I looked back at Great Hawk. "You sure?"

"I want his horse. It will get Lena Smith to safety faster."

A roll of the eyes. "Aye, aye, chief."

The scope appeared, the reticle went where it needed to go, and the right index finger gave a steady squeeze. *Crack.* The head in the crosshairs snapped backward and its owner toppled out of the saddle. The horse glanced back at him, sniffed, and continued on as if nothing had happened.

The brief rush that materializes before the trigger-pull faded. Adrenaline. The knowledge that I was about to end a life willfully, with malice, and in so doing would live a little while longer. It's callous, tragic, stupid, and wasteful, but when you take up a gun and set out to war, those are the rules of the game. You kill me, or I kill you. Be quick, or be dead. And this time, it was the other guy who made the mistake. Sorry, pal. Nothing personal.

"Nice shot," Gabe said. I turned to see him looking through his own scope.

"Thanks."

"Stay here," Great Hawk said. "I will be back shortly."

He stood up, stepped around a couple of trees, and was gone. There was no way I could track his movements—he was too skilled for that—but I knew exactly where he was heading. So I watched through my scope, and a minute or two later, the Apache reappeared. The horse seemed mildly startled, but did

251

not run. Great Hawk approached it slowly, kept his hands low, and let the animal sniff his palm. His other hand came up and gently scratched the horse's neck until it relaxed and went back to snuffling the forest floor. Mission accomplished.

Great Hawk then turned his attention to the dead insurgent, searched him, and produced a radio. He held it up to make sure I saw it.

"They have radios." I said.

Gabe hissed something four-lettered and not intended for polite company. I felt like doing the same. Repeatedly.

Great Hawk swung into the saddle and rode back to us. "I will proceed ahead," he announced upon returning. "Tie the duffels together and load them on the horse."

We did, and secured them to the saddle with para-cord. Once done, Great Hawk turned his mount and rode away.

"Fucking Lena Smith," May grumbled. "Hope she knows how lucky she is."

"Look on the bright side," Gabe said. "At least we don't have to carry the duffels anymore."

"Good point."

I flipped my NVGs back down and looked in the direction of the insurgent I shot. His presence was a disturbing development. It meant some of Samson's men, probably outriders, had escaped the horde we put in their way and were tracking us. Which meant they must have had a general idea of where to begin looking in the first place.

"They're tracking her."

Hicks looked at me. "What?"

"Lena Smith. Has to be."

"I was just thinking the same thing," Gabe said. Hicks caught our meaning and nodded in understanding.

"We need to pick up the pace," May said.

We started running.

TWENTY-EIGHT

Dawn came.

LaGrange found the device hidden in the hem of her jacket. Great Hawk held it in his palm and stared hard at Lena Smith.

"Did you know about this?"

"No."

"Any idea how it came to be hidden in your clothes?"

Lena gave the Hawk a withering glare. An impressive feat, considering she was wearing a thin wool blanket as a poncho and her feet were wrapped in nylon fabric that used to be a duffel bag. Hard to muster a convincing level of scorn under those circumstances, but she pulled it off.

"I don't know how I got it. But a lot of things are starting to make sense now."

"Such as?"

"Such as how General Samson always seemed to know where I was going to show up, the smug bastard. I thought he had a network of spies..." Her gaze went distant, the look of someone who had been trying to solve a riddle for a long time and had finally figured it out.

"Where would he have gotten this?" Great Hawk prompted. "It is a complex device. Not the kind of thing one finds lying around."

"Probably from Sandoval. He was the head of our secret police. Ex-NSA. If anyone within the Alliance's inner circle knew how to find or make those things, it was him."

"But why do it at all?" Gabe asked. "Why spy on you? Did Samson suspect you were a double agent?"

"We've been enemies since the beginning, Mr. Garrett. Our visions of what the Alliance should look like as a nation were very different. His included slavery, and torture, and rule by intimidation. I wanted no part of that. Others chose differently."

"Like the people we assassinated?" I said.

The steady green eyes swiveled my way. "Yes."

Great Hawk dropped the tracker against a large river stone and ground it under his heel. "At least you managed to break this thing before Samson's men found you. Must have happened sometime after Anderson called me and before we met here at the stream."

"I fell a few times along the way," Lena said. "The ground was muddy, and I was barefoot."

A nod from the Hawk. "That might have done it, but we cannot be sure. We need to leave this place. Hicks, you are the best horseman I have. Take Lena and go south as fast as you can. Stop for nothing. If anyone approaches you, assume they are enemies. Take this." He handed Hicks the ruggedized laptop. "I will notify Central of what is going on. They will be able to track you using the computer's GPS signal."

"Any clue how long until evac?" Hicks asked.

"My best guess is thirty-six hours, give or take. Go now, and ride fast. *Ka dish day*. Good luck."

Hicks nodded, swung into the saddle, and helped Lena up so she sat in front of him. The former vice president of the Midwest Alliance, a powerful and dangerous woman until yesterday, looked small and childlike next to Hick's tall, broad-shouldered frame.

"Watch your asses, fellas," Hicks said before leaving. "Hope to see y'all soon. First drink is on me."

"We'll hold you to that," Gabe said.

A kick, a pull of the reins, and the horse was off at a gallop. I was jealous. I wished I was going with them. My job was done, and I wanted to be away from this place. I wanted to be home with my wife. I wanted a stiff drink and a hot meal. I wanted to cut out General Samson's withered black heart with a rusty nail.

I settled for watching Hicks ride out of sight. When he was gone, I looked at Great Hawk. "What now, chief?"

The obsidian eyes were calm. "Now we run, my friend. Far and fast."

*****

Twenty minutes later, three reports split the air in rapid succession.

"Well that's not good," Bjornson said.

"They must have found our trail," I said to Great Hawk.

He signaled for everyone to stop. We had been running at a steady pace since leaving the campsite. At best guess, I figured we had covered a little over two miles. I had at least eight miles left in the tank before I would need to slow down, so my endurance was not an immediate concern. My body's reaction to sleep deprivation, however, was. It had been over forty-eight hours since I had slept last. The longest I had ever gone was five days, and at the end of it I was hallucinating and talking to my long-dead father. Right then, my brain felt like it was made of scrambled eggs, I had sandpaper for eyelids, and a gaping hole occupied the space where my stomach once dwelled.

"We cannot outrun them," Great Hawk said. "We will have to set up an ambush."

A grin split LaGrange's face. "Now you're talkin' my language."

The pilot from the other helicopter, whose name was Faulkner, leaned against a tree and slid to the ground. "I have to

256

rest," he said. It was the most he had spoken since we found him.

Anderson handed him a spare radio and extra batteries. "Keep going south. Don't look back. We'll call you when evac arrives."

The pilot looked conflicted. "I have combat training. I can help."

Anderson shook his head. "You're too important, Major. Get going. We'll hold 'em off."

The pilot took the radio, pushed himself to his feet, and said, "Good luck."

Anderson wished him the same, and off the pilot went.

Gabe pointed back the way we had come. "I say we double back on our trail. Me and Eric up in trees, the rest of you on the ground. Set up a few claymores, hit 'em with a LAW when they're in range. Snipe as many as we can."

"We'll have to move fast," Anderson said. "If they're on horseback, they'll be here shortly."

Great Hawk checked his rifle. "Then we had better get moving."

*****

I hate waiting for a fight to start.

I also hate sitting in trees. There is no comfortable way to do it, and something always stabs me in the ass. Nevertheless, I remained still and quiet and grateful that Gabe had grabbed my rucksack after the helicopter crash. If he had not, I would be without my ghillie suit. And while the ghillie was heavy and made me sweat in the growing heat, the concealment it afforded was too valuable to go without.

The sounds of men shouting to one another were getting louder. I peered through the scope and saw them coming over a

257

ridge, about twenty of them, all on horseback. No infantry, which made sense considering how far we were from Carbondale. It was unlikely they would arrive for at least a few hours.

I keyed my radio. "All stations, Irish. I have visual on hostiles."

"Irish, Hawk. How many? Over."

I told him. He acknowledged. Gabe gave a report from his position confirming what I had already seen.

We had chosen a natural chokepoint for the attack, a cleft between two sloping hills that met at a shallow ravine. Our backtrail ran through it, as we had used the cleft earlier in the day to cross the hills without skylining ourselves. My perch was on the eastern side, and Gabe had taken position to the west. Everyone else lay under ghillie suits in the surrounding brush, arranged in a crescent to create a crossfire covering a fifty meter area.

The horsemen came steadily closer. A few of their trackers followed our trail in the low-lying sections, while the rest had fanned out into a broad skirmish line. Each rider held the reins in one hand and a rifle in the other. Their posture, expressions, and firm tones of voice suggested confidence, belligerence, the arrogant swagger of those who know they are the hunter, not the hunted. Good. It would be all the more satisfying when a well-coordinated hail of lead and explosives sent them scrambling for cover.

"Irish, Hawk. Range? Over."

"Two hundred meters and closing. Over."

"All stations, stand by."

In a hundred meters, no less than seven of the horsemen would be right in front of the two claymores we had planted along our trail. They were the remote detonation variety, set off by a simple radio frequency trigger. Great Hawk held the button, and had instructed me to notify him when there were hostiles in range. We had been hoping the riders would

258

approach single file so we could hit them in the middle, but no such luck.

Seconds ticked by. The riders were cautious, alert, eyes scanning the brush and the trees. I was well hidden from them, legs wrapped around a maple trunk with my rifle steadied on a branch. This caused the slight disadvantage of having to shoot through foliage, but considering the ranges I would be dealing with, as long as I did not hit any tree limbs, it would not be much of a problem.

"Hawk, Irish," I whispered into the mic. "Enemy at one hundred yards standoff."

"Distance from the claymores?"

"In range. Should hit seven or eight of them."

"Irish, Wolfman, fire at will. All other stations, stand by."

No more waiting. Two deep, calming breaths, and on came the rush that occurs in these moments, a sharpening of the senses, a clarity of thought. Every twist and crevice of bark under my legs became its own singularity of discomfort, each birdcall a distinct, clarion trumpet. The rough texture of the trigger was gritty as sandpaper under my finger. I centered the reticle on a horseman outside the range of the claymores. Gabe was probably doing the same.

Slow release of breath, squeeze, squeeze, squeeze, nice and steady, and … *crack*. The shot surprised me, so I knew I had done it right. A hundred and fifteen grains of copper-jacketed lead rocketed downrange at over 2500 feet-per-second and hit its target in the sternum with close to 1700 foot-pounds of force. The man I shot looked surprised, then in pain, and then his face went slack and he felt nothing at all.

Next target. Big guy, dark brown skin, red headscarf over long hair, beard down to his chest. I aimed just below the beard and fired twice. *Crack, crack.* He fell out of the saddle.

I wondered if the insurgents could hear the shots from this range. Suppressed fire is not the same as silent fire, meaning even a suppressed rifle still makes noise. But between the steady drizzle of rain falling from the sky, birdsong, and the other natural sounds of the forest, there was a lot to cover it up.

I made one more kill before the shouting began, the signal Great Hawk had been waiting for. He knew Gabe and I would take out at least a few hostiles before the others noticed, and when they did, he triggered the claymores.

The explosion was enormous, a shockwave of force that hit me like a giant, invisible hand. Thousands of small metal balls tore into the insurgents and their mounts at incredible speed, ripping flesh, breaking bones, tearing off limbs and whole sections of faces and craniums. Horses screamed and reared and dumped their dead or dying riders, then bolted away, iron-shod hooves stomping a tangle of blood-soaked bodies. The ones who could not run fell where they stood, crushing fallen riders beneath their massive weight. Other horses nearby, those not hit by the blasts, began to panic, their riders struggling to control the beasts and, in many cases, getting thrown to the ground.

I had never seen a claymore detonate before. The guys in First Platoon had told me plenty of horror stories, but hearing about it and seeing it in person are two different animals. For a few seconds, all I could do was stare. The sheer volume of blood was staggering. The men who had been closest to the mines when they detonated were unrecognizable shreds of bloody meat. Organs and entrails and amputated arms and legs lay scattered like windblown leaves. The horses were in no better shape.

So deep was my shock, I nearly fell out of the tree when Bjornson fired the LAW.

This was a more familiar explosion, one I had seen and felt before. The blast killed two riders and their mounts and injured another. When the smoke cleared, of the twenty well-armed SS troops sent to find us, only four remained alive. And one of them was badly hurt.

Static. "All stations, do not let the survivors escape."

A quick breath. Picked a target. *Crack*. A rider fell from his mount. Shifted to another one, but Gabe got him first. The survivor who was injured fell from the saddle when his horse stopped and started bucking. Gabe got him too. The last rider was at the top of the hill now, about to go out of sight. I aimed and fired four times. Maybe two caught him, high and to the right. I heard staccato cracks of the others shooting, and realized they were aiming for the horse. It screamed, thrashed sideways, and fell over the other side of the hill, tumbling out of sight.

Great Hawk sprang up from the ground and gave chase, running faster than I had ever seen anyone run. He seemed to flow over the terrain like water, trees and roots and fallen logs no obstacle at all. I did not see his rifle, but he clutched his knife in one hand and a pistol in the other. In less than twenty seconds, he was over the hill. I sat still, not sure what to do next. Maybe half a minute passed, and then Great Hawk walked back over the ridge carrying the insurgent's radio.

I climbed down from the tree and started checking for survivors. Two of the troops caught in the claymore blast were still alive, barely. The first one I came upon was missing an arm from the elbow down, his right leg looking like a pride of lions had been chewing on it, and his torso was perforated like some sort of grotesque sieve. Blood frothed from blue lips and small, agonized screams tried to rip free from shredded lungs. I put two in his head and considered it a kindness.

The second was in even worse shape. How he was still alive, I could not fathom. Gabe walked over and stopped beside me.

"Jesus."

"Yeah," I said.

"You wanna do it?"

"Sure."

I leveled my rifle and fired twice. The twitches and gurgling and blood-spitting stopped. I walked away, set my rifle against a tree, and dry-heaved for a few minutes. Nothing came out but a few long strands of sour-tasting spit.

I needed to eat. I needed to sleep for a month. I needed someone to reach inside my memory banks and delete the

261

carnage I had just walked through. Most of all, I needed to get the hell out of this forest and back to civilization, back to my life.

When the retching subsided, I walked back and joined the others. Gabe and Anderson were in conversation with Great Hawk, while the rest had gone to chase down horses. The possibility of riding out of this place appealed to me very, very strongly.

"We're only a few miles from I-57," Great Hawk said, eyes fixed on the ruggedized tablet. "We will continue south, parallel the highway, and then scavenge for boats along the Ohio River."

"Then we can follow it south to the Mississippi," Gabe said. "Take that all the way down to Tennessee."

"That will not be necessary. Evac will show up before then."

"Yeah, well, it never hurts to have a back-up plan."

Anderson tapped Great Hawk on the arm and looked over his shoulder at the ridgeline. "We only got half of Samson's cavalry. The rest of his troops won't be far behind. And I sincerely doubt they'll stop at the Union border."

"No to mention every ghoul between here and fucking Mexico is headed our way right now," I said. "Those explosions must have echoed for miles. We'll be up to our ears in undead by nightfall. We're going to have to find shelter."

Great Hawk put away the tablet. "I will scout ahead. Anderson, you are in command until I return." He handed Anderson the sat-phone. "I will find shelter and radio in. If you are out of radio range, I will text you from the tablet."

"Works for me," Anderson said.

"Here," I said, taking a magazine from my vest and giving it to Great Hawk. "Just in case. You can never have too much ammo."

The Hawk took the mag. "Thank you, my friend." He accepted another spare from Gabe and Anderson each. After

262

thanking them, he said, "I have a plan to slow Samson's men, but I will need volunteers."

"What's the plan?" I asked.

He told me. I liked it so much I smiled. "Count me in."

"Me too," Gabe said.

A nod from the Hawk. "Good luck to you, then."

A few minutes later, Bjornson, May, and LaGrange showed up on horseback with four more mounts in tow. Great Hawk selected a tall mare with a brown coat and little splotches of white on her face. Then he wished us luck again and rode away at a gallop.

I looked at Gabe. "You ready for this?"

"Not really."

"Yeah, me neither."

A shrug. "Never stopped us before."

I swapped the partially depleted mag in my rifle for a fresh one. Pulled the charging handle. Caught the expended cartridge. Loaded it into the half-empty mag. Checked the safety.

"Nope. Never has."

TWENTY-NINE

We had a few known quantities working in our favor, and a few making our job a pain in the ass.

As to the former, we knew Samson's men had radios. We knew they were smart enough to check in periodically, and when the dead outriders did not, Samson would know something had gone wrong. There was also the possibility he heard the explosions. Either way, he knew the game was afoot.

And since he and his men had survived the Outbreak as long as Gabe and I, they knew the sounds of fighting were going to bring ghouls. Lots of them. Nightfall was fast approaching, meaning chances were pretty good they would try to find shelter for the night. Furthermore, if they were as smart as I gave them credit for, they would assume our group was being forced to do the same. Which meant they probably weren't worried about Great Hawk and the others running far enough away that Samson's scouts couldn't find them.

As to the latter issues, the rain had picked up again, the hordes were starting to arrive, and since our job was to follow the outrider's backtrail, locate the rest of Samson's forces, and harass them guerilla style, this did not create ideal conditions. It did, however, give me the opportunity to field test the MK 9 Anti-Revenant Personal Defense Tool. Or Rot-chopper, as it is affectionately known in the Army, Rot being an increasingly common slang term for the infected.

The trail led just over two miles back to the stream near where we had set up camp the night before. Which made sense, considering the water consumption a hundred-and-twenty men are capable of. They would need an abundant source to fulfill their needs.

Along the way, we encountered two small hordes. The first one, we skirted by urging our horses to a gallop and outrunning them. The second was larger and spread out over a wider area— no getting around them—so we dismounted. I let Gabe hold the reins of both horses and approached the undead with the MK 9.

"Work fast," Gabe said, a pistol in his free hand. "No showing off. Just cut a path so we can get out of here."

"Will do."

The first three ghouls were all children. I hate fighting infected children. Not just because they are faster than their adult contemporaries, but because they are freaking *children*. Or used to be, anyway. Looking at their wasted, evil little faces awakens a dread, a sense of violated taboo, which cuts me to the bone. It's a reminder that the Phage, like death, spares no one, has no pity, no remorse, and if given the opportunity, will consume us all.

Not today.

I kicked the first one, barely a toddler when it died. As the ghoul-baby went flying, I hit the tallest of the three with a backswing. The MK 9 cleaved through the skull so easily I thought I had missed for a moment. But then the dead kid fell, the top of its cranium coming off like a slice of cantaloupe, and before I could stop to admire my work, the third one lunged and forced me back a step. I put the point of the blade against its throat and shoved hard, expecting it to knock the little ghoul over. Instead, the point penetrated all the way through and hit the spine. A lethal cut to a human, but only a minor inconvenience to a ghoul. I pulled the blade free and chopped downward with a strike called a pear-splitter. As the name implied, it cut the ghoul-kid's head in two neat, even sections.

By the time I recovered, the first one I kicked had gotten back to its feet and was coming in at a slow trot. This time I swung with less force and more careful aim. The result was a

265

neat, clean decapitation. I held up the MK 9 and looked at the sweep of its blade.

I could get used to this thing. The ghouls began to converge from all directions, but slowly, more like the steady ingress of high tide rather than a flood.

The MK 9 was surprisingly easy to use. By the eighth or ninth kill, I had the hang of it. The best technique was to use the full length of the handle to my advantage, one hand at the bottom, the other high, just below the bolster. Swing from the hip, follow through with the shoulders, keep the blade in a continuous arc, and be careful not to swing too hard. If my aim was true and I set my feet properly, about three-quarters strength was all it took.

The blade became stuck few times, but was easy to dislodge due to the leverage afforded by the long handle. Hacking and slashing wasn't as quick as my old choke-and-poke method, and was significantly more tiring. Oddly, however, I found it intensely satisfying. There is something visceral and elemental about defending one's life with a big sharp hunk of metal. I won't say it was fun—it wasn't—but it spoke the language.

Twice, Gabe had to shoot ghouls who got too close while I was occupied fighting others. But only twice. The MK 9 worked well enough I had little trouble keeping the horde at bay. If they had been more tightly packed, it would have been a different story. But with an interval density of about thirty feet, I could handle it.

After twenty minutes of steady work, there were very few ghouls ahead of me, but on the trail behind, they had bunched together and formed the now-familiar teardrop shape. The faster, less damaged ghouls made up the narrow pointy part, while the slower ones fell behind and formed the larger body.

Once Gabe and I were out of danger, or as out of danger as one can be these days, we mounted up and set off at a steady trot. An hour passed. We saw no more ghouls, and it became obvious the horses were getting tired. I knew how they felt. I ached in every bone and was starting to get lightheaded from hunger.

"We're not far from Samson's camp now," Gabe said, startling me. I had nearly fallen asleep without realizing it.

"You think?"

A nod. "Tracks are fresh. Looks like they turned east here and headed for the stream. We should veer west, ride out behind them, and come in from the north. They won't be expecting an attack from that direction."

"I hate to say this, Gabe, but I could use a rest. I'm about used up."

"I know. If the bags under your eyes got any bigger, I could use them for luggage."

"Thanks, asshole."

"Horses are tired too. Need a drink and a chance to forage."

"Same could be said for us."

Another hour of riding brought us to the bank of the stream somewhere north of Samson's force. Gabe said they were less than two miles away, and lacking better information, I took him at his word.

While the horses drank, Gabe said, "We'll have to let them go."

"Let who go?"

"The horses. If we tether them, they'll be sitting ducks."

"So will we, after we attack Samson's troops."

"They'll have more horses. We'll figure something out."

"Improvise and overcome, right?"

"Exactly."

The two of us found trees with limbs in the right configuration, made sleeping platforms from trimmed down saplings and branches, and lashed them securely in place with

267

para-cord. My summer bedroll consisted of a black yoga mat that was long enough for me to stretch out on, a rectangular pillow I had made with tough fabric and foam harvested from a car seat, and a thin camouflage blanket scavenged from an abandoned house. I rolled it out over my rough pallet, tied myself to the tree with more para-cord, and lay down. Gabe tied the horse's reins under his palette, but made sure the knots were loose in case the infected showed up. I hoped the horses would be smart enough to bolt if that happened.

It was the last thought I had before I fell asleep.

*****

The rain woke me up.

I had gotten used to the soggy pitter-patter of the last few days, but this rain was different. A strong wind hurled it at the forest, rocked the trunk I had lashed myself to, loosened the structure of my sleeping palette, and sent water cascading down in sheets. I shielded my face from it and sat up. There was no light to see by. My hand groped in the dark, freed my fighting knife, and cut the para-cord holding me in place.

I sat up, swung my legs so I was straddling the trunk, and assessed my situation. I could feel my vest and everything in it. Soaked, but still there. Pistol in its holster. Rifle lashed to my chest. Blanket was a lost cause, but I wanted to save the yoga mat. Rubber dries just fine.

"You all right over there?" Gabe called to me.

"Just dandy," I replied. "Needed a shower anyway."

"Glad you realized that. You were starting to get a little ripe."

"Yeah, and you smell like fucking roses. Any clue where the horses are?"

"Gone."

I let my head drop. "Wonderful."

"Oh, it gets better. Put on your NVGs and look down."

My rucksack was hanging just below me. I had been sensible enough to put the rain cover over it, so when I extracted my night vision goggles, they were dry.

"Shit," I said, looking down.

Gabe, not hearing me, said, "You see what I'm talking about yet?"

"Yes." Louder.

What he was talking about was a horde passing beneath our feet. A few looked up at me when I spoke, but kept moving. Strange. Ghouls weren't usually so blasé when they spotted a living person. "They're like lemmings. What the hell is going on?"

"Listen," Gabe replied.

So I did. And I heard it. Gunfire. Not small arms, but the kind that comes from aircraft. Big, thudding, booming shots, and rapid fire at that. My heart lifted.

"Got your radio?"

"Yeah. You?"

I pulled it from my pack, shielded it from the rain as best I could, and stuck the earpiece in. "That one of ours?"

Static. "I think so."

"How?"

"Great Hawk had two tablets. Remember? One he brought from Hollow Rock, and the other he got from the supply drop. I jury rigged a couple of radio batteries we took from Samson's outriders and made a charger."

I laughed. "You clever son of a bitch."

"I have been so accused."

"You called in Samson's position?"

269

"Texted, actually. Took a long time to transmit, but yeah."

"What'd they send?"

"AC-130 is my guess. Heard it pass. Definitely not a helo."

I processed that and said, "What the fuck is taking so long with the evac anyway? It's like Central *wants* us to die."

"Not sure, brother. But the next time I see General Jacobs, we're going to have a nice long talk about it."

"I want to be there."

"We get out of here alive, you will be."

"Speaking of getting out alive, you got a plan, Stan?"

"My name ain't Stan. And yes, I have a plan."

"Care to enlighten me?"

"I was thinking we'd hang out here in these nice safe trees until the ghouls pass, then hump over to Samson's camp, or whatever's left of it, and see what we can see."

"Wow, Gabe, I stand in awe of your intellect. No way would I have ever thought of that on my own."

"Blow me, smartass. You asked."

I sighed. He had a point. "What time is it?"

"Three-hundred hours."

Three in the morning in civilian time. I had actually managed six hours sleep. "You think an MRE tastes any better in the rain?"

"I doubt it. No harm in trying, though."

So I ate an MRE. The main course, side dish, crackers, cheese spread, and cookie bar. The chemical heater pack and the baggie with chewing gum, Tobasco sauce, utensils, wet napkin, sugar packets, and instant coffee, I stashed in my pack. All that stuff was valuable trade. And while I often serve my country as a mercenary (*ahem*, private security contractor), I am first and foremost a business man. And a good business man never tosses away easy money. Especially when it is small, light, portable, and worth much more than the cost of carrying it.

Belly full and feeling somewhat rested, I clung to the tree, prayed none of the lighting in the distance found its way closer to me, and rested my head against my arm. There was nothing to do now but wait.

At least my seat was not too terribly uncomfortable.

*****

The AC-130 had wreaked havoc.

A circle of trees covering two acres had been thrashed and chopped to pieces by large, airborne cannons. The infected had shown up during the bombardment, evidenced by their corpses lying in various states among the remains of once-living men. Some of the infected lay permanently dead, while others crawled through the mud and shallow holes left behind by the Union artillery, their bodies horrible to look upon, entrails streaming behind them as they pulled themselves along with bloody, skeletal hands.

"How many killed do you think?" I asked Gabe. We were perched in trees less than fifty meters from Samson's camp.

"Hang on." A minute ticked by, and then he said, "Eighty-eight dead, best I can tell. Most of the horses with them."

"So Samson's down to thirty-two, all on foot now. How the hell did they get away?"

"Your guess is as good as mine."

We had moved in when the infected thinned out to the point it was safe to travel, and then made our way closer to the encampment, taking to the trees. The undead had stripped most of Samson's men and horses down to blood-crusted bones, and the others were nowhere to be found. I shifted position in my perch, and a thought occurred to me.

271

"Think they're in the trees?"

Static. "Could be. Or they may have run for it."

"Still got your IR scope?"

"Wait one."

I waited. A few minutes later, the earpiece crackled. "Nothing."

"So they escaped."

"Yep."

"How long until dawn?"

A pause. "Two more hours."

"First light?"

"First light."

I clung to the tree, looked to the eastern horizon, and prayed for daylight.

THIRTY

When Gabe and I had first arrived in Hollow Rock, I had a newly minted gunshot wound in my side that damn near killed me. Doctor Allison Laroux, now Doctor Allison Riordan, who was the only doctor in town at the time, saved my life. Later, she fell victim to my masculine charms. Or maybe it was the other way around. My memory of that time is a bit hazy.

Anyway, after I recovered, Gabe insisted I stop lifting weights and instead focus my physical training on muscular and cardiovascular endurance. I considered it an ironic suggestion coming from a man boasting two-hundred and fifty pounds of solid muscle, but I took the advice anyway. Most of my workouts since then have involved body-weight exercises—more commonly known as calisthenics—and a hell of a lot of running. And when I am in the field, rarely does a day pass when I do not look back on my decision to follow Gabriel's advice and feel a profound sense of gratitude. Especially when being out in the field involves running for a prolonged period of time.

It was not long after dawn when the infected got bored and wandered off, leaving a smattering of flesh-stripped corpses in their wake. I followed Gabe while he walked a wide circle around the carnage, and somewhere near mid-morning, he stopped, crouched, and traced a line on the ground with his eyes.

"Got 'em."

"You sure?" I looked where Gabe was looking and saw nothing out of the ordinary. I'm not much of a tracker, despite my old friend's attempts to the contrary.

"Yep. They went that way." He pointed southward. "Tried to cover their tracks, but didn't do too good of a job."

"On the run?"

The big man looked over his shoulder. "They were surrounded by infected and taking heat from a fucking gunship. What do you think?"

"I'd have run away too."

"Looks like you still have a chance." And with that, Gabe started running.

My oldest and best friend has long legs and insane endurance, but he is in his early forties, built like a brick shithouse, and I am only in my early thirties. He outpaced me the first few miles, but his size and the oxygen requirements of all that muscle eventually slowed him down. By mile four or five, we were side by side. At mile seven or eight, Gabe slowed and signaled for a halt.

"What is it?" I asked between labored breaths.

"We're close," Gabe said, hands on hips, chest heaving.

I reached back, undid the Velcro strap holding my rifle barrel to my web belt, and checked the weapon. Safety off, round in the chamber. "How close?"

"Passed through here not more than an hour ago."

I looked down at the moist earth, the dead leaves, pine needles, and small crawling things and considered our options. "We should move in slow and quiet."

"Agreed."

Ghillie suits. Slow, deliberate crouch-walk through the forest. Twenty meter interval between the two of us. Another mile, and we heard gunfire.

I keyed my radio. "Hawk, Irish. How copy?"

274

A few heartbeats passed, then static and Anderson's voice. "Copy Lima-Charlie, Irish. Hawk is indisposed at the moment. Twenty on Wolfman?"

Gabe keyed his mic. "Right here."

"Good. Damn glad to hear from you. We are under fire, holed up in the Pulaski County Sheriff's Office."

"Christ," Gabe muttered, referencing the map in his finely-tuned head. "We're just outside Mound City, almost at the river."

"Sitrep?" I asked over the radio.

"Surrounded by a fuckload of infected and a bunch of pissed off SS troops. These bastards just don't give up."

Gabe looked at me, the gray eyes flat and cold. I knew what he was thinking. I nodded and checked my carbine again.

"We are inbound, Shorty." Gabe said. "Hang in there."

Anderson sounded harried, gunfire chattering in the background. "Sooner is better. Shorty out."

We headed toward the sounds of fighting.

*****

Mound City was a small town hugging the Ohio River at the border of Illinois and Kentucky. The Pulaski County Sheriff's Office was at the northeast corner, backed by overgrown fields and a thin strip of old-growth trees. Gabe and I took position in the thick greenery where we could commune with branches, leaves, birds, and bugs, and peer at the town through dialed-up scopes. It was mid-afternoon, and the hot sun had turned the last few days' rain into a fume of stifling humidity. The stench of the undead was strong on the wind.

"Ever seen that many infected in one place?" I said into my radio. We were on our own channel, the rest of Task Force

275

Falcon unable to listen in. For the third time in the last ten minutes, I had to wipe condensation from the lens of my optics.

"Yeah, but it's been a while."

There were thousands of them, clawed hands scraping uselessly at walls of brick, cedar, and vinyl siding. The sheriff's office was an oasis in a sea of undead. Our friends and allies were inside, fighting a large-scale sniper duel with more than thirty of Samson's men. The enemy troops had taken position on houses and other buildings across the street, lying on rooftops.

I focused on one of them, a youngish man with a dense brown beard, long hair, and tired eyes. Despite his role as aggressor, he looked like a hunted thing. I shifted the scope and took in a few more gaunt visages. The young man's compatriots did not look much better. I got the distinct impression their heart was not in this fight. It gave me an idea.

"Hey," I said into the radio mic, "you remember what Samson looks like?"

When Gabe spoke, I could almost hear the grin on his face. "Kill the head of the snake and the body dies. Right? If only I had a bigger gun."

"I have faith in you, old friend."

"Could use a spotter."

"Got nothing better to do."

It took Gabe a few minutes, but he finally found what he was looking for. "Got him. Red rooftop, corner of Ohio Avenue and Pearl Street."

I scanned until I located the street signs, dialed up the scope's magnification to its highest setting, and focused on where Gabe directed. Sure enough, I saw General Samson's narrow, hateful face behind a pair of long-range binoculars. He had dark hair where his scalp had not gone bald, a reddish beard, strong jawline, and a straight, aristocratic nose. If the ocean of infected howling for his flesh affected him, he gave no indication. He stared through his binoculars with singular focus, his attention wholly consumed by his desire to kill the men in the Sherriff's Office.

"You know," I said over the radio, "he probably thinks Lena Smith is in there with them."

Static. "The thought occurred. Probably explains why he's being such a tenacious son of a bitch. Vengeance is a powerful motivator."

"Right, and I'm thinking if we get him out of the way, his men won't be too motivated to keep up the fight."

"One way to find out. Give me a range."

I did, using the reticle on my scope. Approximately two-hundred and forty yards. Tough shot with a standard M-4 carbine chambered in 6.8 SPC, but not impossible.

"Concur," Gabe said. "Stand by."

There was a part of me that wanted to take the shot myself, but I told it to shut up. Gabe had taught me everything I knew; he was the real sniper, the one with the crazy Quantico training. I'm good, but I'm not better than my mentor. So I concentrated on my role as spotter, looking through the scope with my non-dominant eye closed, gaze unfocused.

"I have a shot," the earpiece said.

"Send it."

The first one missed, impacting against the asphalt shingles a few inches to the right of General Samson. One of his men jerked in surprise and looked around, did not seem injured, but had obviously heard the impact. Samson continued gazing through his binoculars, unaware and undeterred.

"Correct to the left. Azimuth off by less than a foot. Elevation low by about six inches."

"Copy."

I watched and waited. Seconds passed, and then I saw Samson's head jerk backwards, a neat little hole in his forehead.

The binoculars dropped from limp fingers as he began rolling down the rooftop, his men watching in stunned horror as their commander fell into the waiting arms of the infected. In seconds, he was torn limb from limb. I peeled my eye from the scope. No need to make further additions to my already ample collection of nightmares.

"Got him."

"Yeah, I noticed."

"What now?"

A pause. "Now we wait, amigo."

I rolled my eyes. "Sure. Why not?"

So we waited.

*****

As they are wont to do, the undead took their sweet-ass time before giving up and wandering away. Probably did not help that Samson's men kept firing for another ten minutes after the demise of their fearsome leader.

Gabe and I began actively sniping them, but they figured out what was happening and quickly got their asses behind cover. I got two, and Gabe got four. Typical Gabe. I clicked the button on my radio and told him no one likes an overachiever. He told me not to be jealous. I suggested he perform an anatomical impossibility and settled in to wait for the infected to leave.

By nightfall, all but a few dozen had wandered off. The ones left behind were mostly crawlers and those too mechanically non-functional to manage more than a slow shuffle. Gabe and I discussed moving in and trying to take out more of Samson's men, but they saved us the trouble by emerging from their hides and scattering into the forest.

"You seeing what I'm seeing?"

Static. "Yep. I'll call it in."

I switched back over to the command net and listened while Gabe gave a sitrep. Great Hawk was back on the horn. "Do you still have batteries for your radios and NVGs?" he said.

"Affirmative," Gabe replied. "You guys got transportation?"

"Negative, Wolfman. Had to let the horses go."

"Same here."

Great Hawk was silent a few moments, then said, "I am thinking a few things. I am thinking Samson's men do not have batteries. I am thinking they are operating in the dark and dodging infected. I am thinking they are low on ammunition, food, and water. I am thinking we could track them, just a few of us, and determine if further action is needed. The rest of us can proceed south to await evac."

"Speaking of," I asked. "Any word from Tex?"

"Package has been delivered, Irish. Safely. Along with the pilot from the other helicopter."

I let out a breath. All four targets dead, Lena Smith safely in Union hands, one indispensable pilot saved, and all it cost were the lives of three pilots, two aircrewmen, Stewart, Taylor, McGee, and Liddell, all highly-trained warriors our country could ill afford to lose. I swallowed my bitterness and resolved to give General Jacobs an earful the next time I spoke to him.

"How about Tex?" I asked. "He all right?"

"He is on the transport with Lena Smith."

"Lucky him."

"Let's stay focused, people," Gabe said, "We still have a job to do. The last thing we want is Samson's men dogging our trail until evac arrives. How much longer, Hawk?"

"Dawn tomorrow. Allegedly."

"I'll believe it when I see it. So who wants to volunteer for the night's festivities?"

"I'm in," said Bjornson.

"Me too." Gabe this time.

"You know me, brother," I said. "Your fight is my fight."

"I will go as well." Great Hawk said.

I checked my rifle and ammo. Good to go. "Okay, fellas. How about we stop flapping our gums and make this shit happen? The longer we wait, the farther the enemy will run."

"Meet me behind the courthouse," Great Hawk said. "We will find their trail and give chase."

I climbed down, found Gabe, put on my NVGs so I could see in the quickly falling gloom, and followed the trackers.

THIRTY-ONE

Samson's troops regrouped half a mile north of Mound City, then turned southeast and made a beeline for the Ohio River. Along the way, we came upon the recently reanimated corpse of one of the fleeing troops.

"Rot got him," Bjornson said, staring at the walking dead man.

No shit. Figure that one out by yourself? "So they're down to twenty-four men. Or less."

"Better and better," Gabe said.

I decapitated the ghoul with my MK 9 and proceeded on mission.

We found them scouring the river bank, gathering canoes and anything else that would float. I counted eighteen. Gabe concurred. None of the insurgents had night vision.

"We got the drop on 'em," Bjornson said into his radio. "I say we ambush 'em, hit 'em hard, take out as many as we can."

"Any objections?" Great Hawk asked.

I thought about the last few days, the gunfire, the fighting, and the bloodshed. I thought about how many people were lost during the Outbreak and everything that happened after. I thought about the guilt riding my conscience, and what kind of a father I was going to be to my child.

When he or she was old enough, what would they think of me? I wanted them to love me, respect me, and when I am gone, I want them to be able to say their father was a good man. But

281

to do that, I had to *be* that person. I had to be someone worth loving, and respecting, and saying nice things about after I left the world.

I searched myself and decided that the kind of man I wanted to be, the kind of man I wanted to raise my children, was smart enough to learn from his mistakes. Smart enough to turn away from a fight if there was an alternative. Smart enough to speak up against needless killing, and, when he could, try to find a better way.

"Hold on," I said. "Let me move in, get a read on their disposition."

"The hell for?" Bjornson demanded. "We got 'em dead to rights. Let's take their sorry asses down and get the fuck out of here."

Great Hawk said, "Wait, Sergeant. The Irishman has a point. I will go with you, Irish. We will gather more information and then decide how to proceed. Viking, you and Wolfman remain behind as fire support."

"Copy," Gabe said.

"Sure. Fine." Bjornson did not sound happy.

We moved in. Great Hawk was a ghillie-suited ghost in the shadows of the trees, his steps silent, rifle at the ready. If I had not been wearing NVGs, I would never have known he was there.

At the riverbank, the foliage thinned and we went down to our bellies. Samson's men had gathered in a loose cluster behind a house that had burned down years ago. A small pier in the back yard was still intact, jutting out into the river. There were several small boats tied to it, each with a pair of oars. The Hawk and I crawled slowly and quietly until we were in earshot of the conversation.

"...it's over, Jason. Do you understand? It. Is. Over. Samson's dead. The president is dead. So is the council speaker and the secretary of defense. The vice president is missing.

We're down to just a few men. We're lucky we survived this long. I'm not pushing my luck any further."

The man speaking did so with an air of authority, his voice that of a person accustomed to being obeyed. The other individual stood stiffly, his face a mask of inner conflict.

"But those troops we fought …"

The leader made a cutting motion with his hand. "Those Union troops aren't interested in us. If they were, they'd have sniped us while we ran away. We're nothing to them. They wanted Samson. They set a trap, and the dumb bastard walked right into it. If he'd gone west like I told him to, all the people we lost would still be alive. And in case you haven't figured it out yet, the general was crazy as a shithouse rat. I'm talking in-fucking-sane. What happened to him, he brought on himself. And I, for one, am glad the loony son of a bitch is gone. You want to follow in his footsteps? Go for it. I'll raise a drink for you when you're dead."

The second man shuffled his feet. "So what are we supposed to do we do then, Captain? Stay out here? We'll die of exposure, assuming the infected don't get us first. I still say we should go back to Carbondale."

The leader put his hands on his hips and took a step forward, leaning down so he was in the second man's face. "Go back to what, exactly? There's nothing for us to go back to. We're hated in Alliance territory. If you go back, you'll be strung up by your balls and left for the crows. Is that what you want?"

The second man looked down and did not answer.

The leader stepped back and addressed the group. "Here's what we're gonna do. We're going to climb in these boats, head downriver to Kentucky, and scatter. None of us will tell any of the others where we plan to go. That way, if one of us is captured, he won't be able to rat out the others."

Silence. Worried glances back and forth. The leader ran a hand across the back of his neck and sighed. "Look, fellas, I don't like this any more than you do. But it's time to face reality. Our days in the SS are over. That part of our lives is behind us. It's time to move on. You want to go back? Fine. Go back. But don't say I didn't warn you."

With that, the leader turned away from his men, climbed into a boat, and started unlashing the lines from the pier cleats. After a few seconds hesitation, some of the others climbed in with him. The rest headed for other boats.

"What do you think?" Great Hawk whispered into his radio.

"I think we let 'em go. They're no threat to us now."

We watched the former insurgents paddle down the river until they were out of sight. "Better let them have a head start," I said. "Wouldn't want to run into them on the river."

"Good thinking."

The two of us crawled back to the treeline and briefed the others. Bjornson was not happy about letting Samson's men go, but relented when Great Hawk explained it was not fucking optional, and this was not a fucking democracy.

"I am sorry for the men we lost," the Hawk said, softening his voice. "I understand the need for revenge, but our mission is over. Killing those men will not bring your friends back. It is time to go home, Sergeant."

Bjornson looked down, nodded, and began walking southward. The rest of us followed, the Ohio River to our right, a narrowly avoided war behind us, and an increasingly uncertain road ahead.

*****

The helicopter showed up at dawn, as promised. A Chinook this time, not a Blackhawk. I was not exactly thrilled to be riding in a chopper of *any* sort again, but it was the fastest way home. Thankfully, no enemy aircraft showed up to shoot us out of the sky.

None of us spoke much during the flight. Just a few comm checks, but no real conversation. Task Force Falcon had lost four men, and the survivors were beginning to feel the loss. There had not been time to mourn when we were running and fighting for our lives, but now that we were safe, there was time for reflection.

I felt bad for the lost men. I felt bad for their friends. But it was a distant, generalized sort of grief, nothing sharp or acute. More like the pang of concern one feels when hearing about some distant tragedy, an earthquake or hurricane or other disaster. I felt it, but was not truly affected by it. Not the way Anderson's men were. I wondered what it said about me. I wondered what kind of man I was becoming. I wondered if pre-Outbreak Eric would approve of this version of me. I wondered if he would even recognize me. Somehow, I doubted it.

When we landed, I said a quick goodbye to Anderson and the remainder of his team. I told them I was sorry for their loss, and wished them luck. Then we shook hands, Anderson first, followed by May, LaGrange, and finally Bjornson.

"You know," Bjornson said, "I was wrong about you. You're all right, Riordan. Sorry for giving you so much shit before."

I waved the apology away. "Water under the bridge, amigo."

He clapped me on the shoulder and followed his brothers toward the command building. Great Hawk remained behind with Gabe and me.

"So what's next for you, chief?" I asked the big Apache.

He shrugged. "I think I will stick around for a while. This place seems as good as any, and better than most. I will need to find a job. Know anyone who is hiring?"

I smiled. "I think I could find something for you."

A pat on the shoulder. "Thank you, my friend."

THIRTY-TWO

The summer passed and gave way to October, and the harvest, and my child growing steadily in my wife's belly until the most nerve-wracking day of my life finally arrived.

I stood next to Allison, her hand gripping mine like a steel vice, and held on for dear life while she pushed and screamed and pushed some more. I was wearing blue scrubs, a clear plastic bag on my head, and dearly wished I was anywhere but in this hospital room with all these people, my wife uttering some of the vilest sentences I had ever heard, most directed at me, calling into question my intelligence, ancestry, and my odds of surviving the day. Which, according to her, were not very good. She seemed to be under the impression her intense suffering was entirely my fault, and boomed out her reasoning thereof at great length and with ear-burning eloquence. I wanted to point out she'd also had a hand in things, and I had certainly never heard her complain during any of the sessions that led to the conception of her current misery, but prudence and good sense told me this was not the time to bring it up.

"It's okay, honey," I said lamely, not knowing what else to do. "Just keep pushing."

She looked at me fiercely, face sweaty and flushed, hair a damp tangle. "What the fuck do you think I'm doing, you moron! What have I been doing this whole shit-sucking time!"

"Okay, okay, honey. You're doing great. Just-"

"Shut your goddamn mouth you brainless idiot!"

So I shut up, and held her hand, and prayed the baby would come soon. There was more pushing, and screaming, and a lot of people moving around between my wife's legs. Finally, one of the scrub nurses uttered the most beautiful sentence I had ever heard.

"It's breaching, Doctor."

"Okay," Doctor Khurana said. "Almost there, Allison. Give me one last push."

The nurse motioned for me to help. I put an arm behind Allison, lifted her up, and said, "Come on, honey. You can do it."

Her eyes went hard, she took several quick breaths, clenched her teeth, and pushed with everything she had, culminating in a scream of raw, primal effort.

"He's out, Allison," the nurse said.

My wife collapsed on the pillows and struggled to catch her breath. I stepped around the side of the bed and looked at my child. Doctor Khurana's eyes held a smile behind his surgical mask as he held up my baby.

"It's a boy. Congratulations, Mr. Riordan."

I had to wait while the nurses cleaned him up, suctioned something out his mouth and nose, cut the umbilical cord, and put some kind of clear goop in his eyes. Blue eyes, just like mine. Then they wrapped him up and handed him to his mother.

Allison smiled through the pain and exhaustion and cried tears of joy onto her little boy's face. The little fella started crying, and his toothless, baby mouth was the most adorable thing I had ever seen. Allison glanced up at me.

"Say hello to your son, honey."

I took him from her and added a few tears of my own to the growing collection on the little guy's cheeks.

"Did you decide on a name yet?" Allison asked me.

We had chosen on a middle name already. Kenneth. It was Allison's grandfather's name, whom she had been very close with before his death over a decade ago. The baby's first name, however, she had left up to me.

As I opened my mouth to speak, there was a knock at the door. Gabe poked his head in. "Is it okay to come in now?"

Doctor Khurana looked to Allison, who nodded. Gabe stepped in, dressed equally as stylishly as I was, and smiled down at my son.

"He's beautiful," the big man said.

Allison touched my arm. "He still needs a first name."

I cleared my throat, wiped the tears from my cheeks, and smiled at the best friend I have ever had.

"His name is Gabriel. Gabriel Kenneth Riordan."

*****

"You should stop listening to that thing."

I looked across the kitchen table at my wife. Her shirt was unbuttoned, one side of her bra pulled down, little Gabriel suckling at her breast. It had been three weeks since we had brought him home from the clinic, but it still creeped me out to see my son's mouth on my wife's boob. I wondered if I would ever get used to it.

The little guy's eyes blinked slowly as he drank, his bright blue irises contrasting sharply with his mother's olive skin. I reached over and turned off the emergency radio.

"You're right."

I stood up and walked over to the window. My reflection looked pensive in the early morning light. The President had just made her weekly speech, and as usual, it was not good news.

As expected, the Alliance had fallen into anarchy with the death of its highest-ranking officials. The KPA troops stationed there, never terribly popular to begin with, had been driven out of the city-states. At first they had scattered, hiding in the woods in small bands, but then managed to regroup in northern Kentucky and launch a counter-offensive. Their problem, however, was they were isolated, unable to re-supply properly, and unable to call in reinforcements.

The President, who wanted to work quickly to mend fences with the people of the former Midwest Alliance, committed thirty thousand troops to the fight, including most of the troops stationed at Fort McCray. Only the Ninth TVM had remained behind.

The North Koreans never had a chance. Trapped between the hammer of former Alliance soldiers and the anvil of Union troops, they were slaughtered to a man.

In the months after the fighting, all but a few former Alliance city-states signed treaties with the federal government, essentially making them part of the Union again. The response from the ROC was predictable. Their best and strongest ally had turned against them. They had their collective backs to the wall. War was imminent.

There had been opportunities to take part, being that General Jacobs thought that me, Gabe, and Great Hawk were a bunch of steely-eyed bad-asses, meaning he had no shortage of missions for us. The pay was very high. Gabe and the Hawk took a few contracts. I did not. I'd had enough of fighting for a while. I wanted peace, and quiet, and to spend time with my wife and son. Having a family was a new experience for me, and it suited me just fine.

"What are you thinking about?" Allison asked.

I turned to look at her. The sun coming through the window lit her amber-colored eyes like flames, highlighting her thick, wavy hair in golden cascades. The warmth in my chest that had been growing since the day I met her flared to a heat so intense

I thought it would burn me alive. It did not. I sat down next to Allison and took her hand.

"I was thinking of something Thomas Edison once said."

She tilted her head. "And that would be?"

"'Non-violence leads to the highest ethics, which is the goal of all evolution. Until we stop harming all other living beings, we are still savages.'"

She nodded and was quiet for a long moment. The little guy fell asleep, a small stream of milk and drool dribbling down his chin. Allison wiped his face with a cloth and tucked her swollen breast back into her shirt.

"Is that what you think? We're all just a bunch of savages?"

I sat back in my chair and ran a hand over my jaw. "I think we all have a bit of savagery in us, Allison. I think anyone can be pushed to it. And I think the more often we resort to that sort of thing, to violence, the easier it becomes. When your only tool is a hammer, everything starts to look like a nail."

"You haven't reached that point, Eric. Not even close."

"I used to have nightmares. I thought I would again after the mission in Illinois. I thought it would be like after the Free Legion."

"But it isn't."

I shook my head.

My wife put the baby in his crib, poured herself a cup of water, and sat across from me.

"For whatever it's worth, Eric, I'm proud of you. I think what you did took a lot of courage. I think you're strong, and brave, and not afraid to stand up for what you think is right. I think the world could use a hell of a lot more people like you. And I think you need to stop with all the self-recrimination and armchair psychoanalysis. Life is what it is. Not good, or bad, or anything else. It just is. One person's tragedy is someone else's triumph. The only difference is which side you happen to be standing on. This time, you picked the right one. So just be who

290

you are, turn into whatever you're going to turn into, and remember that no matter what happens, we'll get through it together. As a family."

I pulled her onto my lap and held her tight. Outside, southbound geese flew overhead, fleeing the coming winter. I nodded my head in the direction of the window. "Still think they have the right idea?"

"What do you mean?"

"I remember you mentioning something about leaving Hollow Rock."

She laid her head on my shoulder. "I may have changed my mind about that."

"Good."

We sat together in our home, held each other, and for the first time since the Outbreak, I could say in all honesty, without reservation, that I was happy. And with this realization came the understanding that all the other things I had worked for in life— trade, freedom, shelter, food, all of it—nothing compared to this. Nothing compared to being with a woman I loved, a woman who had given me a son, and with whom I could truly enjoy a moment of peace. Whatever else the future held, I would always have this memory. I would always have this light inside me, no matter how dark the road ahead.

For now, it was all I needed.

Epilogue

Caleb Hicks pulled the morning watch.

Unlike most of the other soldiers at the north gate, he did not mind getting out of bed early. He liked mornings, the way the dawning sun passed through trees in bars of lemon-gold, the crispness of the autumn breeze, the smell of cold in the air, and the sky-shades of copper and burnt amber painted across the eastern horizon. He stood with his hands in his pockets, rifle hanging loose on its tactical sling, and scanned the field below for infected. He did not see any.

"You notice there aren't as many ghouls coming around these days?"

Caleb turned to look at the other guard on watch with him. His name was Vincenzo, one of Sanchez's men from the Ninth TVM.

"You know, I was just thinking the same thing."

"Wonder why that is."

Caleb shrugged. "Don't know. But I'm glad for it."

"Yeah. No kidding."

The two soldiers continued their patrol along the wall, reached a watch tower, and turned back. Caleb thought he saw movement near the treeline and raised his binoculars.

"Got incoming."

Vincenzo checked his rifle and brought it to the low ready. "Living or dead?"

"Not sure. Hang on a minute."

Caleb switched to his rifle, dialed the magnification on the scope to six power, and peered through it. The figure in the distance wore thick layers of mismatched clothes, a hood over its head, and a scarf wrapped around its face. Caleb relaxed. Wearing thick layers, and lots of them, was a common tactic travelers used to protect themselves from ghoul bites.

"Living. Let's go see what they want."

Vincenzo lowered his rifle, but held it so he could bring it up quickly if need be. Caleb did the same.

The two men descended a ladder to ground level and waited while the figure approached. The closer the person came, the more Caleb knew it was a woman. Or a girl, more likely. The gait was distinctly feminine, but had a touch of the awkward clumsiness of early adolescence. She was tall, maybe five-foot ten, and did not seem to have fully grown into her body yet.

She came to a stop not far from where Caleb stood. She wore a pack with a short crowbar lashed to one side, a small pair of bolt cutters on the other, and a rifle over one shoulder. The rifle was a Marlin Model 60, .22 caliber.

Good choice, Caleb thought.

A pouch on her belt, which looked to have been hand-stitched from thick nylon fabric, hung heavily against her hip. By its obvious weight and the slight rattling it made when the girl moved, Caleb guessed it was full of ammo.

"Good morning," he said pleasantly. "I'm Sergeant Caleb Hicks. This is Private Vincenzo. What can we do for you?"

The girl stood and stared. Only a small part of her face was visible, the eyes obscured by the hood and scarf covering her face.

"Is this town called Hollow Rock?" she asked.

The voice was young. Caleb guessed the girl at no more than fourteen. Tall for her age. "Yes ma'am, it is. Are you here to trade, or are you with a larger group?"

She hesitated. "Um … actually I'm looking for someone. I was told I might find him here."

"Okay, we might be able to help you with that. But would you mind pulling down your scarf, though? It muffles your voice, makes it kind of hard to understand you."

The girl did as Caleb asked. She was neither pretty nor ugly, her face long, square, straight nose, sharp angles to the cheeks and jaw, and a pair of striking gray eyes. Greasy strands of long black hair blew on the breeze as she pushed back the hood. Oddly, she looked familiar. Caleb had the feeling he had met her before.

"This is who I'm looking for. The man, not the woman. She's dead."

The girl slowly pulled a picture from a jacket pocket. It was inside a small freezer bag, ostensibly to protect it from damage. Caleb took it and felt his heart skip a beat. He understood now why the girl looked so familiar. The picture was of two people, a man and a woman, the woman in a wedding dress and the man standing behind her in a Marine Corps dress uniform, his hands on her waist, obviously taken on their wedding day.

"The guy in the picture's name is Gabriel Garrett," the girl said. She reached out a nervous hand and Caleb numbly gave her the little plastic bag.

"I know that guy," Vincenzo said. "He's kind of a big deal around here. Why are you looking for him?"

Caleb knew the answer but let the girl speak anyway. His mind swirled with thoughts of how his friend was going to handle the shock headed his way.

"My name is Sabrina Garrett," the girl said. "Gabriel Garrett is my father."